First Edition published July 2021
Published by Indies United Publishing House, LLC
Cover art designed by Damonza

Hardback: 978-1-64456-328-1
Paperback: 978-1-64456-329-8
Mobi: 978-1-64456-330-4
ePub: 978-1-64456-331-1
AudioBook: 978-1-64456-332-8

Library of Congress Control Number: 2021940248

INDIES UNITED PUBLISHING HOUSE, LLC
P.O. BOX 3071
QUINCY, IL 62305-3071
www.indiesunited.net

To the three Bs. Long may you run.

Thanks again, Jayne!

LOOKING FOR DON

D. KRAUSS

INDIES UNITED PUBLISHING HOUSE, LLC

Chapter 1

Déjà vu all over again.

Sitting in Mom's car on Washington Avenue checking out Don's house to see if the coast was clear before coasting down the road and up Don's driveway in prelude to days and nights of hijinks and peril… how many times had Butch done this? A hundred? A thousand? It's like he never left.

But he had.

Butch shifted irritably in the seat, drumming fingers on the wheel. Thought you got away, huh? Yet, here you are, right back at it. Only things different are the details: Mom's car is a Pontiac, not a Duster. Thank God for that. And Butch is no longer in high school; he's in the Air Force. Let's not thank God for that. Still, Mom's car, and he was using it to look for Don.

Which was a bust: Don wasn't home. Don's mom's Buick was out front, but the Batmobile wasn't, so what's the point? Came all this way for nothing. Could say "hi" to Mom, at least.

Don's mom, that is. Not his own mom whom he'd already said "hi" to this morning when, fresh off the plane and out of a taxi, he'd knocked on the door at Ridge's house over there in Rest Haven and hi Mom I'm back from basic training and no, I don't want any breakfast can I borrow your car, please? as Ridge glowered at him from the living room. And she'd hemmed and hawed and cast fearful glances back at Ridge, who said nothing because, really, what could he? It's not like Butch was his kid or anything, and she'd relented — finally — while looking all put out and hurt that he didn't want to stay and have breakfast and tell her all about basic and why did you join the Air Force just like that out of the blue without telling me and seriously, Mom? Seriously? And took the offered keys.

Guilt is a wonderful motivator.

Some wretched Abba tune screeched from the dashboard speakers and Butch sighed and wished he still had Buggy, his 1961 baby-blue VW Beetle with porthole windows in the back, no working instruments and only one functioning windshield wiper (the driver's side, fortunately), air-conditioned in summer through a combination of open window-wings and speeds of 60 mph, and heated in winter by a valve underneath the driver's seat he unscrewed to let in the engine fumes.

But you know what it did have? FM radio. Which meant he wouldn't have to listen to this top 40 WIP-AM radio crap. Gawd, Mom, you have FM in the house, why don't you have it in the car?

Easy; because Ridge is a cheap-ass, at least when it came to Butch's Mom and her kids. Ridge's kids probably had FM in their cars, probably cassettes, too, which they didn't pay for, like they didn't pay for their brand-new-special-ordered Mustangs and Camaros and GTOs. Ridge paid. With Mom's money.

Butch paid for Buggy with his own money; half of Buggy, that is. Cindy and he split the $100 price. "Now you both will have to share," Mom said as she did the paperwork while he and Cindy danced around Buggy, already planning cross-country drives or, at the minimum, a visit to Seaside. Sharing didn't bother either of them. They shared a lot.

A lot.

He shivered.

The sharing came to naught because, shortly after, Cindy got herself an idiot Piney boyfriend who drove a Nova SS and they were out all the time doing stupid Piney things, effectively leaving Butch as Buggy's sole proprietor. Butch had acquired an FM converter in a dubious transaction with Pee Sea (which, upon reflection, should have been his *last* dubious transaction with Pee Sea) and spent a subsequent afternoon under the dashboard trying to figure out which wire hooked to what. It was about the only time he wished idiot Piney boyfriend was around because the guy did know cars; but Butch managed, leaving the converter on the floor in front of the passenger seat because dismounting the AM radio and setting the converter in its place was a bridge too far. That made changing stations while driving a hazardous proposition but he'd never needed to change stations after he tuned in WYSP…

"What's this shit?" Don picked the tuner off the floor, examining the hard-to-read dial like a doctor checking for gangrene.

"YSP." Butch downshifted while peering hard through the half-assed wiper, which was losing its battle with the snow. "A new station. It's better than MMR."

Don snorted. "Nothin's better than MMR," and he spun the dial wheel looking for it but no way could MMR or YSP or any other Philly radio station be acquired or re-acquired in the middle of a snowstorm somewhere on the other side of Mt. Misery. It took Butch a couple of days to get YSP back and he'd threatened Don with dismemberment if he ever, EVER, touched the converter again. Which he did, anyway…

Butch chuckled.

Feel free to change Mom's crappy AM radio the moment you get in, Donny boy. Like you're going to find anything good on it.

First, though, had to find him. So let's knock on the door, ask Mom where he is, go to that location, and acquire his hijinks-and-peril sidekick.

Looking like this?

Butch ran his head over his skull. Not hair; skull. Some bristles up there could technically be called hair but they were nothing compared with what he'd sported before that mule skinner laughingly called a barber at Lacklaaaaand Air Force Base! (always said in *Firesign Theater* accents) had his way with him. Butch's beautiful white-'fro fell in waves down his front and back and all over the floor and it had not grown back. Not a whit. Eight weeks later, he still looked like a shorn Basic Trainee. Butch still mourned. He would never get his hair back. Don wouldn't recognize him. No one would recognize him.

Maybe that was a good thing.

Boarding that plane at Philly airport eight weeks ago with sixty other loser idiots too stupid or too broke to do something worthwhile, such as attend college or grow dope, meant he'd escaped unpaid debts, old scores, unresolved complaints, and even a murder attempt or two. It also meant he was now a full-fledged member of Loserville (the military. Oh God) but a full-fledged *breathing* member of Loserville, at least.

And yet, he came back.

The dog returns to its vomit.

Butch accelerated the drumming fingers to Keith Moon levels and frowned and considered alternative courses of action.

Take the car back. Right now. Have Mom drive me to Philly airport. Grab the first thing smoking for Chicago. Get on the Chanute Air Force Base bus and report early for Weather Observer school.

They'd probably make him paint toilets or haul garbage the two weeks before the school started, but it was better than hiding at the apartment sans car or hiding at Ridge's house sans sanity.

Forget it.

Instead, keep Mom's car, risking vehicle theft charges (courtesy of Ridge), and tool around the Barrens heading towards the inevitable run-in with old enemies and girlfriends who would stop and stare and bust out laughing when they saw Butch the Skinhead. "You loser! You sellout!" and there'd be fights, half of which he would lose.

What the heck is a Weather Observer, anyway?

Butch didn't know. He'd put it down as his third career choice, after X-Ray and Lab Technician, the counselor at Lackland saying, "Ah, you'll get your first choice anyway. Just finish out the form with this" – tap of the finger on the line displaying the Weather AFSC (Air Force Specialty Code. He was larnin' the lingo) halfway down the list of available Air Force technical schools – "and then I can submit it and there you'll be, on your way to a Medical Career!" The guy actually smiled when he said that. Butch did, too.

You idiot.

Little too late now, my friend.

I'm locked into four years of observing the weather.

What's that entail? Run outside a couple of times an hour, stick a hand out, see if it's raining? Butch shook his head. Only the Air Force would have a job like that.

So, after four years, I'll be a highly trained and skilled rain spotter. Big call for that in the outside world.

'Outside world.' Listen to you. You're already making distinctions.

"Are you going in or what?"

Butch did not immediately leap straight through the top of the car because he knew that voice. Instead, with a calmness he really shouldn't feel, he glanced at the rearview mirror. Yep, Frank Vaughn, sitting behind him.

"I thought you were in Oklahoma."

"I am." Frank pushed his cheek back into place, closing the hole in the side of his head. Butch shuddered. "Just paying a visit."

"I haven't seen you in a while. You look… older."

"So do you."

"But you can't get older. You're dead."

Frank dismissed that with a shrug and fiddled with the jaw some more. "Question remains, you going in?"

Butch stared at the house. "What's it to you?" he asked and turned for the answer but Frank wasn't there. But he did have a point. Didn't get dressed up and come all this way for nothin'.

Butch shifted into first and drifted down the road and pulled into Don's driveway and shut off the engine, listening as the after-knock ran for about thirty or forty seconds.

Think you need a tune-up, Mom. Like Ridge is going to spring for it. Like I am?

He scowled. No, he wasn't. Mom owed *him*; he didn't owe *her*. Hence, possession of the car for the day. Or a couple of days. Or maybe for the rest of his life if he simply avoided Ridge's place and tooled around the Barrens getting into fights before heading to Illinois.

Could I? Butch mused.

Well, yes, he could, with impunity; his sense of being owed eliminated any guilt twinges and Mom's sense of guilt obviated any stolen car reports except ... he'd left his duffel bag, filled with his entire issue of Aaaaair Farce uniforms, at Ridge's.

Idiot.

He stepped out, pulling the cunt cap off the right side of his belt as he yanked and tugged at his 1505s until they were straight and proper, gig line in place. 'Gig line'. Only the ate-up military would create an actual term to describe the lining up of the pants' fly with the edge of the *buckle, belt, chrome, one each*. And here he was ensuring said gig line was, indeed, gigged. And here he was, walking around in full-blown ate-up uniform.

Butch'd thought of changing into his civvies when he got off the airplane, but then he'd be walking through the airport in overalls and T-shirt and Earth shoes, his shiny-and-bright skinned head proclaiming to the world he'd either recently escaped from a concentration camp or undergoing chemo… or some military guy pretending he wasn't in the military. So which was worse, the pretense, or the reality? He'd opted for the reality and got a few nods and friendly waves from some old farts, and lots of sneers and flipped birds from the young. Get used to it. Besides, 1505s were comfortable. Too bad the Air Force was doing away with them.

He walked up the porch and knocked on the door and glanced up and down the street to see if anyone had spotted him yet; specifically, anybody he used to hang out with; more specifically, any of the guys (or gals) still pissed at him. Didn't want to get any blood on his spiffy and properly-gigged 1505s.

The door opened and Don's mom stood there blinking at him.

"Hi, Mom," Butch said, cheerfully.

Startled, she glared hard at him through her blue-plastic *Our Miss Brooks* glasses, trying to associate this skinny bald fascist on her porch with someone who could call her that. Glared UP at him, more accurately, because she was about four feet nothing, less than a hundred pounds nothing, slight and wispy and myopic and the best mom in the world. Just was.

"Butch!" she trilled in the perfect mom voice as a perfect-mom smile threw her heart-shaped face, framed by brown curls (natural curls at that), into the perfect-mom expression, "So glad to see you, son, please come in and have some cookies," and Butch warmed, because how many times had he knocked on Don's door at all hours and days and Don's mom greeted him in exactly the same manner, no questions asked, "C'min c'min." Now, if Don's *dad* opened the door, as was sometimes the case, he'd get an instant growl of, "Grab a rake. We got work to do," and propelled off the porch and to the backyard where they spent hours doing yard stuff. And that was okay, too.

"Oh, my!" she thrilled, gazing at his egg-smooth skull and reached up and rubbed his head, knocking off the cap, which Butch caught in a deft display of reflexes, and she giggled and it was "C'min! C'min!" and he followed her into the perfect-mom living room: couches and chairs all covered in knitted afghans and throws. All her handiwork, so many that the original upholsteries revealed themselves only through various knitting gaps. Family photos of Don and his brother at various stages of growth between oil portraits of mom and dad at various stages of aging and random watercolor seascapes – which Don's mom painted – covered every available wall space, the original wallpaper peeking shyly here and there between frame gaps. The smell of roasted coffee and potpourri and string beans boiling on a distant stove blended with the perfume of welcome and stability and home. A home.

"Oh, my!" Don's mom beamed at Butch, who stood in the middle of everything and absorbed it all and felt weights and stresses and concerns simply melt away. "They certainly did a job on you, didn't they?"

Butch made an exaggerated swipe at his hairline, or, rather, where his hairline used to be. "They certainly did."

"And look how skinny you are now!" Her hands clutched her collar in mock horror.

"Yep!" Butch made an exaggerated sweep down his body. "Lost twenty pounds."

"You didn't have it to lose to begin with!" She took a ferocious step and pushed him into an armchair padded with afghans across from an afghan-padded couch, unfinished knitting on the table between them. "Now you sit right there while I make you a sandwich. Two sandwiches!"

"You really don't—"

She raised a "nonsense!" hand as she flipped around the corner and there were sounds of plates flung about and drawers opened and Butch grinned and sat back and all was right with the world. He browsed the pictures while Don's mom committed assault on lunch and look at this one right here, Don and Dooby and Butch, the Three Musketeers, in front of the house, Don sitting on the hood of the Batmobile, his '59 salmon-colored Impala with the gigantic fins, hence the name, Butch and Dooby flanking him, all long hair and beards (in Dooby's case) and hippie overalls and plaid shirts and looking so young and teenaged and carefree.

Carefree.

"Now, let's get some of that weight back on you!" Don's mom turned the corner with a serving tray that she dropped onto Butch's lap: two gigantic Wonderbread sandwiches piled high with turkey and ham and lettuce and tomato and Charles Chips and Oreos. She placed a cup of steaming coffee on a flank of the unfinished knitting and a glass of milk on the other, all in one motion.

"Gee, Mom, you really didn't—"

"Nonsense!" Spoken this time, not gestured. "Your mother must have passed out when she saw you."

"I don't think she even noticed."

"Oh." She dismissed that with an irritated wave. "Of course she did. And your hair looks fine." Said in the voice moms used when things didn't look fine. "Dad" – Don's dad – "had his hair that short about the whole time he was in the Army, so I think it looks nice."

"Thanks." Said without enthusiasm but Butch actually felt better. Of course. Mom's superpower was making her sons feel better.

She chose to read his pseudo-skepticism. "No, I mean it. You look very handsome in your uniform."

"Handsome?" Butch straight-out laughed. "That would be a first."

She flourished a handful of knitting. "Oh, stop fishing for compliments. I always knew there was a handsome boy under all that hair. So how was it?"

"Rough," was all he said, slightly stung because yeah, he had been fishing, hadn't he? Couldn't help it: there weren't a lot of people with good things to say about him. Not even his own mom.

And whose fault is that?

She gave him a sideways glance. "Rough?"

He blushed a bit. "Well, not as rough as the Army or the Marines I know, but rough enough." And blushed a little more because, geez, her husband was a Major and fought in Korea and here Butch was complaining about creampuff Air Force basic training.

She threw him a lifeline. "It's rough if you're not used to it."

"I wasn't," he said, grasping at it, "I thought I was, you know, with all the karate training but, wow." He shook his head. "The running damn near killed me."

She bent over the needles. *Click clack click clack.* A scarf, Butch guessed. "Imagine doing all that with a fifty-pound backpack and a rifle," she pointed out.

"Yes." He nodded vigorously. "I am quite grateful I went into the right recruiter's door."

She laughed. "The Air Force *is* a lot better. They treat their people very well. I wish Donny had gone with you." That last spoken with a bit of ruefulness.

"Speaking of which… where is he? At work?"

An exasperated expression crossed her face. "I wish I knew. He hasn't been home in a while."

"Oh." A pause. "That's nothing new."

"I know, which is why I'm not worried," she said, worried. "At least not yet."

"Give him two weeks before you call the cops," Butch said. "Is he still working at the printing plant?"

"Well, yes." She gave him the fisheye. "You know, you've only been gone a few weeks."

True, Mom, but a week in New Jersey is like a year anywhere else.

Parents don't know that, so he said nothing.

She gestured at his shorn head. "So what *did* your mother say?"

"Eh." Butch waggled his hand. "Nothing really. Ridge said something about me no longer being a hippie and Mom laughed, but I think she was just shoring up her position."

Don's mom gave a dismissive *tsk*. "You really need to get over your mom marrying him. It's not like you can do anything about it."

"I know, I know. I just wish she wasn't such a doormat."

"It's a survival instinct," Donny mommy said. "Once learned, it's hard to change."

"I know."

Boy, did he know.

A smattering of images: cringing in the bedroom as Dad roared down on him; cringing in the yard as Dad roared down on him… lots of cringing in those memories.

Cringing in the rain, shovel in hand, Cindy beside him, shovel in her own hands, crying.

He blinked the memories away. "I just wish…" he trailed, not sure what he wanted to say. She needle-gestured for him to go on. "That we were as close as we used to be."

She pursed her lips.

"It's inevitable. A mom's heartbreak. Her boys grow up and leave."

And she sighed, obviously meaning Don.

"That's not it." He frowned, trying to find the right words. "She's thrown in with Ridge's family. I guess she thinks they're better than us."

"Ha!" Spoken derisively. "No mother is going to abandon her children for someone else's."

"Well, I'm not really her child, am I?"

She let out a long, slow breath. "Butch, that's just unfair to your mom. She loved you as much as her own children. You just said how close you were."

"Yeah."

He conceded the point; at least, that he had used those words. But their closeness back there in Alabama, back during Butch's previous and now completely alien life, felt one-sided. Butch sat with Mom after school and watched the boring soaps (except for *General Hospital*; that was good), went with her to the Piggly Wiggly and helped carry bags, and did his homework in the kitchens of strangers' houses while Mom ran Tupperware parties in their living rooms because selling Tupperware was the only job Dad would let her have. Mom feared the long drives over dark country roads to Dothan, which was the closest town containing households prosperous enough to host Tupperware parties, and Butch volunteered to help her navigate. They often didn't return home until close to midnight. Dad liked that. It left him to his own devices. For hours. So he never gave her a hard time about the parties and she scheduled as many as she could in a given week and Butch passed 7th and 8th grades with flying colors because of all the time he spent completing homework assignments on strange kitchen tables. The strangers gushed admiration for his scholarly diligence and his filial dedication to mom's welfare as they passed in and out of the kitchen collecting brownies and pigs-in-blankets for the party attendees, letting Butch have one or two in passing. Butch took their regard in his stride, convinced he was a good son. In all those instances, from soap-watching to road-traversing, there'd been companionability. Butch felt protective of Mom, supportive.

But a coldness prevailed whenever Butch needed

reciprocation. Say Dad stroked him six or seven times with the bullwhip because Dad had scratched the truck's bumper running into the lawnmower that Butch had not pushed far enough back in the garage and this was obviously Butch's fault (or Dad's for inattentive driving but let's not mention that), so he'd go crying to Mom seeking solace and got, "Serves you right!", instead. Or when the kids at school jeered, "Bookworm! Bookworm!" because he sought the companionability of Heinlein and Alexander Key instead of lewd, cruel games, she'd conclude, "Well, you ARE a bookworm!"

Or when forced to dig a grave… "Don't tell Mom. Ever." Cindy's tearful, panicked plea. And he never had.

A distance, despite his best efforts, and Butch suspected resentments not his fault as their origin. Evidence: that summer in Alabama when she loaded them all in a car because things were out of hand and they needed to hide for a while and Mom told Art that yes, of course, Butch was adopted but Dad was his real dad so he's really your brother, adding with completely unnecessary emphasis, "Yes, that makes him a bastard."

Really, Mom? Really?

Butch was shocked into utter silence by that. Art wasn't. Art used that gem for years after. Thing was, Butch already knew his patrimony, his bastardy, had known since the summer of '65 when they were all supposed to be divorced and Dad had gone gallivanting around the south visiting his girlfriends (and other bastard children, as it turned out) with Butch as reluctant companion and witness while Cindy and Mom and Art (and Dale, don't forget her) remained at the Deats' homestead in Oklahoma preparing for a life post-Dad and post-Butch. Butch and Dad weren't supposed to come back from that gallivant; it was the dissolution of the family, doncha know, but, surprise, surprise, they did go back by the end of that same summer, plans for divorce temporarily shelved and Dad packed them all up and stowed them, kit and kaboodle in the desolation of abomination called Alabama. Where everything else happened.

Cindy briefed Butch regarding his aforementioned patrimony the very day of his return. He hadn't known before. Mom had told her the same day he and Dad had gallivanted, so the sister of the bastard knew he was a bastard three months before the bastard himself knew. Butch guessed Mom thought it was easier to justify the death of this family to Cindy if she exposed the reason for it, Butch being that reason. Didn't expose it to Art; he was too young. But the family didn't die, went on, in fact, like a stubborn cancer patient, in the middle of Alabama swampland suffering occasional relapses like that later summer in which Mom felt it necessary to finally enlighten Art, before the final, terrifying expiration some months later.

So why did Mom think it necessary to tell Art at all? Especially in Butch's presence?

Payback?

"Yeah," he said again, because he still couldn't find the right words.

"Anyway," she said brightly, "I'm very glad you decided to get out of New Jersey. I don't think there's much of a future here."

Butch's brows rose. "Then, why are you guys here?"

"Because we're retired. We don't have a future." She laughed.

Butch's brows segued into full furrow. "But… isn't Dad still working?"

Dismissive tut. "Oh, that's just a bill-paying job. Mad money. Dad's real career was the Army."

In a way, Butch understood that. Only a few weeks in the Air Force and he already felt its uniqueness. If he stayed in, then it would be his life, too, would define him, regardless of anything else he ever did before or after. Which was why he had no intention of staying. Do his four years, get his VA, go to school to study Japanese, move to Japan and study the sword. That's the plan.

"So what do you mean there's no future here?"

She sighed, long and hard.

"Look around. The Arab embargo, that idiot Carter and the bigger idiot Corzine wasting all our tax money, everybody going on welfare, more crime all the time and the drugs, oh my, the drugs. And people are getting meaner."

"Meaner?"

"Well, yes. Just in the short time you were gone, someone shot a sheriff's deputy right over there in Tabernacle. And they found a headless body on Deep Hollow."

Butch started. "What? Deep Hollow?" The mystical mostly-dirt road connecting the back of the Lakes to the rest of the world through the Lebanon Forest.

It was his Street of Joy.

Many of Butch's craziest nights and weekends originated somewhere on that road, a midnight creep under a wizard's moon as the pines whipped by and the three of them, Don and Dooby and Butch in either Buggy, Battleship, or the Batmobile, imbued with the ether of youth and freedom and illegal substances, launched into the woods searching for the spirits and the gypsies and fought wars of magic and song in the forest's netherworlds. Sometimes they got there separately, in separate cars, after a night of running into each other first here and then there, someone having to go do something somewhere with someone else and fine, man, see you back at the Lakes and when the errands and to-dos ended, the various universes placated and sated, then their various gravities spun them back together, rituals and spells ensuring Buggy and Battleship and Batmobile converged at the side entrance of Magnolia at the exact same time, one behind the other in order of arrival, and they raced down the dirt road through the woods with their lights off, bumper-to-bumper, their only cues the sand berm with its shadow pines and the drip of moonlight through the boughs and felt the motion of the earth, of speeding cars, of their lives, the blood pounding in their ears as the girlfriends-of-the-moment screamed, "Are you crazy?" and yes, yes, dear, we are, but the magic saved them and they piled onto the beach laughing and dancing and brothers always, always brothers.

And now, Deep Hollow was tainted. "Do they know who it was?"

"Yes. Some boy from Perkins named Jape."

Butch's heart stilled. "Garfield Jape?"

"Yes, that's him. You knew him?"

"Yes."

Oh yes, he knew Garfield Sinclair Jape, small-time hood and big-time dreamer and even bigger talker. He was one of the reasons Butch joined the Air Force so hastily. One of the reasons.

"Do they know what happened?"

"Drug deal gone bad."

Well, yes. And Butch had a real good idea which specific drug deal went bad. "They catch the guy?"

"No. They have no idea who did it." Her eyes narrowed. "Do you?"

Well, yes...

"No." Poker face. "I just knew Jape around Perkins." Poker face shifted to one of innocence. "So... when did this happen?"

"Last week."

"Wow," Butch said softly. Definitely should not have come back home.

"Well, are you going to eat those sandwiches or am I going to serve them to Dad for dinner?"

Butch ate, even though his appetite had evaporated, and Mom fetched several books from various tables to show him what she was reading now and he was grateful for the distraction.

"Have you heard of this one?" She held up a monster-sized book, *Centennial* by James Michener.

"Think so," he said, although he hadn't. "Isn't he the guy who wrote *The Source*?"

"The very one." She beamed and he beamed back.

Don wasn't a reader, so Butch substituted as the literary son. Not that he minded. It was good to have a parent who shared his reading passion. Lord knows Mom and Dad never did. You bookworm.

"I'll let you have it when I'm done with it."

"Don't know if I'll have a lot of time for reading over the next few weeks."

"Pish," she countered. "You can always find time to read. Stop watching television."

"Haven't much time for that, either."

She laughed. "No, I imagine not. Not that you're missing anything."

"Eh." Butch waggled his hand. "I kinda like *Barney Miller*. And *Baretta*."

"Stick with reading," she said.

They talked about books, past ones and future ones, and Butch finished his sandwiches and Oreos and did not refuse when she offered Fig Newtons and more coffee and an hour went by, maybe, and Don did not show up and it was time to find him, the jerk.

"Don't be a stranger!" she said at the door.

And he said he wouldn't and got into Mom's car and backed up and wondered where to go next. Don's workplace, probably.

In the middle of the street, he fiddled with the radio in the forlorn hope that one of the AM stations had come to its senses and played album rock when a car pulled up next to him. Absently, Butch waved it on, but the car did not move and he looked up. And froze.

A 1969 purple El Camino. And, behind the wheel, Pee Sea. Staring at him, malevolence flowing off his cement-block-shaped head like an overheated radiator, his pig eyes inflamed and ferocious.

"Welcome back, motherfucker," he snarled, made a gun with his forefinger and thumb, pointed it at Butch, pretended to fire, and then peeled out, without breaking eye contact.

Butch watched in the rearview mirror as the El Camino whipped around the corner, convinced Pee Sea would be back in moments wielding a shotgun. He remembered to breathe and realized he needed to get someplace safe.

Now.

Thong's. Now.

Chapter 2

Thong's was safe because no one knew about it. Thong and Kasey bought their house a week before Butch scooted off to Texas. A day before scooting, Butch went over to see the place, vaguely following Thong's vague directions with a lot on his mind so not paying a lot of attention and now look at this, he was lost somewhere on the north side of Braun's Mills. Which was good. If he couldn't find Thong, then neither could Pee Sea.

Not that he was all gung-ho to see the guy. The last visit was a bit of a cock-up. "You joined the Air Force?" Thong had greeted Butch's news with incredulity, his pop eyes popping even more while his big black curls shook in that ridiculous mixed mullet-and-Elvis haircut he thought fashionable, his fish lips forming an "O."

"Well, yeah."

Thong turned to Kasey and they burst out laughing, Kasey's waist-length brown hair waving like a flag in a hurricane as she rocked back and forth on the couch in synch with Thong's spastic bobbing. It was such a comical scene that Butch couldn't help giggling.

"C'mon, guys," he pleaded but all that did was set them off even harder.

That was Thong's superpower: regardless of the tragedy, he could make it funny. Like the initial disaster that had triggered the cascade of even bigger disasters resulting in the current situation.

"Well," Thong said, after Butch confessed the eff-up of all eff-ups, "I guess you'll be getting married," rendering Butch speechless because he'd already rejected such a solution but that didn't stop Thong from humming Mendelsohhn's Wedding March and speculating on possible kid's names as he nosed the Plymouth through the underbrush past the Train Wreck in search of the Leeds' house. They were hunting the Jersey Devil.

"Thong," Butch sputtered when he finally got his voice back, "I can't marry her. I can't marry anybody."

"Why not?"

"I just… can't!"

"Nothing wrong with getting married."

"Well, why don't you, then?"

And he did. To Kasey. Back this spring at the mayor's office in Mt. Holyoke, with a reception afterwards at the Shawnee Lodge in Medford, Thong's friends and Kasey's friends and Butch's, too, Don and Dooby and Jape and others (but not April. Oh no. Let's not give her any more ideas, shall we?), one of those rare times when Butch's friends were in the same locale as Thong. Because the Thong universe was hidden.

Butch roamed several different universes, traveling easily between astral planes. The Don-and-Dooby universe closely resembled a real family, more than his own did, anyway, which was a separate universe consisting of Butch and Cindy and Art in a murky low-income apartment that Mom visited once a week to stuff Ellio's Pizza in the freezer and then beat a hasty retreat to Ridge's universe, which was a black hole of voids and nothingness. The Archway universe was in a house across the street from the apartment, a place where all the neighborhood orphans gravitated for some Mother Archway cookies and tea and advice and subsequent commandeering of Father Archway's basement to get drunk, safe from the eyes of the Perkins police. Butch had myriad other universes, like Oak's karate club of cool black guys who'd adopted Butch as their pet white boy; April and her family's (until all the very bad things happened); Jape and the dangerous crowd. These universes intersected at various points. Everyone knew the inhabitants of the other. But not Thong's.

No one but Butch knew that one.

Thong's universe was odder than the rest and built of layers. It consisted of Thong's parents, both of whom Butch swore worked for the CIA. One managed some obscure airline and was gone for weeks, at times coinciding with various coups in various forgettable African countries, while the other stayed home to maintain cover. Butch wasn't sure who did what and suspected they frequently switched roles. Thong's four brothers were the second layer, all of them certifiably insane of the "hearing voices" type; an evening spent in their company was simply surreal. Thong's friends filled the next layer, a perpetual David Bowie concert replete with spandex and glitter.

Thong was his own layer. He was sometimes a girl and sometimes a man, however the mood took him, and the times he was a girl, he offered himself to Butch but Butch made it clear that he preferred real girls, regardless of the advantages of a girl/man who knew exactly what a man liked. This was no big deal between them and they still ran the streets together in between the times Butch visited his other universes. No repercussions. No judgments, just two guys (or a guy and girl depending on Thong's mood), enjoying the hell out of each other's company, doing rather silly things.

Like ghost hunting.

Thong was insane about ghost hunting. "Look at this." Boy-Thong pointed at a picture in a family album that girl-Thong had pulled from a shelf when Butch showed up one night about midnight while evading the dangerous crowd universe. "See those two?" He tapped on two smiling women hovering in the back of a crowd of maybe twenty-five to thirty people arranged in four rows between two trees; all smiling and dressed up and obviously a family reunion of some type because (a) it was a picture album in Thong's house and (b) ten- or eleven-year-old Thong was in the front row already sporting that amazing hair.

"Yeah?"

"Those are my aunts, Gertie and Libby. They were both crazy old spinsters." A pause. "They died within a week of each other." Another pause. "A year BEFORE this picture was taken."

Cue the *Dark Shadows* theme music.

They went ghost hunting at least once a week, an activity consisting of felonious breaking-and-entering into various abandoned houses scattered hither and yon throughout the Pine Barrens, including the big scary house behind the kill-horses-and-grind-them-into-dog-food factory in Perkins. They were in greater danger from tetanus and vagrants than the supernatural in those forays, but they used their imaginations to give it credence.

"Elementals!" Thong whispered once as they stood in the middle of a yard so overgrown with brush and ivy that approaching the wrecked house in the middle of it was impossible. Thong was speaking of the rustlings and slitherings of mice and voles and whatnot running for their lives from the clumsy humans tramping down their abodes.

Never, ever saw an elemental. Or any other kind of ghostie or beastie. But it was all good fun.

Butch never told Thong about Frank Vaughn, which was odd because, of all the universes, Thong's would be most sympathetic. Butch, though, was never fully convinced that Frank was real, and telling Thong about it might end up relegating him to the same category as Thong's brothers. Butch glanced at the passenger seat, but no one was there.

He pulled over to get his bearings.

All right, where the hell are we?

Butch frowned around.

Okay, looks like the right area, but maybe a little too far south. Thong's house was on the Ft. Dix side of the Hat Dance Motel and this is still the Braun's Mills' side. Okay.

A few moments later, he passed the Dance and yep, there, a suddenly familiar hidden right turn that he swooped into and up the road and missed the next street so back up and took it and a couple of more turns around the block and there, Thong's car, a 1967 Sunbeam without the top, sitting in the driveway.

He pulled up behind it and laughed.

Still have that POS, huh, Thong? Figured you would have replaced it by now.

Thong kept a car for an average of about six weeks. Butch lost count of how many times he'd walked down the apartment stairs responding to the clarion call of a horn blaring outside the door and there was Thong behind the wheel of yet another junker. "Where'd you get this?" "Don't ask. Get in." And off they went, adventures before them.

He stood by the topless car for a moment and wondered if he should prank Thong, wrap the steering wheel in toilet paper or something, but he didn't have anything other than his cunt cap and he needed that.

So let's go in.

He knocked on the door. Moments later, Kasey opened it and

stared at him, befuddled.

"I've changed," he said.

Her eyes widened and a big smile broke her face. "Butch!" and she had him in a bear hug and man, she was great. Just great. If Thong hadn't married her, Butch would have. She smelled perpetually of cinnamon and cloves, her big green eyes framed by an acre of that brown hair and brown freckles spattered all over her cheeks and always wore peasant dresses that flowed and whirled and accentuated her shape. And she was fun. She was always up for a midnight ghost hunt or bar run, she and Thong laughing insanely as the wind tore at them through the shreds of fabric left on the Sunbeam's top, while Butch held on for dear life to the back bar, his legs jammed through the middle and pressed against the dashboard.

She held him at arm's length. "My God, look what they've DONE to you! You look like a fascist!"

"Hey, now, it's not that bad." He snickered as he followed her inside because yeah, it was.

"I wouldn't recognize you walking down the street." She pointed at the chintz couch. "Sit there, I'll get some tea." She bustled off and Butch sank into the cushions, all now right with the world. He savored the room. It was almost an Indian temple, the chintz and brocades and deep piles and plushes swirling with flowers and arabesques and inlays. Stare too long at any one pattern and he'd be hypnotized. Incense and perfumes underlay it all and Butch expected sitar music to break out any moment. This was all Kasey, who was an India nut. She read Herman Hesse and went to Bollywood movies in Philadelphia and wanted to visit the Taj Mahal for her delayed honeymoon. "Yeah, yeah," Thong said and rolled his eyes at Butch because his idea of a honeymoon was a week in Disneyland, where he could be Peter Pan.

Butch couldn't quite remember when Kasey joined their universe. She simply showed up one day, sitting next to Thong in a Karman Gia as Butch struggled to get into the back seat. Geez, what was it with Thong and tiny cars? "This is Kasey," Thong said, with no further word of explanation and really, none was needed. It was obvious to Butch that Thong was head-over, and she with him. Butch approved. They were good together and it was good being with them and apparently, they thought it was good to have him along because he was riding on some Thong-

and-Kasey adventure at some point of every day. Well, that might be an exaggeration but they did spend a lot of time together, almost as much time as Butch spent with Don and Dooby. Seemed like his senior year consisted of him running from the Lakes to Kasey's parents' house hidden somewhere on the other side of Braun's Mills, where they tried to get Butch interested in Kasey's sister, but no; or off to Moorestown and Kasey's private school friends and attempts to get Butch interested in one of them named Molly, who was a real hippie chick, but no. Because Butch was still in shock. Probably for life.

Thong was in shock, too, after Lindsey, and now look at him. Got over it fairly quick, didn't he? 'Course, Butch's shock was at an entirely different level.

Lindsey. Wow.

Butch had completely forgotten about her.

In junior year, Thong was head-over with Lindsey, a skinny freckle-faced sophomore who had Thong's exact same hair. That's how they became an item, comparing locks by the lockers as Butch *tsk*ed his exasperation. Lindsey joined the universe and was with them on many Thong adventures, which Butch did not mind because she was fun and loud and brash and up for anything and anyways, Thong was head-over ... while she wasn't.

Butch saw it long before Thong did. While she circled Thong's sun, the other planets attracted her and Butch saw her gaze speculatively on some of Thong's brothers or the Country Lakes' crazies flitting in and out of Thong's orbit; like Big Dave, whose father owned a junkyard and who Butch suspected was the source of Thong's constantly changing Thongmobiles, or Leonard, a big black guy given to military clothes and nuclear Armageddon. Butch didn't think it much harm because Lindsey lost her virginity to Thong, something Thong happily informed him about the night of the day it happened, his face oddly uncertain and pained during the joyous recounting. The next day at school Lindsey seemed ... different. Still brash and loud but she walked around herself now, as if trying to avoid something, and there was a far-off light in her eyes. She'd seen the possibilities and Butch trembled because, in Alabama, he'd seen the results.

And then someone was pounding on the apartment door one midnight and Butch yanked it open baseball bat in hand and Thong swayed and blubbered his way inside, eyes red from agony and beer and a joint or two. "Lindsey's left me!"

They sat in Butch's bedroom on his cot, drinking pony bottles of Rolling Rock that a bartender down on Magnolia Road was willing to sell to anyone who pretended to be eighteen, and the sordid story came out. Lindsey had secretly been seeing Ollie, a college-aged loser who hung around the Lakes with two of Thong's brothers and who Butch dismissed as a dweeby moron but, look at this: Lindsey told Thong to get lost this very night and while Butch did not think it an actual tragedy, there were forms to be observed, so he listened and sympathized and Thong told him the story of his life. Specifically, his sexual life, beginning with a middle-aged woman in a New York suburb who initiated twelve-year-old Thong into the mysteries and a middle-aged man, an art professor with a Van Dyke and bowler hat, who initiated the year-older Thong into the other mysteries.

That was the first time Thong looked at Butch and licked his lips and made a proposition. Butch merely smiled in confirmation of a tendency long suspected, and said, "No thanks, man, not my thing." And it wasn't. And it was never an issue between them. They were too good friends.

Thong drank himself into a stupor and they both fell asleep in each other's platonic arms. Butch loved Thong like a brother but only as a brother, despite Thong's subsequent occasional efforts. And there were no Thong girlfriends after that, until Kasey pulled him out of it.

Good ole Thong. Good ole Kasey.

She bustled back with a teakwood – of course – tray bearing two steaming gigantic cups and Butch took one. He sipped. "Wow." He winced at the major assault of sugar and spices.

"You need the calories," she said as she sipped her own. "So?"

"It was rough."

Butch regaled her with harrowing tales of basic training, the abuse and terror and physical exhaustion. What he didn't tell her: every night after lights out, lying in his cot wondering what the hell he had done, wondering whether Thong and Kasey and everyone else who'd told him he was crazy and that he would regret this, were right. Because, here it was, a mere few weeks later, and he did.

How much more so in four years?

"We called it the Butler snatch." He was winding down the stories. "Sergeant Butler would see something he didn't like, reach down, grab you by the lapels, and hoist you over his head, shaking you up and down like a rag doll. One-handed."

She was suitably horrified. "Omigod! He must have been huge!"

"Six-foot-five, about 120 pounds. Couldn't cast a shadow. He was just all gristle."

She laughed. "I thought they couldn't hurt you."

"Depends on what you mean by 'hurt.'"

"Omigod." She set the cup down. "So what now?"

He shrugged. "I have to go to Illinois in about two weeks for school. Weather school."

"Weather school?"

"Don't ask."

"Okay. So what are you doing in the interim?"

"Seeing people. You guys, for instance." He stretched and looked around. "So where's Thong?"

She stilled, became shroud and fog. The room did, too. "You don't know."

Not a question. And right then, Butch knew Thong was dead.

Car accident. Had to be. Something this sudden, this out of the blue, could be nothing else. Thong acquired another one of his mysteriously acquired cars and wound it up on some back road, maybe Springfield, and a rod snapped or a cable popped and he sailed through the air and wrapped around a tree and that was… fitting. Thong had been so much in love with cars that to die in one was a tribute.

"What kind of car?" he whispered softly.

"What?"

"What kind of car was it? An MG? Opel?"

She looked at him blankly, uncomprehending, then sat back. "Ah. No. Not a car wreck. Stomach cancer. About a week after you left. He had a stomach ache, went to the ER. He was dead two days later." The fog wrapped her. "I thought you knew."

"No." A pause. "I wasn't in contact with anyone while I was down there." For strategic reasons.

"Oh." The fog swirled. "I'm sorry you found out this way. Although… it's kinda funny."

Startled, he cocked his head in disbelief at her. But, yeah, actually, it was. He couldn't help a small smile. "The ultimate prank. Thong would have gotten a kick out of this."

"He would."

They sat in silence and fog for a moment. "I gotta go."

He left. And knew he would never go back.

Chapter 3

"Ki-YAAH!"

The kids on the floor screamed silly trebled *kiyaahs*! as they turned into downward cat block. Butch kept his face straight.

Must encourage, not ridicule.

A white-belt class of eight- to ten-year-olds dumped here by their parents to kill what was left of summer vacation was nothing but a mob, giggling and acting up, exasperating the red belt teaching them, one of Flirt's students named Wayne. Butch sympathized. He had half an urge to walk out there and thump a few of the little brats.

Not surprising that Wayne and the kids didn't give Butch the customary bow when he walked through the door. Butch passed his black-belt test about three months ago, and these kids were brand new. Wayne didn't know Butch that well, anyway. He rarely showed up here at Oak's studio, spending most of his time at Flirt's dojo in Glassboro. Besides, Butch was now unrecognizable: no hair and no identity, a faceless blob in uniform, some troop visiting from Ft. Dix or McGuire Air Base (for those sophisticated enough to recognize an Air Force uniform). Even more besides, the guy had his hands full. Must be checking off the teaching requirements before qualifying for his black-belt test. Butch had to teach a bunch of white belts for about a year before testing but they were older, some of them older than he was.

Butch grabbed a fold-up chair on the side, smirking in anticipation of Oak diddlybopping through the door saying, "How'ya doin', soldier," then a double-take then, "Oh man!" and throw his big arms around Butch in a murderous bear hug.

God, Butch loved Oak. God, Butch loved karate.

Ever since he saw Kato on *The Green Hornet*, Butch wanted to be a martial artist. As a 98-pound, bewildered, weakling nerd doofus spaz in an Alabama middle school filled with strapping peanut farmer kids who butchered hogs on weekends and knew everything about sex because they watched their cows (and probably their parents) do it, Butch was dead meat. The locals discovered within minutes of Butch's first appearance how naïve and squeamish he was and humiliated him with a gleeful mercilessness worthy of Torquemada. Every single day, as he extricated himself from a locker or pulled his underwear out of his crotch, he yearned to spin and punch and kick like Kato dispatching the Green Hornet's enemies.

So he'd bought a bunch of Bruce Tegner books and filled up one of Dad's old duffle bags with dirt and hung it from a tree in the backyard and beat on it, replicating Bruce Tegner's moves as best he could, and liked it. Really liked it. Downright loved it. He knew it wasn't real martial arts, was a poor collection of odd stuff that would get him killed if he tried it, that he was as far from being Kato as Maxwell Smart was from James Bond, but he kept at it anyway because he loved it, just loved it. And those silly Tegner moves actually paid off. A bully asshole said something about Cindy and Butch's head exploded and the world went red and next thing he knew, the kid's knee was in pieces, as was the kid's athletic future. Butch felt bad about that, but the kid shouldn't have said what he said about Cindy.

A lot of things shouldn't have been said about Cindy. Or done to her.

He stilled for a moment, lost in the rain at the back of the house and then shook himself when Wayne called "*Joom-bee!*" and the giggling kids pulled into a semblance of a line. "Okay, okay, calm down," Wayne sighed, "Let's take a break. You guys can play Pad Baseball."

"Pad Baseball!" The kids all crowed and formed a scrum around an equipment stand and Butch watched, curious, as the kids grabbed protective pads and then formed into a semblance of a baseball team. They played a game that looked like a combination of dodgeball and baseball, except the kids side-kicked the pads across the home plate and the batter kicked them back. He laughed.

"They love this game," Wayne, who'd wandered over to the spectator area, said to Butch.

"It looks like fun," he said.

"It is, and they get to use their techniques."

"Not exactly traditional karate training, is it?"

"No," Wayne agreed, smiling, "not exactly. Master Oak came up with it as a way to keep the kids' interest."

Of course. Another Oak innovation.

The guy was a karate genius on a par with Bruce Lee, keeping the traditions of the martial arts while incorporating techniques from other martial arts like judo, and even medical research. Oak had read articles in some phys-ed journal about stretching and then applied them to the warm-ups. Within a month, Butch's normally stiff legs reached another inch over his head. That his legs reached anywhere above his hip was thanks to Oak, who trained and drilled and yelled at Butch over the past four years: "Get your head outta your butt, white boy!"

God, Butch loved Oak.

He'd met him about a week after escaping up the side of an Alabama road with Cindy and Art, suitcases balanced on their heads to ward off the rain, the three of them terrified Dad's truck would crest the hill and catch them, catch them, and there'd be three more holes dug by the side of the pool, but they made it to the store without mishap. Well, without a Dad mishap. They'd called a taxi and paid their way to the Dothan Greyhound station with Dad's appropriated coin collection and a three-day bus ride later, their shocked Mom collected three shocked kids at the Burlington bus station and ensconced them in Grampop's house in the middle of Perkins. Butch had been walking the streets in a haze when he spotted Oak's dojo on a corner. He'd stolen up to the picture window and peered inside. A handsome coal-black man with a short beard and cropped Afro and decked out in full karate regalia, frayed black belt draped over his legs, sat in a chair next to the window and waved him in.

The place was packed, and Butch was the only white guy in there. Not entirely true: there were a couple scattered here and there alongside a couple of Spanish guys and a couple of Asians but the majority were black. And there was Butch in high-water jeans, black Converses and white socks, paisley button-down shirt, a short yellow jacket that was way too thin for this New Jersey winter, crew cut and tortoise-shell glasses, the poster boy for geeky whiteness. The handsome black guy sized him up, crinkled his eyes in a massive effort to contain a chortle, stuck out a hand and said, "I'm Oak. You interested?"

Boy, was he! As he shook the brick-breaking callous-layered Oak hand, the haze dissipated.

Wow, look at this place.

There was so much going on. One group of *ghi*-clad practitioners in one corner did forms, their *kias* ringing off the walls. Another group was gathered around a chalkboard etched with stick figures and arrows where a short pale-skinned black guy, sporting his own frayed black belt, beat on the board with a wooden staff while he explained a move. Another group threw each other onto mats while others hit bags. Marvelous. Oak led Butch to an out-of-the-way chair where he sat mesmerized for a couple of hours until the students lined up and did some group exercises and bowed out and walked by and said "How ya doin'? Wassup? Hey, man!" to Butch as they left. Oak came over, sized him up, crinkled knowing eyes and said, "When you starting?"

The next day.

Butch paid for those first lessons with his lunch money, with the money he made from cleaning up yards, and with what he could beg from Mom. About three months later, Oak closed the school in Perkins because of rent issues and moved it to Mt. Holyoke, so Butch hitchhiked or caught rides with the other Perkins students who had a car and/or license and were willing to pick him up. Every night after school, every weekend, every chance he got, he was there. He ate and breathed and slept karate 24/7. How he found time for other things like running the streets with Don and Dooby or working a warehouse job on McGuire airbase and going to school and doing homework was a mystery, but he did all those things, too.

Life was great.

Oak became the father he never knew or, more accurately, the father every kid was supposed to have. He was fun and understanding and kicked Butch's ass on a regular basis. "Man, that wasn't cool," Oak said whenever Butch did something very uncool, like tell a dirty joke to a bunch of girls. He taught Butch about music, exposing him to the better Marvin Gaye and

Parliament and the revolution will not be televised and talked about God as something other than an angry Being intent on punishing Butch for his, and other's sins, no, Butch, that's not it, He's a spirit of grace and welcoming. He taught Butch about meditation and chi and force and counterforce and all of it, all of it, applied to life and his war with Mom and Ridge and with himself. Sometimes when Butch was more lost than usual Oak would rescue him, letting him sleep on the floor of Oak's apartment-of-the-moment that belonged to Oak's girlfriend-of-the-moment. Butch worshiped him. Everything Oak said and did was holy writ. It was cult-like, except Butch knew Oak was human. Just a better human than most.

The dojo became one of his universes, the other club members its planets. On Friday nights after class, the brothers would grab him and stuff him into the middle of a car filled with about eighty other people and they would go cruising the black bars of south Jersey, shouting, "He's with us!" as they piled inside. Butch was a source of great amusement to the other patrons, and black girls would sit on his knees or try to teach him to dance, which was a lost cause. Fourteen years old and life was great.

But the karate itself ... well, not so great. Despite all that dedication and work and sweat, he never really prospered, never really excelled. He lacked the grace and elegance that defined the masters, like Oak and Al Dacascos and Tayari Casel. He looked awkward, was awkward, could not, no matter how much he practiced, execute the wonderful spinning and flying techniques that a lot of the others did with ease. Butch was workmanlike, holding his own, able to eke out a victory here and there against much better opponents with much flashier styles but he didn't have a wall of trophies and no one looked to him for inspiration. He was always there and could be counted on to teach a class when necessary or bring drinks when they were doing an all-day tournament and help out at tests or whatever. But lead?

No. Butch was a corporal. Not a captain.

And that was fine. He did better with someone to follow, to support, to work for. Like Oak. Because he had no confidence. None. No matter how well he did in school or at a job or occasionally at a tournament, Butch knew it was temporary, a fluke, that he was certain to disappoint everyone moments later. Unsure and fearful all the time, convinced that everything he did was wrong or stupid and that everyone looked at him with disbelief, their hands clapped across their foreheads. Everyone else knew things and did things correctly while he had not the slightest clue of what constituted acceptable behavior anywhere, anytime. Left on his own, he was rudderless and confused and guilty, oh so guilty.

If it weren't for him, Mom would be happy. If it weren't for him, Dad would be honorable. Cindy would be whole. There would be no graves beside pools.

He shuddered.

"So, are you interested?"

Butch blinked. "Hmm?"

Wayne was standing before him and made an impatient gesture. "In lessons. For you, or for your children?"

Butch smiled. "Wayne, it's me. Butch."

Wayne furrowed a brow then an entire face in astonishment. "Whoa! Butch! Sensei!" and he bowed several times. "I didn't recognize you! Hey, everyone!" He whirled to the kids going crazy on the floor. "It's Sensei Deats!"

The kids froze and looked at each other in complete confusion because not one of them knew who this Deats character was but they heard the word "Sensei" and conditioning kicked in and they all bowed and then went right back to the game. Butch laughed.

Wayne looked him up and down. "Wow, they really did you up."

Butch made an exaggerated head rub. "That they did. So how did you end up with this class?"

Wayne shrugged. "Got laid off. They're closing the plant."

"Oh, man." Butch was instantly sympathetic. "I'm sorry to hear that. You okay?"

Another shrug. "Yeah. Looking for another, but it ain't the only plant closing." He turned to the floor and settled a rising dispute, then turned back. "May have to join the Army myself."

"Don't."

"What, is it that bad?"

Butch let out a breath. "You know, I don't even really know? All I've done is basic, which was rough, and they cheated me out of the job I wanted, so if you want to do this, make sure you have a guaranteed slot before you go."

"What job?"

"I was trying for X-Ray, but I ended up in weather."

"Weather?" Wayne snorted. "You mean like on TV?"

"I hope."

Wayne snickered and excused himself because some parents came in to fetch offspring and Wayne pulled the kids off the game. He ran them through a couple of forms and some ending exercises for the parents' approval and dismissed the class. Parents mingled and argued with offspring and a few of the cuter mothers gave Butch an appraising glance and a tiny smile and Butch thought maybe there was some utility to the uniform, after all. Wayne flopped in the chair next to him as the last of the cute women walked a kid squalling for ice cream out of the door.

"Man," Butch summarized.

"You got that right." Wayne fanned himself with a magazine. "Kids are a handful."

"Bet the moms are, too."

Wayne laughed. "Now, now." He wagged a cautionary finger. "Don't mess with the customers."

"Yeah." How many of those cute moms had ended up Oak's honey of the week? Cautionary tale. "So when are you testing for *chodan*?"

"Maybe the end of fall. I've still got a couple of forms to do, and I gotta get the testing fee together—"

"Whoa." Butch held up a hand. "What testing fee?"

Wayne stared at him. "Oh, that's right, all these changes happened after you left."

"What changes?"

"Well, testing fees for one. Hundred dollars for black belt."

Floored, Butch said, "What? When did that start?"

"After you made it. Of course." Sarcasm not even hidden there.

Butch threw up pleading hands. "Well, I didn't have anything to do with any testing fees! Why did Oak ... are we broke or something?"

"You mean, you don't know?"

"No! This is the first I've heard of it!"

Dramatic pause, and a look of sudden sympathy on Wayne's face. "Not the fees, about Oak."

Dread flooded Butch. Oh no, not another Thong.

"Oak is gone, man. They threw him out."

Dread to utter confusion at the speed of light and Butch gaped at Wayne.

"Oh yeah." Wayne nodded more to himself. "I guess all this happened after you left. They had a meeting and stripped Oak of his position."

From confusion to rage even faster. "Who did?"

"Flirt. Jimmy John, Huck, Boogie Man, the other black belts."

His friends, his pals, his brothers. "They can't do that."

"They did."

"But… they can't! They just can't! This is Oak's school!"

"Not anymore. It's Flirt's. He's realigned with Tang soo Do. Even changed the patch." He slapped the bare side of his ghi. "I haven't put the new one on, yet."

"So what's Oak doing about it?"

"Oak's gone, man." Wayne's tone indicated a different meaning.

"What are you talking about?"

"He left. Went to New England. That's why they voted."

"What??" It wasn't a question.

"Yeah. His girlfriend, what's her name, Genevieve?" Wayne frowned because it was difficult keeping up with Oak's girlfriends. "Yeah, well, she was pregnant or something and went home. Oak went with her."

Pregnant girlfriend. Déjà vu all over again.

"Oh, man." Butch felt very much like he'd just gone three rounds with Chuck Norris. "Is he coming back?"

Wayne shrugged.

"Oh, man."

"Yeah. So are you, like, here? Because a bunch of us aren't happy about this and we'd follow you if you wanted to start another school."

Wayne hovered, expectation on his face. Butch offered helpless hands. "I can't. I have to do this Air Force thing. I have to go to friggin' Illinois. For four friggin' years. I'd love to, love to …" His voice trailed as he watched another opportunity slip away. "I can't."

He looked at Wayne, the disappointment rising in both of them, then stood and walked out because that's it.

That's it.

He looked back at the school, his image reflected in the

windows as it did the first time he stood at the window in Perkins, but it wasn't him looking back. It was someone else. He was so different now. Everything was.

Everything.

Chapter 4

Butch scoped the apartment parking lot three times before he was convinced no purple El Camino idled there. No purple El Camino, or any other car for that matter, in the Archways' circular driveway across the street, either.

Too bad. Would have been nice to scrutinize the apartments from the safety of Mother Archway's kitchen window before making a move. So let's make a move. After all, you're now an Air Force trained killer.

On the fourth pass, Butch whipped into the parking lot and screeched a U-ey around the back to see if anyone followed him in, but no. No one came out of the apartments to shoot at him for waking them up before the noontime beer and/or heroin call, so he eased back up the lot until he was near his place. Mom's place. Cindy's place, actually, since she was the last one standing. He grabbed a parking spot and scurried over, quickly unlocked the door and slammed it behind him.

Whew. Safe.

But, then again, maybe not.

If there was one thing movies like *The Godfather* and *The Friends of Eddie Coyle* taught Butch, it's that going home is a really stupid idea. Home is the first place the Mafia looks. Pee Sea was hardly Mafia, but he watched the same movies and could be sitting up there right now, pistol in one hand, machete in the other. Butch held his breath for a couple of days listening, but nothing.

No one's here but me. I hope.

He stole up the stairs prepared to jump the landing and fly out of the door should Pee suddenly loom. One advantage of his recent basic training, he was in good enough shape to pull that off.

He reached the stairwell top and peeked over the edge, like that Kilroy Was Here drawing, anxiously peering around the living room for any errant thugs but it was empty –

"Whew!"

– and he flipped around the banister and sank into the couch backed against the stairwell, which placed his head in the ideal position for lopping from behind. He shifted out of it and sat in the plush chair opposite, but that left him vulnerable to a lopping from the direction of the bedroom, so he got up and grabbed a kitchen chair and sat at the table. No one can get him from behind now, unless they're hiding in the refrigerator. He took in a deep breath and let it out slowly.

Home sweet home.

The walls were bare whitewashed sheetrock, the standard look of cheap underprivileged housing throughout New Jersey, if not the world. No homey pictures hung here and there because this was a temporary refuge for shell-shocked children who no longer got along with grandparents intolerant of new-fangled ideas like staying up past 8:00 p.m. and running the streets with ne'er-do-wells and maybe it was best we find our own place while Mom got her act together and built up enough savings from her job and alimony to buy a house. That was four years ago and referenced house had never materialized; at least, one that Mom owned and in which Butch was welcome. As a result, the apartment still held an air of transition, more storage unit than home.

Butch hadn't actually lived here for about a year and a half: after high school, he'd gone to San Francisco, returning about six months later when SF didn't turn out very well. Moving back into this apartment put him under Ridge's thumb and well, no, so he'd bunked with Thong and Kasey in a two-room addition on the back of a gas station at the end of Lakehurst Road. Fun times that quickly wore thin because it is one thing to hang out together when everyone still lives with parents but quite another living cheek-to-jowl in the same cramped quarters. He'd graciously bowed out and shared an apartment with April in Mt. Holyoke until that didn't turn out very well, either. And now he was in the Air Farce. Funny how things not turning out well led to major changes in location. And circumstance.

The couch and the chair were Grampop cast-offs. The only things in here owned by a resident were the 13-inch Philco on a Grampop cast-off stand, and an FM radio with two separate speakers on the shelf beneath it. Mom bought the TV; Butch bought the radio and spent more time with it than the boob tube. MMR then YSP, dude, every day and night. He supposed he should take the radio with him to Illinois before it ended up in one of Ridge's kids' houses or pawned by a Cindy idiot-boyfriend-of-the-moment. Not Nova SS-owning Piney idiot boyfriend; he'd disappeared ages ago into the netherworld of Cindy ex-boyfriends and Butch had no idea what addict she was dating now. He wondered how he could get the radio to Illinois. Maybe he could talk Mom into letting him use the Pontiac for the trip out. And for the next ten years.

If he hadn't left his duffel bag at Ridge's ...

Dammit.

The kitchen table was a 60s Formica-and-chrome disaster that Mom snagged from the side of a road one day, along with four mismatched, torn-plastic upholstered chairs in varying shades of green acquired in the same manner. The mismatched dishes and cups and pots and pans scattered here and there on the shelves that passed for cabinets came from rummage sales and sympathetic cousins and aunts and uncles, of which there were myriad in Perkins. The preponderance of evidence indicated he was poor, but Butch didn't feel poor. He'd always had some cash in his pocket because he always had a source of income, usually a job. Some more dangerous than others.

Nervous glance around.

An "Al's at Columbus Market!" pizza box sat on the counter next to the sink and Butch got up, hope springing eternal. Best pizza on the East Coast and he eagerly opened it but no luck, only a couple of crusts that, judging by their color and hardness, were a couple of days old. He opened the refrigerator: half a loaf of Wonder Bread, an almost empty jar of Welch's Grape Jam, an almost empty carton of milk, an almost full bottle of Take-A-Boost (yech), and half a bag of moldy cheesesteak buns.

Geez, Cindy, don't you ever shop?

In the freezer, though, was a carton of Ellio's Pizza, the breakfast-lunch-and-dinner of poor abandoned New Jersey orphans. Butch pulled out two planks and turned on the oven.

Welcome home, son.

He poured a glass of water and sat back at the table waiting for the oven to heat up. It's like he never left. Alone in the apartment again, the only hint that others lived here a two-day-old pizza box and a periodically stocked freezer. It could be an Edgar Allen Poe story: the prisoner never sees his keepers, never sees the other inmates. Mom always made it a point to drop the Ellio's off at times she was assured no one was here, like Saturday nights or during school hours. Butch and Cindy were usually gone from Friday at about three until about sunrise Monday morning, when both stopped by long enough for a shower and clothes change and then Butch off to school because he loved school with its intertwining universes and Cindy back out the door before Mom showed up and caught her with idiot-boyfriend-of-the-moment. Art was the random factor, sporadically in the apartment between visits to Alabama; but he was Mom's favorite so her running into him was not a problem. Occasionally Mom miscalculated and walked in when Butch or Cindy or both were home and all of them would be astonished then flustered, underscored by Mom-questions on how school was going and were they brushing their teeth and getting a good night's sleep, while Butch and/or Cindy stared at her like an invading alien. She bustled out as quickly as she showed up, promising to spend more time with them.

Which she never did, because Butch and Cindy carried the reminders.

Of failure, of horror, of despair, but mostly of failure. She could not keep her husband in her bed. Butch doubted any woman could keep Dad in her bed but Mom lost that battle early on, the result being Butch. Butch once figured out gestation periods and determined that Dad impregnated Butch's real mother, some German housemaid, within a week or two of Cindy's birth, both events occurring on opposite sides of the world, Mom delivering in New Jersey under the care of her parents while Dad, under the care of the US Army, delivered in Germany. Apparently, Dad, upon hearing the news of a second daughter, decided to acquire a first son through any means, illicit or otherwise. You'd think, though, given his predilections, he'd delight in a second daughter's arrival, like a jackal over a lion's leavings.

So Butch was a revenge fuck: take that, woman, for not giving me a son. And Dad got a son. Of course, any time someone messes with the rules of the cosmos, the irony police show up and Art came along a little more than a year later, the first actual son of Dad and Mom. It was one of those rare times that Dad had kids *within* marriage and, naturally, all the attention went to the legit. Butch was left in the cold, peering in through fogged-over windows at the Thanksgiving feast inside.

Okay, it hadn't been that bad but Butch felt a distinct separation from Mom, a lone tree in winter, a spiritual distance the entire time they were in Oklahoma and Alabama, and a physical distance, courtesy of Ridge, ever since moving here. Not that he blamed her.

Butch did not think he was the best of kids. Over the past year or so, he'd had several opportunities to evaluate his behavior and it wasn't pretty. As a littler kid, he'd been obtuse and nerdy and spazzy, a crybaby, selfish, cowardly. Any little cut or bruise propelled him screaming back into the house for Mom to make it all better. He didn't want cupcakes for his fourth birthday and cried when she served them. He threw rocks at cars. He picked his nose. He bounced on the couch and turned the TV way too loud and cried when cartoons ended and threw up his okra and drove her crazy.

Add that he was a kid too far, a kid she shouldn't have to suffer. Dealing with her own kids was bad enough because Dale was defiant and Cindy was wild, but this kid, this changeling left on her doorstep, was a lash, a knife cut, a reminder that she could not keep her husband out of other women's beds. No wonder she lavished Art with all the attention and love that her two other kids and intruder refused to let her express. No wonder Butch hated Art: the little dweeb got the devotion rightly belonging to him, no matter how difficult a kid Butch was. But Mom had no real obligation to him, and he stood on the far shore and watched her slip farther into misty distances until Ridge loomed out of the fog, picked her up and spirited her permanently away.

The summer after running from Alabama, they were at one of Mom's innumerable cousins' houses somewhere over in Woodlane for a barbecue. Butch was wary, uncommunicative, maladjusted to the hardcore New Jersey Yankee Piney culture which was *de rigueur* among Mom's family. Both children of the cousin throwing the party (which meant they were Butch's cousins of some sort) regarded him as some invading alien and spent the party yakking and yukking it up with Cindy and two of Ridge's sons while Butch wandered about. Ridge's sons were there because Ridge was a friend of the cousin and had been invited.

Gee, wonder why?

Cindy was right in there yukking and yakking and downright flirting with the elder of Ridge's sons and Butch stared at her in horror because –

Cindy, do you not remember what happened a mere six months ago?

He'd walked around the corner of the house to get away from the yuk/yak/flirt fest to find Mom and Ridge sitting on the porch holding hands and smiling at each other and Butch stared in horror because –

Mom, do you not remember what happened? A mere six months ago?

Obviously, the cousins had decided that Mom needed a man in her life after fleeing the man in her life who made all their lives a nightmare a mere six months ago. Six months after the barbecue, Ridge and Mom married and they all moved in together as one big happy family of steps, the Brady Bunch… well, no.

Ridge had, early on, expressed in various ways his distaste for Mom's kids, like criticizing Butch's hair and Cindy's boyfriends and Art dropping out of school and Mom thought it a good idea for 'you kids' to stay in the temporary apartment because Ridge's four-bedroom-three-bath-two-car-garage-2500-square-foot house was 'too small for all of us'.

So us kids did.

Mom supplied weekly Ellio's. Cindy supplied idiot boyfriends. Art bounced between Alabama and the apartment and friends' houses in Braun's Mills. Butch traveled his various universes. And Mom was simply gone.

Not that he blamed her.

Ridge was a nightmare: controlling, bullying, disapproving, everything for his kids and none for Mom's, but he was a step up from Dad. She had a choice: the reminders, or the incrementally better.

We fade, we fade.

Butch threw the planks into the oven and headed to his bedroom. Still his. No one else in their right mind would use it. He stepped to the middle and ah, the savor of unwashed sheets, unscrubbed floors, years-old dirty clothes piled up in a corner…

"Hello, Murphy," Butch greeted the pile, "Hungry? Got Ellio's cooking."

Murphy said nothing.

Thong had christened the clothes pile 'Murphy' early in its existence and periodically warned Butch about its carnivorous tendencies, usually after the second or third joint or the third or fourth bottle of Ripple and the millionth ward of Thong's advances and they'd both get to giggling and try to entice Murphy to make a leap at them. After the fourth joint, Butch swore it did.

If Murphy, or these walls, could talk.

Unlike the living room, Butch plastered every square inch of these walls with teenage culture. Right over his cot – yes, a cot, not a bed, loaned by some other cousin – was the Santana *Abraxas* poster; next to it, the *Stoned Agin* poster, *Lost Horizon*, *Frodo Lives!!,* all the hippie psychedelia he could find. No Farrah Fawcett, no Linda Ronstadt, no politics, just black-light heaven and incense and a hash pipe and an album on the turntable.

The albums were all gone; he'd sold them before going off to Lacklaaaand Air Force base, including all his Firesign Theater ("Deputy Dan has no friends") because he didn't want them and his Doors and Big Brother and the Holding Company ending up in whatever house of Cindy's whatever idiot Piney-boyfriend-of-the-moment. The turntable was still there, a fold-down model they'd had in Alabama and that Dad brought up the summer after they'd escaped (oddly enough, a week after the Mom-meets-Ridge party), dragging his latest wife along with him to fetch Art. Butch hid in the woods behind the apartments until Dad left, hoping it was the last time he'd ever see him. Which it wasn't. Saw him just yesterday, in fact, when the bastard showed up, uninvited, to Butch's basic training graduation.

What fun that had been.

Butch was politely pushing through the crowd of parents and siblings and others connected to this latest cadre of newly minted Younited States Aero Farce Airmen, intent on getting to his bunk so he could turn in all the linens and get the hell out of Dodge when "Hello, boy!" boomed out, freezing him in place. Dad materialized like some assassin in the middle of the bazaar, all jovial and happy and smiling and pumped Butch's hand like they were father and son or something.

"The Aiiiiir Force! Ha!" Dad'd bellowed, "You couldn't pick a real service, like the Army?"

Wife number two after Mom, if Butch was counting right, stood behind Dad all beaming and big-haired and Southern because a boy in the military is sumpin' right proud, right proud. She had a couple of little blonde and cute girls, maybe ten or eleven years old each, clinging to her, and Butch was terrified.

"What are you doing here?"

"What am I doing here?" Dad looked downright surprised. "Came to see you graduate! Wacha think?"

"How did you even know?"

"Art told me. Good someone did."

He eyed Butch, the ungrateful son who neglects his poor, loving father, putting on a wounded look that hid something so much worse. Butch spun about and fled into the crowd, quickly becoming one more bald, blue-garbed zombie among hundreds and slipped out the back, Jack, without further incident.

That was the second time he'd seen Dad since hiding in the woods behind the apartment. The first was during his return trip from San Francisco. For reasons he still didn't understand, he'd routed through Dothan and called Dad from the airport to come get him, all the while debating whether he should simply turn around and get on the next thing smoking.

What was he doing here? Why did he come back here? Didn't he know that Dad was the Beast?

The Beast showed up about an hour later with wife number one after Mom (was she the same one who came with Dad to fetch Art? Who knows) in tow and Butch sat in the back with the wife's two blonde daughters a little younger than him, ice engulfing his spine.

Funny how Dad sought wives with blonde daughters, wasn't it?

The wife, whatever her name, was sugary and big-haired and Southern and kept asking about the flight and commenting on how skinny he was and his long hair and his hippie overalls in a joking manner and the girls came to his defense because long hair and overalls were the rage, doncha know, and here was this exotic creature, a former denizen of the hippie kingdom and oh, Mom! All the time, Butch saw Dad's vulture eyes on the girls. He wondered when the girls would find themselves standing behind a pool at midnight with shovels.

Dad was staying at the wife's house, a nice place in Enterprise, because Dad had abandoned his house but hadn't sold it yet because that meant strangers would be poking around and things needed to settle, become obscure, first. As soon as they got to the wife's house, Butch refused numerous offers for cornbread and divinity and said to Dad, "Mind if I borrow your truck?" and took the keys off the cute little hillbilly gap-toothed wooden key holder hanging near the refrigerator.

"What for?" Dad, the volcano rising.

"See some friends." And Butch was out of the door and down the driveway before the volcano could explode, wife's "But we're going to eat!" in his ear and Dad in the side-view mirror, the devil watching him leave. Butch honestly did not know what he would have done if Dad had said no to the truck. Butch was bigger now, stronger, karate-trained and angrier, but it was a coin flip whether he would have killed Dad or just collapsed in terror.

Good thing Dad did nothing. Good thing.

He got to the house about sunset, pulling up the weed-covered driveway, stunned how everything had gone to hell. Weed-covered driveway, for one. Weed-covered everything. Kudzu crept up the sides of the house and laundry shed, the garage had collapsed, the lawns were jungles. It looked like a place abandoned for decades, haunted and brooding.

Haunted.

He did not get out of the truck. He stared at where the pool used to be. It could even still be there but the overgrowth masked it. It was undisturbed. No one had been back there. Nothing had come out.

Looked like everything was settling nicely.

He drove to Yoman, stunned that the school was closed; not for Christmas vacation or AEA holidays, but permanently closed, surrounded by a chain-link fence with a big warning sign, unreadable in the failing light, set in the middle of the padlocked gate. "What happened?"

"Ain't enough kids," said the fat one-eyed unshaven dirty-shirt yokel who took Butch's money for gassing the truck at Atco's Store a block away. "All goin' to Enterprise now. Don't I know you?"

No, you don't. Not anymore.

Butch drove off, heading east and, a few moments later, pulled up to a white one-story farmhouse fronting a barbed-wire electric fence and several sheds, easing his way between two or three pickup trucks scattered across the drive. Some moppet opened the door as he mounted the concrete steps. "Is Becca here?"

The round-eyed and round-headed moppet watched him from behind a blanket held in front of her face and, without moving her head, yelled, "Becca! Visitor!"

Judging by this, Butch concluded the moppet was one of Becca's three or four hundred siblings, a mere baby when Butch made his ignominious escape to New Jersey, or added shortly after. Over the time Butch lived here, Becca's parents produced their own baseball, basketball, and hockey teams, a new brother or sister appearing every six weeks or so, like her Mom was a rabbit or something.

"What's your name?" he asked.

The moppet said nothing, merely hid behind the blanket and regarded him.

"Do you have a name?"

"Yes, she does," Becca, irritated and suspicious, suddenly appeared behind the moppet. "Trish, go on back now." The moppet disappeared. "Can I help you?"

Hep yew. Ah, right there, the southern smothering of the English language that Butch found so endearing. What's not so endearing, the baby on Becca's hip and the obvious extra weight she now carried.

Oh no, Becca, not you, too.

She stood there, eyebrows raised and challenging and stormy, and he remembered a hot night some five years ago, the two of them sitting on her back porch with the stars and the locusts and the fireflies and talking about the world and the future and Butch said he was going to join NASA and she kissed him.

"Becca."

She furrowed a brow. Then it cleared. "Butch!"

Not said in delight but sheer consternation, sheer confusion as her jaw dropped and she once- and twice-overed him. "Oh my God! Oh my God!"

Butch flourished hands down his front. "I admit to a couple of changes."

"A couple of… oh my God! Your hair! Your clothes! Come in! Come in!"

With an adroitness of movement considering baby and the physicality involved, she hip-pushed the door open and he entered and was back in the same narrow little front room as five years ago, with the overstuffed couch and chair and table all close together and moppets of each sex running here and there. In moments, he was pushed back onto the couch with a glass of too-sweet tea in his hands, Becca sitting opposite, baby still on hip, various moppets popping in and out and sitting next to him, rotating turns with each another.

"All y'all just go!" she yelled at the moppets and there was a scrambling akin to a buffalo stampede as the herd ran for the various exits. She kept the baby. "Oh my God," she said, shaking her head at him.

"Yep. Oh my God."

Butch scrutinized her. Same pale blue eyes and brownish hair, no longer in the beehive style of their youth but falling down around her shoulders, thin line of lips and the pert little nose but no longer the pert little body. He raised an eyebrow at the baby.

"Oh!" She glanced at the kid. "Ain't mine. 'Though I wish it was," and she gave him a big wink.

Hmm. Does that mean she likes kids, or likes sex? File for later. "Whose is it?"

"My sister's."

Butch could have asked which sister but, even if she answered, he'd have no idea. Becca was the oldest so, even if the kid belonged to the very next sister, she'd be a girl younger than Butch. Young girls getting pregnant before they graduate seemed to be a theme 'round hyeah.

At least she didn't end up behind a pool.

He shuddered.

"So my, my, look at you!" Still astonished by his distinctly non-peanut farmer look. "Where have you been all this time?"

"San Francisco."

He might as well have said 'Mars.' "San Fran… really?" Thoroughly astonished. "Well, what in the world for?"

He shrugged. "Needed a break. My sister was out there, so I went to live with her."

"Cindy is living in San Francisco?"

"No, my other sister. Dale. You never knew her." Neither did he, for that matter. "She moved out there before we moved here."

In 1965, the summer of murder.

Frank's murder.

"So what'd you do out there?"

He took in a deep breath and thought.

What did I do?

Lived a quasi-hippie lifestyle, smoked dope, dropped acid, sat on the beach tripping, took the trolley to a job in the middle of Haight Ashbury (which lost its peace and love years before and was now Charlie Manson writ large) sweeping up and straightening out a halfway house for psychopaths, the inmates bumming cigarettes off him, even though he didn't smoke – cigarettes, that is – the last bit of their meds wearing off which meant they would start roaming the streets screaming and throwing things and chasing women with evil intent.

The things he saw there.

He got off at 3:00 a.m. and went to the bus stop and stood in the shadows watching the show: a guy with a rainbow Afro and a diaper and nothing else walking down the middle of the street with a parade of nubiles wearing sheets and nothing else following single file behind him. Rainbow would, periodically, turn around and scream something unintelligible at the girls, who didn't flinch. Another time, six huge black guys in a Cadillac, all wearing brown leather jackets and kepis and sunglasses, this time of night, cruised up and down the street glaring at everybody. Then the bus came and Butch rode back to Dale's place in the company of tubercular and drooling winos.

Dale had gone full-bore hippie. She'd gotten rid of her first husband, a cool black guy running a security business, trading him for a Latino then a Korean, kids with each, so that the house was a junior UN. Butch took the kids to the beach and taught them karate, which was a mistake because they would gang up on him whenever the mood took them. Dale fully defended their behavior in some Montessori-type language about them finding their way, but Butch would deck a couple of them and send the whole crew running off crying and, after about six months of this, Butch had had enough of peace and love and used his latest paycheck to buy a ticket back to Philly, via Dothan.

"Nothing."

She blinked, a cursory glance at his current getup putting the lie to that. "So, what happened?"

"Needed another break."

She was confused. "No, I don't mean there, I mean here."

His shields went up. "What are you talking about?"

"Well." She almost lost the baby making a helpless gesture. "You just… disappeared."

Butch sat back.

He had, hadn't he?

They had, the entire Deats family, poof, gone, in one day, into thin air. No explanations, no further contact. His manifesting on her porch a few minutes ago was the first indication to anyone in Yoman that they were still alive, still on this planet and not on the moon being probed by aliens.

"I swear," she said, "I thought y'all got kidnapped by aliens or something."

Twilight Zone music filled Butch's head.

"You and Cindy and your brother were just gone. We got no letters, nothing. Your Dad said y'all had gone to New Jersey."

Butch held up a hand. "Wait. You spoke to my Dad?"

"Yes." She fussed with the baby. "At the wedding."

"What wedding?"

"To his wife."

Butch took a moment to process that. "The woman he's married to now?"

"Yes. She's a cousin and—"

"Wait." Another hand up. "You mean, you and I are now related. By marriage?"

"Yes!" she laughed. "Now we're kissing cousins!"

Out the door in seconds.

"Where you going?" Astonished, she chased him to the driveway and stood, baby on astonished hip, watching as he screeched back down the road.

Kissing cousins, Becca? Seen this movie.

He drove back to the wife's house and gathered his things. Dad was not there. "The truck will be at the airport, key under the mat," he said to the wife as he started it.

She and her daughters stood next to the driver's side window, arms crossed, frowning. "Okay," she said. No "Where you going?" "Why don't you stay?" "What's wrong?"

He pointed at her girls. "Be careful," he said as he backed up.

She only nodded. She already knew.

He slept in the parking lot and got on the first plane heading in the general direction of Philadelphia. The wife divorced Dad a month later.

"Should never have married him," Frank said.

Butch spun about. Frank sat on a short bookcase under the window. "What are you doing here?"

Frank shrugged. He looked around, curious. "This was your room?"

"Yes."

"Same size as mine," he said, his face cracking like an eggshell.

Butch opened his eyes. Apparently, at some point, he'd lain down on the cot. Cautiously, he felt his face but it was intact and he swung his legs down and looked around, but the room was empty.

And smoky.

"Oh, crap!" he yelled. Leaping to his feet, he rushed the kitchen, swiping at the pizza smoke roiling in his way. He yanked open the oven door, enveloped in a fog of burning Ellio's.

"Ouch! Ouch! Ouch!" he yelled as he grabbed the edge of the foil and flung the planks into the sink. He doused them with water from the faucet and then threw all the windows in the apartment open, ending up on the balcony and fanning the smoke away. Any second now, the fire department would come screaming into the parking lot ... but, other than the normal traffic speeding by, nothing. No distant sirens, no people pouring out from the surrounding apartments screaming, "Fire! Fire!" It was quiet.

Butch gazed across the street. Mother Archway's Bel Air sat in the circular driveway.

Might as well go say "hi" while the apartment aired.

Chapter 5

"Hi!" Butch called out as he opened the kitchen door. The Archways never locked it.

"Hello!" A pleasant contralto response from the living room and Butch headed that way. The kitchen was a dark room so narrow all the appliances were lined up on one side, otherwise no one'd ever get through, ending in three too-thickly carpeted steps leading up to the living room, a hazardous ascent and Butch was careful. He'd lost count the number of times he'd fallen flat on his face here. 'Course, he'd usually been drunk.

Mother Archway was sitting in an overstuffed rocking chair at the far end of the room, blinking at him. Even with her old-lady glasses she was myopic, and Butch figured at this distance he looked like a sheriff's deputy.

"Ma'am? You'll have to come with us," Butch said in a lower register, authority-toned voice.

Startled, Mother Archway snapped back in her chair. "What?"

"Contributing to the delinquency of minors, ma'am," he said and then couldn't help it, started laughing.

"Oh! You!" She pushed her elephantine bulk out of the chair, her smock dress flapping around her and threatening to trip her up and Butch braced. She grabbed him with a giant hug so powerful she almost lifted him off the ground. "Butch!"

"Hi, Mother Archway!" Butch gasped as she squeezed his lungs flat.

"You had me going there for a moment." She wagged a finger in his face as she threw him onto the couch, the thirty or forty pillows on top avalanching down Butch's shoulders and onto his lap. "What kind of uniform is that?"

"Air Force," he said as he dug his way out.

"Well, it looks like a prison guard's," she said and shook a pleased head. "You wait here while I get some tea." She trundled off, maneuvering the steps and rolled out of sight.

Butch sat back, happy. He'd seamlessly entered another of his universes, one still intact, thank God, while pulling off a good joke on someone who appreciated a good joke. He looked around. Man, he loved this place. Everything was overdone. Far more pictures than any self-respecting house should endure loomed everywhere, all of them giant framed oils of mountains and snows, the kind of gilt and wood monstrosities expected of fifteenth-century merchants. Giants had designed the couch and its accompanying five or six chairs to encompass their bulk, the beige carpet, which must be at least six inches deep, absorbing the shock. The coffee tables shared the fifteenth-century motif, all elaborately carved and overworked with at least two decks and each holding stacks and stacks of magazines, ranging from *National Geographic* to some firefighting journals that Father Archway studied as if they were religious texts. The TV was just short of being a movie screen, encased in cabinetry as complicated as the tables. Butch grinned.

Home again, home again, jiggity jog.

He was leafing through one of the firefighting journals when Mother Archway lurched back, a giant steaming cup in each ham-hock fist and a plate of Fig Newtons balanced across the top of them. Adroitly, she laid everything on the table and dropped on the couch next to him, slamming his leg with one of the ham hocks so hard it almost tipped him upright.

"I am so glad you made it!" she said and pinched his cheek, almost ripping off his face.

"Ow," he said, pleasantly, and took a Newton. "I'm glad, too."

She beamed, saying, "My, my," over and over, exclaiming over his hair and uniform and skinniness in the manner of all mothers (except his own) until Butch had finished about half his tea. "So how was it?"

"Good," he said, sipping a bit more.

She slammed his leg again, chortling. "I don't mean the tea, funny guy. The Air Force!"

"*Ow*," he repeated then told her about basic training, embellishing a bit because Father Archway never did service, his firefighting exempting him, so she didn't have anything to compare. Her "My my's" became "Oh my!" on a few occasions as he described the Butler snatch and exaggerated the mile-and-a-half runs into death marches, earning a few *tsks* along the way.

"So when did you get back?" she asked as she munched a Newton.

"This morning."

"And I'm one of your first stops. Isn't that nice?"

Butch let that fiction stand. "So what's everybody else doing?"

"Well, Pop is at the firehouse. You should go by and say hello. He'd love to see you in that uniform. Elaine is at Seaside, one last summer fling before school starts. You know she's going to Stockton State?"

"I didn't. She was still waiting to hear when I left."

"Well, wasn't her first choice but she got in, for child psychology."

Appropriate, given all the crazy things that happened in Elaine's basement, unknown to her parents. He hoped.

"That's nice. Sorry about missing her graduation."

She waved that away. "You were a little busy."

Certainly was. About the time Elaine was walking across the Perkins High football field, gown flapping in the wind, Butch was flapping in the wind from the top rail of some torture device on the Laaackland obstacle course. "There's a couple of guys from my class at Stockton if she wants the names."

"Oh, I think she'll be fine."

"Sure." He paused. "I heard about Thong."

"Oh, oh," and she was mournful. "I'm so sorry about all that. He was special." He was. Thong was one of the original Archway orphans.

Butch and Thong became pals here. Previously Thong'd been merely one of hundreds of familiar faces up and down the school hallways, a grade ahead and they didn't share any classes and didn't know each other's names until, sitting next to each other in the back of the room during the first meeting of newly minted journalists for the school paper, they discovered a mutual delight in bedeviling Mr. Years, the paper's advisor. The next evening

Butch trundled down the Archway's basement steps and found Thong sprawled there, suffering from the first of several periodic exiles imposed by his CIA parents for some violation or another (although Butch suspected mission requirements necessitated Thong's absence).

Kismet.

How Thong ended up in Perkins all the way over from Country Lakes, Butch never figured, but it probably had to do with Elaine Archway, a freshman who felt it her duty to adopt all the Perkins Township High School orphans, especially those living in the apartments across the street. That's how Butch ended up there; Elaine recruited him mere moments after Mom moved them in.

Serendipity.

The Archway universe consisted mostly of the wounded from the apartments: Butch, Pepsi, Pepsi's brother C-Note, Elway, and Truck. Add Thong and Elaine and various girlfriends (and boyfriends) of one or the other, and the basement turned into a rather rollicking hideaway. Just about every Friday night the universe formed as the ever-changing cast of Perkins orphans and loners gathered down there, flipped on a black light, piled their various albums next to the console and rocked out, laughing and grabassing as Father and Mother Archway made periodic appearances, bringing sandwiches and chips and fairly good advice, studiously ignoring the various bottles of MD 20/20 and Boone's Farm surreptitiously placed here and there. No drugs. Father would not stand for it and they all respected him too much. So, outside, in the woods that bordered Rancocas Creek.

It went like that for most of high school, Butch circulating between the Lakes and Don-and-Dooby's and Thong's (during periods of reconciliation with the CIA agents) and the Archways. Sometimes he hit all these places in a single night, putting three to four hundred miles on Buggy before dawn. Even after the seismic break of his graduation and subsequent West Coast odyssey, he resumed his place in the basement with pretty much the same people. No one wanted the parties to end. They were too good.

Like New Year's Eve, the most memorable party of all. Memorable?

Infamous.

It was the catalyst of so many things that had gone so wrong, a black hole opening in the middle of the universe, at first innocuous and ignored but growing and growing and finally swallowing all. Two black holes, actually, with two overlapping event horizons: Jape met Truck. Butch met April. And existence ended.

Butch had returned from San Francisco about two weeks prior and was in the apartment tallying his failures when Elaine knocked on the door and gave him a big hug and asked how long he'd been back and why for goodness' sake was he hiding up here? Well, Elaine, trying to keep everybody from knowing what a loser I am I guess and she tutted and said, "New Year's Eve party" and everyone was going to be there and they'd be happy to see you again.

"Yeah? Who's everyone?"

Thong and Kasey, the remaining orphans, and a few outliers, including Garfield Jape. "Really?" An askance glance. "You know Jape?"

"From around."

Askance glance maintained because, if there was one person in Perkins who Elaine should NOT know, it was Jape.

Jape was ... Jape. An oddball in a population of oddballs, half-Piney and half-greaser and half-assed at both. He was usually found on various Perkins street corners goofing around with traffic or passersby in an almost criminal manner, falling just short of getting arrested. Much the same way in school, that sickly freckled-and-pale redhead suddenly popping into the middle of a group and throwing in a completely inappropriate remark for the topic under discussion and then sounding out a laugh akin to a mule's bray, to the astonishment of the entire group. He had an almost genetic ability to irritate anyone he encountered but, at the same time, could make anyone laugh because he was weird and manic and so out there, he earned tolerance.

Up to a point.

Butch wasn't sure how long he'd last at an Archway party before the genetic irritation made someone slap him silly. Which was probably why Elaine invited him: she collected the broken and tried to make them better.

Still...

"Okay." He conveyed enough doubt in his tone that she patted his arm and smirked and turned and left but added over her shoulder, "Oh, and a friend of mine from Mt. Holyoke named April. You'll like her." A wink and gone.

Prophecy.

Butch diddlybopped in around ten. April, camped by the punch bowl, looked him right in the eye.

Hamana hamana!

She was part Asian, had that beautiful red-black hair of the species, thick and full and falling past her hips, delicate features and huge brown eyes. "Hi," she said.

"Bwa," Butch said back.

What happened later that night spoke even more of how instantly and intensely both of them were attracted to each other.

Moments after midnight and the requisite throwing of beer and Boone's Farm on each other, Butch and April strolled hand in hand across the street and found an empty apartment, Cindy off somewhere with a Piney and Art somewhere in Alabama, and they made love until New Year's sunrise, stopping every once in a while to make Ellio's. And it was "making love," not Butch sex, the cruel taking, replete with bellow and roar which characterized his normal performance, the quivering victim staring at him in horror afterwards as he leaned over the bedside and cried in full-blown agony.

No crying, this time. None. My God.

They finally slept, curled into each other, and woke up a few hours later and made love again and had Ellio's and, finally, talked.

She was the fifth daughter of an American Army sergeant and his war-bride Japanese wife who still did not speak English. Her dad was typical Army, rough and disciplined and demanding and refused to let the girls date or go to college and micromanaged their waking hours by assigning daily chores on a minute-by-minute schedule, like the girls were a bunch of privates in a barracks. Her eldest sister got pregnant and ran away but, with dad's urging, married the guy who then quit college to work in the dad's construction business. Also at dad's urging. Her next oldest sister had secretly attended Burlington County College until dad found out after a bill for the first year's tuition mysteriously appeared at his office. He thought she was going to a job every day so he paid the bill and forced her to work in the construction company office to pay him back. The third had demanded a car and dad loaned her the money, in exchange for working at the construction company.

At this point, Butch should have recognized a pattern. But, he was in love.

She went home about noon and Ridge came to the apartment about six and demanded that Butch start paying rent if he was going to stay there and that was a demand too far, so he'd called the by-then permanently exiled Thong (guess the CIA agents thought he knew too much) who had, two days prior, taken the two rooms in the back of the gas station and made an off-hand comment sometime during last evening's festivities that Butch should consider moving in with him because Thong needed a roommate. Or, more accurately, the roommate's half of the rent. Thong picked him up about an hour later.

Kasey moved in about a week after that. By that time, Butch and April were full-blown lovers and, the same week that Butch was becoming increasingly uncomfortable with the gas station living arrangements, April's dad demanded to meet him, so he went over there. Without belaboring the point, they did not get along.

The next day, Dad delivered an ultimatum: "April, stop dating that hippie asshole or get out."

So she got out. And they got an apartment.

It said something about how instantly and intensely he had fallen for her that, upon delivery of the dad ultimatum, he was immediately willing to share a place with her, or, at least, that's what he had told himself. There were other factors, such as his mounting discomfort, no pun intended, over Thong and Kasey shagging in just about every available nook and cranny of the gas station's mechanic's bays. Ad infinitum, ad nauseam.

He could have moved back into the apartment but there was that whole rent thing and the subsequent scrutiny of Mom and Ridge and now Art, who was back from one of his Alabama forays. And Cindy spent a lot more time there now with her current boyfriend, some bartender from Mt. Holyoke, shagging in every available nook and cranny and Butch had already seen this movie.

And April's dad had pissed him off.

So, the scene had been set, the machines put in motion. Jape and Truck came together, Butch and April came together.

And then everything happened.

"So sad he went so quickly."

Huh?

Butch shook off the reverie. Oh, right, Mother Archway is still grieving Thong.

"I wonder how Kasey's doing?" She placed a worried hand on his forearm.

He shrugged. "I just saw her. Okay, I guess."

"Oh, that's good to know. Elaine drops by there every once in a while. Is the house for sale?"

Butch furrowed a brow. "I don't think so. There wasn't a sign or anything."

"Well, maybe she's changed her mind. She said something about going to Pennsylvania or Michigan or something."

Kasey is leaving? Of course. Another universe dissipates. Change the subject. "So what's everyone else doing?"

Genuinely baffled. "You know, I don't really know? I really don't! I haven't seen Pepsi since the summer started. C-Note graduated with Elaine and he's got a job at one of the truck stops on the Turnpike, so he's never home. Elway moved to Mt. Holyoke, works at the Safeway. Truck… it's odd, but I haven't heard anything of him since shortly before you left."

Butch kept his face blank. "Oh, you know how he is, a rambler and a gambler. He told me he was going down to his father's in Florida and work on the boat."

"Did he?"

Of course not, but it was as good a story as any, should anyone come around asking questions. Plausible deniability would keep her safe. "I think so."

"Look at this." She hung her head mournfully. "All my children are leaving me!"

"Isn't that a sign of a good mother?" Or a bad one?

She smiled. "Oh, you," and slammed another fist into his leg and got more tea and Newtons and told him firehouse stories, all of which were hilarious, and, after a while, Butch said, "I gotta go."

He really didn't, but he'd worn out all of what he would consider safe conversation. She understood and said she would always be here and drop by anytime and see if you can get over to the firehouse and Elaine will be back next week and would love to see you, here're some Newtons to munch on, bye.

He came out of the door as a neon lime-green Challenger with a ridiculous ten-foot-high spoiler on the back fishtailed out of the apartment parking lot, tires smoking.

"Heeey, brooo!" Someone waved at him frantically out of the passenger window.

Cindy.

Astonished, Butch halfway raised a hand to wave back as the Challenger roared down the road towards Mt. Holyoke so fast Cindy was a blur. "Welcome baaaaaaack!" and she was gone.

"Thanks," he said, and idly glanced towards Perkins. There was some kind of commotion down there, a lot of cars skewed in odd directions and a set of emergency red lights blinking in the middle of it.

"Father!" Mother Archway shrieked behind him as she burst through the doorway. Butch leaped almost three feet in the air and spun about as Mother hit the driveway and bulldozed down it, waving her massive arms over her head, her face tear-stained and wretched. "Father! Father!" And she was rumbling down the shoulder towards the commotion.

"What's going on?" he yelled.

"Father! Father! Father!" all the way down, her massive figure growing smaller as she ran as fast as her bulk allowed.

Butch stared for a moment, then crossed the street and went back into the apartment.

Chapter 6

The burnt pizza smell had dissipated into a mere suspicion, and Butch scrutinized the two planks he'd left in the sink.

Not bad.

He brushed them off, put them on a plate, and took them to the table. Crunch, crunch, crunch.

Carbon is a food group, right?

He glanced around for evidence of Cindy's visit, but nothing gave it away. 'Course, if he went into her bedroom, there might be plenty.

No thanks.

He wondered who the Piney boyfriend was, but realized it didn't matter. They were interchangeable, the only common theme some ridiculously souped-up and over-accessorized muscle car. Must be the style.

Must be the danger.

Not from the boyfriends, she could handle them easily, but from the mortality their uncontrollable cars offered. What better way to go than wrapped around a tree at 100 miles per hour? The stuff of teenage legends, like that guy during Butch's freshmen year...

What was his name... oh, yeah, Cornell...

...who drove his Mustang and four of his friends into a tree at better than 100 miles per hour, turning all five of them into hamburger. Go to any party anywhere in the Barrens today, it was guaranteed that someone at some point would repeat the oft-told tale that Cornell's brain was driven right through the tree and out the other side. Doubtful, given the physics, but it was now an indisputable urban legend about someone who wasn't all that legendary. From what little contact he'd had with Cornell before the kid drove his brain through a knothole, Butch concluded he was a dick. Now, he was a famous dick.

Fast cars, fast death.

Maybe Cindy wanted the same legendary status. Better a spectacular story than a cautionary tale. For decades to come, local partygoers, eyes rounded and tones hushed, would describe her rapid transition through a windshield and subsequent oak tree, instead of sneering about a pool and a shovel and the rain at midnight.

Or, maybe she just liked fast cars.

Butch was no longer sure. Their drift apart was fairly complete. They still acknowledged each other, evidenced by her calling out as she sped by, and they still retained the trappings of sibling love, but it was an act for public consumption. An impassable gulf opened when the two of them were alone, the other standing on a far shore, barely recognizable.

Because they carry the reminders.

Much of it now blurred.

Thank God.

Butch suffered impressions more than details.

Thank God.

But still, that was enough: a night of blood and screaming, and then whimpering and slapping around and Dad's murderous tones, and then a night of actual murder. He did not see the murder because he'd turned about, ignoring sheets wrapped around a mewling, tiny form, and concentrated instead on Cindy's hand clutching desperately to his. Then the snap of small bones. "Come on," Dad growled at them, the threat of slightly larger bones getting snapped compelling them to move, although Cindy, still too weak from blood and trauma, should have stayed where she was.

Terror is a great motivator.

A typical Alabama winter night, raining and cold, perfect for evil acts requiring gloom and fog as a curtain. No one could see them back there, with their bloody sheets and clay-covered shovels and Dad's gently motivating slaps to the side of the head. Butch did the majority of the labor because he was the only one of the two kids strong enough to actually dig. Dad has to hold the lantern and direct efforts, doncha know.

Slap, slap, hurry, hurry before someone comes along. Not Mom, she was in New Jersey attending Nana, which was excellent timing on her and Cindy's part. Art, maybe, although the little twerp was asleep, like always when there was work to do…

God, what is wrong with you?

He stared at the table.

What is wrong with me? What you got?

Because I could have stopped it.

Long before that night, sometime during the first week of school, Butch was in the upstairs garage room quietly reading some sci-fi book – *The Forgotten Door* or *Knee Deep in Thunder* – when Cindy materialized in the doorway at the top of the dangerous stairs. She told him what was happening. She told him of her recently discovered condition. She expressed her panic and terror, hammering Butch right between the eyes.

"I am going to kill him," he promised her. "Tonight."

They both went back to the house and Butch fetched the .38 from the silverware drawer and she went to her bedroom and Butch went back up the dangerous stairs and resumed reading, waiting for Dad to get home. Art was somewhere, Mom was somewhere, but it didn't matter. The moment Butch heard the truck pull into the garage below, he planned to close his book, walk down the dangerous stairs and up to the driver's side and empty the .38 into Dad's head.

Instead, he fell asleep.

Which was a broken promise and, sometime later, Cindy ran away from Yoman school in the company of a peanut farmer slattern named Shorty. Butch suspected Shorty also suffered forced attentions from depraved family members, specifically her brother, the poster boy for depravity.

Cops got called and searches began and Butch was interrogated but said nothing because telling the cops what was really going on would highlight Cindy's shame and his failure. Some hours later, the cops located Cindy and Shorty at some dive in Daleville and a rather sympathetic State trooper brought Cindy back to the house, Mom almost collapsing with relief and Dad… did nothing.

Nothing.

Did not reach for the whip, did not forgo the whip and beat her half to death with his fists, didn't even unstrap his belt. All he did was hug her and say don't do it again, which was the most un-Dad response ever. Should have been a big clue for the two people in the house who didn't know what was going on.

But it wasn't. Not for Art, not for Mom; at least, no more than all the other clues that Mom chose to ignore. And when she could no longer ignore them, to absolve them. Example: that summer in Alabama when she loaded them all in a car because things were out of hand and they needed to hide for a while at one of her Tupperware friends' house, that same drive-away in which Mom felt the urge to explain Butch's sordid origin to Art because, you know, that must have been important or something.

Butch did not know what specifically caused this particular drive-away but it, no doubt, involved a combination of Dad's nightly wanderings and his near-murderous beatings of them all, including Mom. It was the second time Butch had packed suitcases and fled, the first being the big gallivant during the summer of 1965, also caused by Dad's nightly wanderings and near-murderous beatings of them all. That first time, though, he had fled in the opposite direction, with the wandering and near-murderous Dad, leaving Mom and Art and Cindy and Dale and sanity and safety behind because… because he was stupid. It had turned into a rather bizarre trip seasoned with abandonment and terror and near murder. And, yeah, a couple of cool things: Butch had learned how to turn invisible – a talent he wished he still retained – made good (and not-so-good) friends and developed a decent rapport with the deceased Frank Vaughn. All during that trip, Butch saw nothing to redeem Dad's behavior; indeed, the danger was reinforced.

But Mom did. Somehow. Inexplicably.

By the end of the gallivant summer, all was forgiven, glossed over, and Dad and Butch returned to Oklahoma and packed up the household and the dogs and cats and parakeets and they all moved to Alabama where 'everything is different and we start afresh.'

For about a day.

Predictably, inevitably, and unsurprisingly, the dangerous behavior resumed, escalating to a point requiring a second escape, this time everyone but Dad to the safety of Tupperware friend. Behavior drastic enough to cause a family to flee from each other twice within a five-year period should have led Mom to declare, "That's it! This is ridiculous, we're outta here. Let's go somewhere safe, somewhere far away from murderous Dad."

Say to Grampop's house in New Jersey. Say to the moon.

But they didn't go somewhere else. They stayed in friggin' Alabama, in Tupperware lady's house. Within hailing distance. Within reach. Guess all Mom wanted to do was signal a little displeasure at Dad's escalating behavior, maybe get Dad to say he was sorry and he'd never do it again, and then everyone go back home, happily ever after. Which is what happened, sans the happily. And then everything else happened.

Mom's fault, then. For ignoring signs and portents and boatloads of clues that this marriage was a disaster, this family was not a family, was actually a hostage situation and any God-given opportunity to escape should be seized. But she didn't escape. She returned to Auschwitz. What did she think would happen?

All the Jews who boarded the trains, what did they think would happen?

In the face of authority and system, most people trusted the better angels: Yes, these Nazis are horrible people and say terrible things about us, but let's go along to get along and things will sort themselves out. Board the train, Miriam. Yes, kids, Dad is violent and crazy and increasingly more dangerous, but he is your father and my husband so let's go along to get along and things will sort themselves out.

Foolish mortals.

Ignoring the still small voice, the sense of unease, common sense itself, even the biological urge to protect her children (and the one not her child), Mom nodded at the forms and the standards and what church and society and grandparents said about a good wife's conduct. The better angels smiled encouragement, and she reluctantly, but with a sprig of hope, boarded an eastbound train.

She called Dad from Tupperware friend's house and told him where they were and said we want to come home and there he was, at the end of the driveway, alone and facing the four of them while the well-meaning Tupperware woman stood on the screened-in porch, watching with horror.

Don't get on that train, Jewish people.

But they had, Butch and Art getting in the truck, Mom and

Cindy following in the car and, right after Dad started the engine, Art found the Luger that Dad had taken off some dead Jerry stuck down the seats and he pulled it out and held it up in confusion as Butch's eyes bulged and Dad gently took it and in Satan's voice said if they had not agreed to come back with him, that he intended to kill himself right there, in the driveway, right in front of them.

Left unsaid: and all of you, too.

A parent killing a child? A father slaughtering his entire family? Unconscionable! Unheard of!

But Butch had heard of it. From Frank Vaughn.

On the last day of fourth grade in 1965, Frank Vaughn's mother had beaten him to death with a baseball bat, simply because Frank had forgotten his final report card.

How... trivial.

A week later, Butch and Dad gallivanted, with Frank Vaughn in all his massacred glory riding along high and merry in the backseat of the station wagon, face peeling, cheekbones falling out, uttering wry commentary about the goings-on. He kept Butch company until the summer ended and the trip ended and Dad and Butch reunited with Mom and Art and Cindy as if nothing had happened. Frank figured he'd done all he could to save Butch and went off to haunt the playground of their mutual elementary school. The big happy family left Oklahoma for Alabama with Dad at the wheel and Mom next to him chattering gaily as if nothing had happened and Butch knew, from his summer-long conversations with Frank, that parents were the Beast.

The Beast.

And the Beast roared for years after, until there was a rainy night behind a pool.

Mom's fault.

But... no... no, it's not. Mom's as much victim as the rest of us, because there's something more visceral than logic and common sense and that was… attachment.

Not the best word, because attachment indicated favor and Butch was ill-disposed towards Dad but it did convey connection, a link, like the handcuffs between prisoners. Let me illustrate.

About the third day of hiding at Tupperware lady's house, Butch was in the living room listening to a Roger Miller album.

Dang me, too, Roger, and they *should* get a rope to hang me.

And he sang along, giggling, because Roger Miller was the best. And then a Roger Miller song he'd never heard before came up, "One Dyin' and a Buryin'." The song was about a Dad losing his family and heading towards the river to do himself in. Butch lost it. Completely lost it.

Because, despite everything, Butch still loved his Dad.

It must be atavistic, a regard among people sharing genetic material. Knowing how dangerous Dad was, how cruel and violent, did much to lessen the regard, but there was still a heartbeat of it, a shadow of connection – of attachment – that made Butch bust out crying halfway through the first chorus of Roger Miller's damnable song. Because of Dad's pain. Dad's family had run away and he was alone and bereft and no one loved him and Butch understood that better than most. Imagine how much worse it was for someone like Dad, who had never imagined being alone.

Mom came in and held him and asked what was wrong but Butch could not answer because he didn't want to say that the idea of Dad being alone was tearing him apart, because, how stupid. The thought of Dad being alone had already led Butch into foolish decisions, like accompanying him on the big gallivant, even though every instinct had told him what a bad idea that was. As it turned out. That same feeling paralyzed him now and later, during the upcoming three-day bus trip from Dothan to New Jersey, awake the whole time and strangling under waves of imagined pain, Dad's pain, when Dad came home and found his kids gone, just a note saying, "Call Mom."

It's called empathy. And it is a horror.

So, does that mean, if I had stayed awake and heard the truck pull in to the garage, that I would have stayed in the room? No clumping down the stairs and up to the driver's side window and emptying a .38 into the side of Dad's head?

No.

I would have shot him.

Because Butch's vestigial regard for shared genetic material was strongest with Cindy. They were bonded, beloved, two against the world, and he would kill for her, had once broken some jackass's knee for her, and was more than willing to shoot their shared provider of genetic material five times in the head. But he didn't. And Cindy ran away. Which strongly indicates that you,

Butch, not Mom, are to blame.

He stilled.

Yes. Yes, it does.

"It's my fault, too."

Butch whirled. Frank glowered at him from the couch, a look made more terrifying by an eye hanging on his cheek. "What?"

"You didn't shoot your Dad, so everything happened. I forgot my report card and died."

"No." Butch rubbed his eyes hard but Frank was still there. "It's not the same thing."

"Why not?"

"Because ... you didn't deserve it."

Frank smiled, half his cheekbone falling out. "We all deserve it."

And he was gone.

Butch jerked his head off the table, repulsed by the pool of drool on his chin. He stared at the empty space where Frank had been. "Cindy didn't," he whispered.

Chapter 7

The balcony angled just enough to give Butch a clear view towards Perkins. A bigger mess down there now, more red lights and vehicles canted across the road while approaching sirens meant more medics were joining the party. The Archway's driveway was empty, so Butch figured Mother had trundled back and recovered her car. He could guess why but no, please no, not this, too, and then went back inside.

He collapsed on a rickety orange-upholstered mess of a chair across from the TV.

What to do?

Could turn on the tube and watch the soaps but he was so behind he had no idea what was going on. Not that it mattered; it was all recycled plot and if he waited long enough, the story resumed where he left off. When Butch went to Basic, Jesse had lost another man and Howie was being a jerk. Bet if he turned *General Hospital* on right now, Jesse is losing another man while Howie is being a jerk so, really, what had he missed? But *GH* came on at three, so *Match Game* and *Password* and whatever else would have to do until then.

Or he could find Don.

Butch vaulted into the kitchen and dug through the crap on the table until he located a Yellow Pages. Let your fingers do the walking.

What was the name of that printing plant, again? No idea.

Butch had never been there and Don wasn't one for details but it was in Braun's Mills and there was only one listed under the

"Printers" heading so, let's assume. He picked up the wall phone and dialed the number. After about six rings, some guy answered, "Printing."

"Is Don there?"

"Don? No, he didn't come in today. Can I help ya?"

Butch hung up. All right, one can now conclude that little Donny was off with some girl getting off or had kicked the girl out the door and was sleeping it off.

Where would that be?

To narrow that down, needed to identify the girl. Let's go down the list of possibilities, beginning with the one Don was seeing before Butch left…

Hmm, what *was* her name?

Butch wasn't sure. He'd glimpsed her only once or twice and Don wasn't one for details but she lived in PL and was a sophomore, which made her a little too young for Butch's tastes but Don never made such distinctions. She had that curly brown hair Don preferred and a bit of a too-big nose for Butch's taste. Don called it a dick canopy. Funny line, but Butch doubted Don had done her, let alone got a BJ. First, she was a bit young. Second, Don talked a good fight but he'd turned a bit gunshy. Recent experiences had made him wary of entanglements.

"So you moved in with that April girl, huh?" Don sniffed as the two of them munched on Red Lion Diner cheese sandwiches and downed coffee in a futile attempt to shake last night's hangover.

"Yesterday."

"And yet here you are," Don noted, licking his fingers free of mustard.

Butch lick-freed his own fingers. "She gets it."

"Yeah, sure she does." Don gave him the stinkeye. "None of 'em get it. Just a front."

"No, man, April is cool."

"Yeah, sure she is." Don demolished a crust remainder. "First chance she gets, stab you in the back."

"Oh, c'mon, why would you say that?"

"Because that's the way they are." And he looked through the picture window at the blowing snow, bitterness wrenching his features into a hate mask.

"Look." Butch dabbed a napkin. "Just because Sherry

screwed you over, doesn't mean they all do."

"*Pfft.*" Don glared at him. "She fucked around on me and ended up with half my shit. I'd say 'screwed over' is an understatement."

"You shouldn't have married her."

"And you shouldn't have moved in with her."

Butch said nothing, simply eyed the remaining crumbs, unease creeping up his spine. Don's disastrous right-out-of-high-school marriage to Sherry Baby was disastrous only in hindsight; it had seemed cool at first. Dooby had written him a letter about it, saying how cool it was and how cool Sherry Baby was and included a couple of Kodaks and Butch had sat under the Golden Gate Bridge, stoned out of his mind, and laughed and laughed over the pictures of foxy Sherry in a white split-thigh dress – hubba hubba – and shit-eatin'-grin Don dressed in a baby blue tux and concluded that yes, indeed, it was very cool that Mister I-Ain't-Ever-Gettin'-Married was the first of them to bite the dust, with a gorgeous redhead from Trenton he'd met in a diner the week that Butch flew off to San Francisco. And they were divorced a week before Butch came back from San Francisco.

And here Butch was, living with April, which was also starting out cool.

"Snow's lettin' up," Don pointed out, "You should be getting home to wifey."

Butch frowned. "Dude."

"You might as well be married. You're living with her."

"Didn't have much choice, ya know. We both had to get out of where we were."

"Yeah, yeah," he dismissed that and broke out a Marlboro, offering one to Butch, who declined. "Roommates. Purely platonic." He put on an innocent air. "By the way, did you call her last night and tell her you were crashing at my place?"

Well, no, he hadn't. Hadn't felt the need. She was cool.

His unease deepened.

Don had chuckled. "Boy, are you in trouble."

And he was, as it turned out. But not for staying out all night. Oh no. That would have been a relief.

A month later Butch was back at Don's house, formulating the plan that would end all of their respective lives, and the PL-dick-canopy girl was there. Déjà vu all over again…

Jackie. That's her name.

"Yay!" A cheer for memory.

Now, how do I find her? She was somebody's little sister, but whose? Derrick? No, she hung *out* with Derrick but wasn't his little sister; she was… yay, a cheer for memory, Eggie Bowman's little sister… Jackie Bowman, that's it.

Quick check of the white pages, bingo. A Bowman family in PL.

The phone rang and rang and rang. Butch hung up after a bit.

Hmm. Where does Eggie work? He was some kind of cement guy, either in a plant or on a truck. Start with the plants.

He found him on the fourth listing, a concrete mill in Tabernacle. "Yo, Bowmie! Got a phone call!" hollered by the answering Piney into what sounded like a hollow cavern that echoed and re-echoed with air hammers and trucks running and other Pineys yelling "Yo!"

After a minute, "Yo!" in the phone. Different Piney.

"Eggie?"

"Yo!"

"This is Butch."

A silence.

"Who?"

"Butch! Deats! Remember, we ran around the Lakes a bit."

"Oh…" Doubt. "Okay. Why you callin' me?"

"Do you know where Don is?"

"Who?"

"Don. You know, your sister was dating him."

"What?"

"Don, from PL. Lives up from the beach. Plays guitar."

"My sister was dating him?"

Oh, great. Butch may have let a surreptitious cat out of a bag.

"Well, not really dating I don't think. She just hung out."

"My sister's at the shore, man."

"Did Don go with her?"

"Why would he do that?"

Butch counted to ten.

"I don't know if he did or not. Do you know where he is?"

"Not a clue. Say, didn't you join the Army or something?"

"Air Force."

"Hmm. How is it?"

"It sucks."

Eggie laughed. "Ever work in a cement plant?"

Butch laughed back. "Can't say I have."

"Well, trust me, you're better off. You know Pee Sea's looking for you, right?"

Butch chilled. "I know."

"Best stay out of PL, man."

Too late.

"So I guess you don't have a number for your sister down at the shore."

"Nope. She'll be back next week." There was some yelling in the cavern, the only discernible words being "Bowmie!" and several choice curses. "Gotta go!" and a hasty hang up.

Butch sighed and also hung up. Now what?

Call Dooby.

He slapped his head. You idiot. The third musketeer always knew where the second musketeer was. Should have been the first guy you called.

So, why didn't you?

Well… because… Dooby is the third musketeer. Kind of remote, more perimeter than center because he lived in Groveville, a Trenton suburb, and roamed the environs of northern Jersey, which was terra incognita. Butch and Dooby linked through Don, who used to live in Groveville, and it was a rare moment when Butch and Dooby hung out without him. Very rare. The muskeeters assembled only when Don arranged it, or as a result of Don and Butch heading up to Groveville on some spur of the moment adventure that Dooby was always game for.

And maybe because Dooby had, like Don, done everything he could to talk Butch out of joining the Air Force and Butch just didn't want to hear it. Again.

"Man, you can't DO this!" Dooby's four-foot-long black strings of a mop mistakenly called hair whipped and waved like streamers in a hurricane, sure sign of his agitation. Occasionally, the hair parted enough to reveal neon blue eyes perched like binoculars over a nose the size of a ship's prow before the next tidal wave of tangled yarn washed over his face again. "You just can't!"

"I'm not seeing a lot of other options here, man."

Butch, sitting in the back seat of the Battleship, was keeping an eye on Deep Hollow Road about ten yards behind them. Drew had whipped the Battleship into one of their numerous Lebanon Forest hiding spots, this one a screen of trees where Deep Hollow bent towards Springfield Road. A 1968 primer grey Belvedere station wagon couldn't be seen in there, especially at night, unless someone – specifically, Pee Sea – was looking for it. And he was. Hence the reason Butch watched the road.

"You could stay and be a man about it," Don sneered from the front seat.

"And you should come with me," Butch sneered back, but with sincerity.

Don was in as much trouble as he was.

"I don't run from a fight, man."

A pulse deep in his temple. "There's fights you can win, and those you can't. We can't win this one."

"'Specially if you run away."

Butch leaned forward, about to demonstrate the difference between a winnable and non-winnable fight when Dooby shouted, "Knock it off, idiots!" and Moe-slapped them both, a particular Dooby talent only lacking the "boink!" sound effect. "Ow!" from both of them and, in any other circumstance, they'd be laughing. But this wasn't a laughing matter.

"Look, you're stupid to stay here." Drew finger-jabbed Don. "And you're stupid to join the Air Force!" Butch finger-jab. "Why don't you guys stay up at my place until all this blows over?"

"Your mom will kill us," Butch pointed out.

"And this ain't gonna blow over," Don further pointed out.

"She'll be fine. And everything blows over."

Both may be true. Dooby's mom was a loud, crazy arm-throwing Italian who screeched at them as though they were the biggest pains in the world, but who always made them spaghetti and meatballs. And things did tend to calm down, given enough time. In this case, about forty years.

Butch blew out a breath. "I've already signed the papers, man."

"Unsign them."

"Doesn't work like that. They'll put me in jail."

"Sounds like you're already going to jail."

Butch waved an impatient hand.

"It's not like that. I can go out and stuff... wait."

Impatient hand turned to cautioning palm as a set of headlights appeared through the screen of trees off towards the PL side, slowing as it reached the turnoff and then slowly banked away. The red tail lights shone through as the driver rode the brakes but receded, although far more slowly than Butch would have liked.

"What kind of car was that?"

"Duster." Dooby, who knew every car ever made, said.

"Do we know anyone who drives a Duster?"

"Your mom," Don replied and he wasn't being funny; Mom did. Hardly an observation applicable to the moment, though.

"Other than my mom."

"No. No one else we know is that uncool," Don said.

Butch dropped it because it was another true statement.

"Look, Dooby, I appreciate it and I would love to hide out at your place for a couple of months—"

"Especially with your sister living there," Don leered and then went "Ow!" as Dooby head-slapped him. No one disrespected Dooby's sister, Ann, who was kind of a babe, in a slightly overweight Italian way.

"—but I gotta get out of here. And not," Butch threw a cautioning palm in Don's face to stop the editorial comment, "because of Pee Sea. We can handle him." He paused. "Because of April, man."

April, man.

Butch stilled and things roiled like ice through his stomach and he dialed the number.

"Dooby," he said.

"Butch! You made it!" and Dooby burst into that insane rise and fall horse-laughter that punctuated every Dooby utterance. "I thought you got sent off to Vietnam shooting commies for mommy!" The laugh resumed.

Butch couldn't help laughing in response. "That's the Army. We drop bombs."

"Okay, okay, that works, too. So what kind of airplane you fly?"

"Can't fly. I can read and write."

"Is that some kind of Air Force joke?"

"So I've been told."

"Well," and the laugh continued, "good, man, good. So when

you'd get back?"

"This morning."

"So where you at?"

"The apartment."

"So whatcha doin'?"

"Looking for Don."

"I ain't seen him in about a week, man. He's working and stuff. There's some doings down in PL he's avoiding, too."

"Like what?"

"You know."

Butch scowled. Yeah, he did.

"Humor me."

"Sheesh, man, it is all fucked up down there. That friend of yours, Jape? Got his head cut off and dumped back on Deep Hollow. You believe that shit? Somebody else shot an Ocean County deputy out at the Train Wreck. You believe that?"

"I believe anything where Pineys are involved, man." He paused. "You think this is all to do with our present troubles?"

Dooby snorted.

"Yeah, yeah." Butch chewed a lip thoughtfully. "I already had a little run-in with Pee Sea this morning."

"No shit?"

"No shit. I was at Don's place."

Dooby was incredulous. "You crazy or something, man? What were you doing there?"

"Looking for Don."

"Dude, don't go back there. I'm thinking of canceling our gig there tonight."

"What?"

"It's getting crazy. Pee Sea's still at war with the Stilt brothers, and they've brought in some Pagans while Pee Sea's got some Breed. Story is, they're the ones who did Jape."

"Wait." Lots to process. "What gig?"

"We're playing the bandshell tonight."

"You are?"

"Yeah, I'd say come because I'm pretty sure Don'll be there but so will everyone else."

"Don helping you set up?"

"S'posed to be."

"What time?"

"Ah, you know."

And he did. Dooby's band, Merlin, was notorious for its loose interpretation of start times.

"All right," he said, "I'll be there, too."

Dooby chuckled. "You got a death wish, man."

"Maybe. But I want to see you guys before I go."

"Where?"

Butch explained.

"Well, that sounds fucked up," Drew concluded, "Did I tell you what happened to Opie the other day? He was driving down Perry Street—"

"What the hell was he doing on Perry Street?"

"Dunno. Guy's crazy. When he spots this full-blown Ludwig set on a dumpster. Like a five-piece with the pedals and throne, man, just sitting right on top. So, he stops, because, you know, drum set and he's looking it over and everything when these guys come out of the house next door and surround him and want to know what he's doing in this hyeah neighborhood, know what I mean?"

"Know what you mean."

"So Opie says he's just out and saw the drum set and figured what the hell and the locals said, man, no, you can't take it unless you can play it, so Opie climbs right up on top, grabs some sticks, and does the entire drum solo from 'In a Gadda da Vida.'"

"No shit."

"No shit. And the brothers are laughing and dancing and a bunch more people come out and before you know it, Opie's got a street party going. Cops show up and the bros help him load the drums into the truck and, ya know, Opie's got himself a brand new, although slightly used" – punctuated with the horse laugh – "drum set. For free. Wacha think of that?"

Butch shook his head. Another Dooby story. The guy had a million of them.

"I should be so lucky. Is he bringing it?"

"Don't think it's tuned yet. So, you're definitely coming?"

"Yep."

"Your funeral. Later, man!" and he hung up.

Yes, it certainly was.

But what better way to depart this Earthly vale than smack in the middle of a Merlin concert? They were good, really good.

Dooby was, hands down, the greatest guitar player in America, at least since Hendrix croaked. The guy could play anything. The first time Butch heard Dooby was sophomore year. Butch had called Don to see what they were doing this weekend. "Running with the band, man. My buddy from Groveville I told you about, Dooby? He's here."

Butch heard electric-guitar noodling in the background.

"Yeah?". Don had extolled Dooby's prowess for months but Butch had his doubts. "Have him play something."

"Waddya want to hear?"

"'Smoke on the Water.'" Like some Trenton dude could do that.

And Dooby launched right into the epic opening chords, note for note, and Butch was dutifully blown away. Even over the phone, the guy's genius came through so he hitchhiked to PL and spent the rest of the day listening as Dooby thrashed Eric Clapton and Robin Trower while Don manfully tried to follow along on his cracked acoustic. Butch had tried to learn guitar but ham fingers and no instrument sense defeated him. He did, though, have the gift of musicality and could discern a true arteest. Conclusion? Dooby was a true arteest.

"Where did you learn to play like that?" he shouted, half deaf, at a break.

Dooby shrugged, threw his yarn hair around like a gladiator net, and said, "Just picked it up."

A natural.

Don's mom flew in and out with sandwiches and sodas and Don's dad yelled every three seconds to turn down that damn crap but he didn't mean it, grinned the whole time and tapped his feet and, after some time, made noises about the yard and they put the guitars and audience criticism away and trooped out and grabbed rakes and blades and did a respectable job and then piled into Dooby's Battleship, amps and all.

"You've got a driver's license?" Butch asked.

"Nope," Dooby said, and they were off.

Merlin had a gig at the Polish-American Club that night and Don pulled out a baggie and they rolled and smoked and Dooby told Dooby stories. Said his father was one of the Del Vikings; which one, he didn't know.

Butch was impressed.

"The white guy?"

"Hope not."

Dooby's mom was a backup singer and gave him up to her friend, the crazy Italian arm waver, so she could keep singing.

A bastard given up for adoption… my brother.

Dooby and Butch and Don became the Musketeers that night.

They got to the Club about a half-hour late, Opie and the rest of Merlin already there and impatient and the guy running the place yelled something at them in Polish but it didn't matter because, as soon as Dooby took the stage and hit the first notes of 'Are You Ready?', the crowd screamed and filled the dance floor without a break for the next three hours of riff and improv and heavy metal and even some Beatles. Butch danced all night long with some pretty Polish girl named Karen who wanted him to call her sometime but he never did. They piled back into the Battleship and drove to an all-night bowling alley in Carteret to get fried chicken, Dooby's string hair scaring the locals and Don almost getting into a fight with a bunch of hardguys over a girl and the guy at the Turnpike booth overcharged them and Don almost started a fight with him but Dooby calmed it down and paid the thief, saying "Eat me!" as they roared off, heading to the Villa down on 206 and got past the bouncer with no problems and ended up on the basement floor of Don's house at around dawn.

The first of many such nights.

That was his life for the next few years, in the best of all the universes. Sometimes he wished it was the only universe and he could settle into orbit around Don's home planet with Don's mom feeding him and Don's dad cuffing him and Don and Dooby and him out every night, forever and ever. And why not? There were physics governing universes, right? Einstein said the proper lever could move them. Or maybe some Greek guy said that but the point: there are ways to suspend time, to make Don's universe cease its inevitable entropy and dissolution and, instead, restart, repeat the same four years over and over, high hilarity and shenanigans over and over forever and ever and who would tire of that? In the unlikely event Butch did so tire, then a push of the lever and alter some of the events ... say it's Butch and Don who put the tin pots on their heads and sing 'New Country Corn Flakes' to a very stoned Dooby, instead of those two at him ... for purposes of variety, forever and ever, world without end, amen.

But it had ended. It had. But now it looked like the Einstein lever had flexed and he'd been granted another run at it. Tonight. One last crazy night with the Musketeers before the Air Force swallowed him whole and spat him out, digested and eviscerated and not the person he used to be. One last chance to be the person he used to be.

He looked down at his uniform.

Hmm. Maybe wearing this wouldn't be the best of ideas.

The mass of drunken Pineys in attendance would take umbrage, while the various angry factions looking for him would have an easy time of it.

Damn, why'd I leave my duffel at Ridge's? So, let's go get it…

Whoa, hold on, chief, there's a real danger that Mom will reclaim her car, especially if Ridge is there shimmering with disapproval. Forget it. Let's see what kind of civilian ensemble you can assemble from what's here.

He went into the bedroom and dug around in his closet and pulled out a respectable Piney get-up: Led Zeppelin T-shirt, straight-leg jeans, plaid shirt, white socks and black Converses. Quickly, he changed… man, he'd lost a lot of weight. Everything fit him like burlap bags. If he turned to the side, it would take his pants three minutes to catch up. Forget dancing; he'd look like cats fighting inside a scarecrow.

This won't do.

Frowning, he changed back into the 1505s and gave himself the critical eye. Not going to work, either, for the aforementioned reasons of Piney and murderer interest. Maybe if he took off the blouse, exposing the tidy whitey T-shirt ... there. He stared. All right, he looked like an off-duty prison guard but that was better than an Aaair Farce member. He'd get a lot of odd looks but there was little chance anyone would recognize him.

Okay, set.

He trundled down the stairs and tossed the blouse and the cap into the back seat, then stood, undecided. Hours to kill. Where to?

Let the road decide.

He got in, started the car, and idled for a moment seeking engine inspiration, then backed up and slowly pulled to the road, undecided. The mess down towards Perkins remained. Don't want to know, don't want to see. so go t'other way and he pulled out without thinking and was headed towards Mt. Holyoke without thinking but…

Oh no no, let's not go there, either.

Let's go to Mason's.

Chapter 8

Mason's dad owned a warehouse about a mile down the road and there was an excellent chance Mason was there because the guy had worked for his dad ever since graduating three years ago, an employment characterized by a very loud and public self-debate, with occasional quiet input from daddy, whether to go to school or not, a debate unresolved when Butch joined the Air Force and, no doubt, still going strong.

Mason, go to school, man, because the alternative is joining the Air Force and, dude, you don't want to do that. Better to sling boxes for your dad. Or work in a cement plant.

Butch whipped into the parking lot and followed it around to the big warehouse in the back, a couple of the larger trucks parked at one or two of the open bays, a few people in "Family Housemen" work uniforms running here and there and, yep, there was Mason's bright yellow Continental, top down and wheels shining, sticking out of an office parking space. Butch grinned.

If that Continental could talk…

It was actually Mason's dad's car, but daddy bought a De Ville sometime during Mason's junior year and the Continental had fallen into Mason's hands and, by default, Butch and Don's. After school, they'd pile into it and, even in chilly March, put the top down and go cruising Perkins and Lake Valley and Mt. Holyoke with one of the most urbane, handsome, stylish black kids for counties around driving it with an exaggerated pimp lean, two scurvy white boys riding shotgun and back seat, all of them nodding to Earth, Wind and Fire. The yokels stared. How could they not?

Mason's father was one of the richest people in the country, never mind the state, owning a giant company that moved and stored the greater Philadelphia area. He owned seven or eight facilities in Burlington County alone, dozens of trucks, and the craziest, happiest workforce in America. Whenever Butch needed a little pocket money, he'd call Mason's dad and ask for a slot and walk down to the warehouse where Bentley, an eighty-year-old bald, wrinkled black guy with the greatest set of teeth, razzed him and called him names and threw him in with a crew that Mason was working and it was always a good time. Mason was a junior; Butch was a freshman, so how could they be pals?

The friends from high school are the friends of circumstance.

Fresh from the trauma of escaping dad, dressed in bell bottoms and a Nehru shirt and those godawful nerd glasses, Butch walked into the Perkins Township High School gym in the middle of freshmen year and said, "Hey, y'all!" in his dulcet lower-Alabama tones. The black kids rose as one to eviscerate him but Mason stepped between, fascination on his face. "Say something else," he'd commanded.

"Sumpin' ay-lse."

Mason then took him by the shoulders and marched him all over the school, demanding that Butch say 'sumpin' ay-lse' to everyone they ran into, including teachers. At the end of the day, Mason plopped Butch into the Continental and took him to meet his dad. They'd been running partners ever since.

But Mason was a different kind of running partner, a unique one with no known allegiances, sort of like a part-time rustler who joined the Clantons from time to time. Mason didn't really fit in anywhere. He wasn't regarded as authentically black. The militants hated his wealth and cars; the jive-asses did, too. It distressed Mason that Butch was more accepted by the militants and the jive-asses than he was, even if that was due more to Oak than any latent coolness on Butch's part. Mason circled Butch's universes like a rogue comet in the Kuiper Belt but never really merged and Butch and he remained pals mostly because Mason didn't really have any others. Which was fine. He had a cool car.

Mason did, though, have girlfriends. Lots of them. Of every shape, color, creed and religion, ten or twelve at any given moment. The jealous boys attributed that to his wealth and cool cars, but that wasn't entirely it: the guy was devastatingly handsome, Rock Hudson handsome or, more accurately, Billy Dee Williams handsome. If Butch was a girl, he'd have joined that harem. On the few occasions Thong and Mason crossed paths, Thong shamelessly flirted. Couple that with Mason's excellent fashion sense and, yes, wealth, and the women lined up. Gorgeous women; Butch's favorite was Libby , a mid-toned black Amazon, built like the Commodore's brick house over six feet tall with three feet of beautiful loose-curled hair topping that, luminous and brilliant and Butch was in awe of her and in love with her, as was everyone else. Mason and Libby walking down a school hallway arm in arm parted the masses before them, the peasants knuckling to royalty. They were actual royalty, both voted Homecoming King and Queen over the standard whitewashed football player and head cheerleader fare. But despite the stunningness of their couplehood, she was interchanged regularly with the other harem members, a blur of gorgeous women of whom Butch quickly lost track, Libby being his lodestone and point of reference.

Because Butch lost his virginity in her presence.

Not literally, of course: Mason and Libby were in one room of the Mason mansion and Butch and Joan were in another. Joan, a pale nebbish of a girl Butch knew from church. Somehow they were boyfriend/girlfriend. He walked to her house once a week or so and surreptitiously played kissy-tit with her on the living room floor while her dad pretended to sleep in the easy chair next to them.

Joan and he happened to be walking along Perkins's main drag one afternoon when Mason and the Continental cruised by, Libby in the passenger seat, and Mason stopped and said, "Let's go," and Butch and Joan hopped in and the next thing you know, they were in separate bedrooms and what else were you supposed to do?

So they did. About an hour later, Butch hated her.

Because sex was evil.

Sex was horrible. Sex destroyed everything.

It possessed him.

Butch was periodically seized by a sex frenzy that forced him to sit in the bathroom and masturbate for hours and then cry and cry for hours afterwards, so helpless and overwhelmed and out of control. Which is what happened with Joan. He'd taken her with roaring and bellowing and no fumbling, no hesitation, just straight raw power and lust so unlike what everyone said the first time was supposed to be and fell down the long hot whirlpool of sex and ejaculation and then sat on the edge of the bed stunned and cried and cried and shook her worried hands off him. The power of dad compelled him. A midnight grave-digging party haunted him. He did not look at her and said nothing to her when Mason drove them back and did not call her and did not talk to her nor walk over to her house again and she was devastated and he did not care because the Beast, the Beast.

There'd been girls since, the one-nighters or the spur-of-the-momenters, strangers, friends of Oak or random PL girls or tag-alongs picked up during one of Mason's excursions and Butch roared and bellowed and took them for hours and left them stunned and afraid, but not half as stunned and afraid as he was of himself.

Sex is evil.

And every time Butch saw Libby in the hall or driving by in the Continental, he was seized with panic and looked wildly about while hyperventilating because the memory of roar and bellow and the sheer power of it led to a midnight grave in December rain. And he had to have more and he ran into the bathroom and cried and asked God to remove this curse, please God, I do not want to be the Beast.

Unlike Mason, who wore his profligacy like a medal and pointedly ignored the hurt on Libby's face, pleased by Butch's odd reputation as a dangerous boyfriend, and insisted Butch accompany him on as many harem forays as possible. And Butch did. Mason's precipice-dancing juggle of girls should have annoyed him but it didn't. Butch felt a sense of absolution towards Mason because the guy understood and accepted the power of the Beast, and as much as Butch wished to be shriven of it, he could not condemn someone who'd mastered it. Besides, Mason was fun.

Often, Mason would drop by when Butch and Don were in the apartment sleeping it off and the three of them would go to the red-neckiest diner they could find just so the waitresses could look upon them with pure astonishment. Butch and Don would nurse their hangovers while Mason beamed and played and ordered food by the platterful, spending his dad's money like it was never-ending, which it wasn't. When Butch and Don sobered up enough, they would go outside and wipe the Continental down with towels and clean the windshield and hold the door open for Mason, which drove the waitresses insane. Good times.

And despite all of this, Mason never became a universe. Not completely. He was, at best, a side galaxy, a trip to the outer planets when other universes were engaged. Mason remained a rest stop on a major highway, good for a recharge, then head out. A lot of that had to do with Mason graduating when Butch ended sophomore year.

There was less truck with each other after that, the impropriety of an adult like Mason associating with a mere high schooler being the main cause, but there was still truck, a lot more than warranted. That's because Mason had the trappings of adulthood but not an actual membership. He was still too much Daddy's Boy, still living in the netherworld between child and grown-up, and so he showed up at the apartment or at the Lakes and was, over the next three years, often in Don and Butch's company. Not so much Dooby's and rarely Oak and the other karateka, that whole inauthenticity thing. But, surprisingly, he flitted through the Archway universe, and Butch had, on several occasions, tripped down the basement steps and there Mason was, flirting with Elaine. Which was fine. Butch wondered sometimes if Mason considered Butch and Don his universe; that would explain the frequent contact.

When Butch got back from San Francisco, Mason was still working for his dad, still driving the Continental and still servicing what amounted to a harem of girls, each convinced they were The One, not knowing that Mason considered all girls The One. Libby was long gone, earning a full-blown scholarship to Princeton and a full-blown realization of Mason's nature and that was a bit of relief. For her, and for Butch's memories.

Butch toyed with the idea of permanently joining Mason on the warehouse crews. Might be a blast working with the guy day in and out, but, given the hierarchy, he'd be working the crews day in and out well into his nineties. Mason would take over when Daddy stepped down, and Mason's little brother would assume second-banana status and maybe, just maybe, Butch become Bentley if the old guy ever died, but this wasn't a future he saw for himself. Not that he saw any kind of future when he came back. And then everything happened and a whole, unanticipated future opened up.

Life sucks.

Butch got out of the car and walked up the ramp and into the dim interior, blinking at the dust clouds and dark and hoping he didn't walk into a forklift. A couple of Family Housemen stopped what they were doing and regarded him. "Office is over there, soldier," one of them said, waving in some murky direction.

Great. Even just wearing the pants was a giveaway. "Airman," Butch corrected. "Is Bentley here?"

The guy's brow furrowed because who was this skinny white soldier – airman, whatever – invoking the name of such a revered person but he continued waving at the office. Like Butch needed the directions. He weaved his way through pallets and boxes and pulled the knob of the frosted-glass door and almost walked into Daddy Mason, who turned and frowned at him.

"Mr. Mason!" Butch said, pleased, and held out a hand.

Old Man Mason wore the thickest pair of glasses ever constructed, so Butch was not put off when he wasn't immediately recognized, but then Daddy smiled his billboard-wide smile and crowed, "Butch! How ARE you?" and pumped his hand like he was seeking water.

It was easy to see where Mason got his handsomeness. Daddy was a medium brown, fine-featured, fine-haired black man, the only unfortunate aspect those glasses. Ebullient and glad-handed in a sincere way, not a politician's, and that genuineness served him well as he began moving in political circles. There was talk of him running for mayor, something Butch enthusiastically supported because this guy knew what he was doing. Who else could build a successful tri-state warehouse business in the middle of redneck Piney country, let alone a black man?

"Well, look at you, now." Daddy sized him up. "You lookin' like a soldier—"

"Airman."

"Yeah, yeah." He brushed that away. "I did my time, too. Korea."

"Really? My dad did, too."

"Most of us did." Said simply, a summary for a better generation.

Butch caught the implication: the way Butch and the rest of

the whiny babies viewed service was less than heroic.

Our wars aren't heroic, Mr. Mason.

Old Man cocked his head owlishly. "See you lost the hippie hair."

Butch rubbed his skull. "Sort of a requirement."

"I hear that!" Daddy laughed. "So what are you doing back here? You looking for a job? I got a crew going out to Seaside in about five minutes if you want to tag along. Bentley!" He shouted back along the passage. "Got ya another strong back."

"Uhm—"

"Who you got?" And there he was, short and built like a dwarf bull, his shiny head catching the fluorescents like sparklers as he grinned that Cadillac grill of teeth. "Well, lookee here! So you came crawling back, didja?"

"Well—"

"Well, nuthin'! You get your sorry white ass outta them Uncle Sam pants, put on some overalls and get your butt back to the dock. We about to go!" And Bentley rolled rheumy old-black-guy eyes at him and spun on his heel, arched eyebrows and a 'get moving' look on his face.

Butch chuckled. Vintage Bentley. "Really," he said, holding up placating hands, "I can't. I've got to go. I just stopped by to see if Mason was here."

"Mason?" Bentley snorted. "That lazy ass nigger ain't ever here anymore." And he turned accusing eyes on Old Man, who shrugged. Bentley was the only one who could get away with talking about Mason like that.

"Mason's gone off to the State Police Academy," Old Man said, with almost an apology in his voice.

Stroked Butch with a hammer. A funny hammer, because he couldn't help it, started laughing. "You're kidding. When did that happen?"

"Damn fool signed up about the same time you left," Bentley said, the accusing eyes now turned full on Butch, like it was his fault. Butch raised querying eyes to Daddy.

"Yeah," he said, "guess he saw all you guys leaving and he wanted to do something, too." Old Man looked sadly around the room. "Didn't want to do this anymore."

"So… who's going to take over?"

Old Man was puzzled. "Take over?"

Butch waved that away. "So how long's he been gone?"

"Gone? To the Academy? Oh no." Old Man waved it back in. "He doesn't report for a couple more weeks."

"So he's here." Butch craned around Bentley, scrutinizing the murky passage for signs of Mason.

"Said he ain't." Bentley looked at Butch like he was stupid or sumpin'.

"But the car's outside." Not stupid, Bentley, observant.

"His girlfriend picked him up." Daddy, examining exquisite fingernails, was mournful. Oh. Butch grinned. Of course. "Which one?"

"Some white girl from Mt. Holyoke," Bentley sneered. "Name of June or July or somethin'."

Ice ran down Butch's spine. "April?"

Bentley nodded. "Yeah, that's her. You know her?"

Oh yes. Yes, he did.

Chapter 9

Butch sat in the car.

What to do? What to do?

His first inclination was to drive out to Tabernacle, borrow a shotgun from Art's pal, Tim, head over to April's and what-used-to-be-his apartment and shoot Mason in the knees. Or, shoot April in the knees. Shoot them both in the knees. But, really, why?

What did you expect?

Mason was a hound dog. Always was. Butch hound-dogged right alongside him. Once, Mason and he drove into Lake Valley and picked up a girl named Tessie and her sister and went back to the Mason house, did them, and then switched. That had been a pleasant afternoon, discounting the roars and bellows and subsequent crying. Two days later, they went to Country Lakes and picked up a girl named Laurel and her sister, wash, repeat.

"How are you not dead?" Butch asked when they'd returned the Country Lakes crew.

Mason laughed. "Just gotta keep a step ahead, man."

Apparently, Mason was a step ahead of Butch.

And why do you care?

Which underscored his second and stronger inclination: forget it. Just forget it. He and April were *hees twa*, irrevocably so from about the beginning of April (no pun intended but unavoidable since everything had gone TU in April. Because of April) when all these various wheels were set in motion, culminating in Butch's hasty enlistment. Wasn't his secondary but still important reason for said hasty enlistment the need to get as far away, as fast as possible, from her? And knowing her inclinations, why be perturbed that she's already taken up with a rich kid? Not that Butch had been a rich kid, but she was seeking someone to make it all better and would settle the details once the victim had been secured. In Butch's case, those details involved marriage and working for her dad for the rest of his life.

No. Thank. You. To marriage, to construction work, to April.

But, Mason, this is just not cool. Not cool at all.

Butch started the car and backed all the way through the lot to the road and inexpertly swung it around and, looky here, pointed towards Mt. Holyoke. Almost a portent. Now, where would April be at noon on a workday? Working at Gino's, of course, but would she be there now? After all, she had reduced her hours in proportion to Butch's corresponding increase in hours at her dad's, putting more of the financial burden on him. Like any good wife. Yeah, but, he had recently skedaddled obviating said financial advantage so she would need those hours back because Lord knows, she can't live off her dad's grudging charity. So she was there. Maybe.

Who knows, but it's a good place to start.

"Not a good idea," Frank said, from the back seat.

Butch glanced into the mirror at Frank looking back at the warehouse. "I can't just ignore this," Butch said.

Frank shrugged. "Sleeping dogs." And he faded away.

Butch frowned. Sleeping? These dogs hadn't settled down yet, were downright growly and snappish. Needed smacking. Man up, Frank, and he pulled out.

Fifteen minutes later, he was at Gino's. Place was packed – lunchtime – and Butch had to park in the rear lot which was actually good because he didn't want anyone identifying him later. Butch had no doubt the upcoming conversation with April would quickly escalate into a scene, one requiring official intervention, with subsequent referral to his future commander in Illinois. That should make for a rather memorable reporting-for-duty, sir, with Captain Stick-Up-His-Butt glaring at him from behind some sheet metal desk and waving a paper while screaming, "Airman, what's this?"

Why, I do believe that's a stark rendition of a very public argument with my ex-girlfriend who decided shagging a former good friend was an excellent means of payback, sir, or are you a pilot and, therefore, unable to read?

He smiled. Second Air Force joke he'd made today. If you want to keep making Air Force jokes outside of Leavenworth, bud, perhaps you should skip this step.

But intervention by authorities and subsequent referrals were hallmarks of his relationship with April, especially as things escalated towards the end, so avoiding the inevitable was no reason to avoid this. Besides, he planned to exit the Air Force at the first opportunity — first legal opportunity, that is — which meant a bad rep was inconsequential.

He got out of the car and reached in the back and grabbed his blouse and slipped it on and settled his cap. Perhaps the uniform will give him some kind of invulnerability. The cops will merely club him to the ground, not shoot him. He walked in, holding his breath and took a position at the end of the line. A few patrons ahead of him and at scattered tables glanced his way, but Mt. Holyoke was used to soldiers – airmen, whatever – so no special reaction other than standard hostility.

He scanned the counter but April wasn't there. Okay, so there's a good chance she was not working today, having put in her grueling thirty-minute-or-so shift and was out with Mason making plans. Funny, April's dad never struck Butch as the enlightened type. Indeed. he'd made a couple of disparaging comments regarding persons of darker visage.

Wonder if he knows about Mason? Mayhaps give dad a call?

He savored the idea as he shuffled forward in step with the line and craned his neck to see if she was in the back and, yeah, there, standing near the fryer…

Oh no. Wait. Not April. Someone worse than April.

Her little sister, May.

"What are you doing here?" May, all four feet nothing, ninety-eight pounds of nothing, braced against the counter, glared at him. Her voice was loud and hostile and quite a few line-dwellers turned to stare at the object of her ire. "And what are you doing in that uniform?"

Butch's face flamed, but if that's how she wanted to play it…

"Ordering lunch. Why'n't you get me a couple of Gino Giants there, toots?"

Made *her* face flame as a couple of line apes said, "Hey, man, wait your turn!" while a couple of others chuckled and turned to watch her next move. Oh boy, lunch and a show.

"Order from the counter when you get here," she said and flounced off. Butch grinned as he stared down the more hostile apes until they turned around, muttering, and everyone else lost interest and Butch was relieved. No intervention by authorities. Yet.

He ordered the Giants from a suspicious black girl with an amazing Afro and even more amazing blue eyes and a stacked body wrapped in the rather sexy red Gino's uniform.

Hubba hubba.

A couple of times, he'd had April put the uniform on before they headed to the bedroom. He aimed the grin at the girl, identified by name tag as 'Alisha,' who became even more suspicious, and then moved with the grin to where a couple of line apes stood awaiting their food. They inched away from him, equally suspicious. Alisha slid over to another black girl so heavy of features and body, no sexy red Gino dress was going to help. The two conversed in low accusatory tones while giving Butch shared snake eye.

"So what are you doing here?" May, towing a pudgy manager sporting fine straw hair and an unbelievably thick moustache, rushed at him with all her tiny ferocity, the apes stepping back in some alarm. That the stainless-steel counter barely came up to her little boobies made the ferocity laughable.

Butch was about to launch into a discourse about public restaurants and their duty to provide advertised products to everyone who entered, but he was suddenly tired.

"Where's April?" he asked.

"She hasn't worked here since you ran out on her."

"Wasn't the question I asked."

"It's none of your business where she is."

"I think it is."

"Well, I think it isn't." She tried to look threatening and Butch had to restrain himself from finger-thwapping her across the head.

"Is there some problem?" the manager squeaked.

"No… Bill." Butch lifted the name from an oversized plastic tag skewed across straw hair's sweat-stained white shirt. "There is no problem. However, I am finding that one of your employees is evincing a level of hostility that it simply not in keeping with good customer service. Why do you keep such an employee on the payroll, Bill?"

Smacked Bill with a wet tuna, he did. May, too, apparently, as she went dark with rage.

"Look you!" She pointed a baby finger in his face. "You leave my sister alone! You had your chance. You blew it."

"Matter of perspective, that," he said, "blackmail being one of the top five reasons that couples break up."

She spluttered incoherently. Bill was thoroughly confused. Take advantage. "Is she with Mason?"

Advantage lost.

May smiled, all the evil in her shriveled little soul hanging from her baby shark teeth. "Oh, so that's it. Jealous, huh?"

"Not at all. Frankly, I've come to warn the world about this unholy alliance, before they spawn the anti-Christ."

"Well, it's too late. They're together. And he's treating her better than you ever did."

Butch blinked. "Have you met Mason?"

"Of course!"

"Then you weren't paying attention. By the way, does Daddy know about the Dark Prince?" Her sudden blanch answered that and he smirked then spun on his heel and stalked towards the door, then spun back and stalked to the counter.

"My Giants?" he said and May practically smashed the bag into his outstretched hand, probably squashing them but the hell with it. He backed away, the apes making noises along the lines of, "Why did he get served before us?" but even those two idiots could see the tension and let it drop. Bill stood there, confused.

"Thanks, toots." He waved at May. "Say hi to April." He walked out.

"Can I have one of those?" Frank asked from the back seat as Butch flopped behind the wheel, fuming.

Without a word, Butch flipped one of the burgers to him. He watched as Frank tried to take a bite out of it while holding his jaw together.

"Don't you have food in heaven?"

"What makes you think I'm in heaven?" Frank was manually working his jaw around the burger, which was an ugly sight.

"Fairness."

Frank laughed, which caused his jaw to slip onto his chest and Butch looked away, drumming his fingers on the wheel. "I can't believe this."

"Told ya to leave it alone."

"Yeah, yeah." He glanced back but Frank was gone, so he retrieved the Giant and ate it, saving the other one for later.

So if April doesn't work here anymore, then where is she?

Easy. The apartment.

He pulled out the back way and drove past the hospital, took a right and headed through downtown, keeping an eagle eye for April and/or Mason traversing the streets and managed to get through the other side without clipping some parked car. He cut down the Grant's lot and in and out a couple of turns and then back down Woodlane and there, Easthampton Arms. He bounced past the oversized broken sign and pulled right up to the apartment's front door. Which was wide open.

Cautious, he leaned into the windshield and peered up the darkened stairwell wondering if this was some kind of trap, May having called April to set it up, when he noticed the "For Rent" sign in the top window.

Well, whaddya know, April absconded.

He got out and cocked an ear and heard the sound of someone vacuuming.

That's obviously not April, so coast clear.

He walked up.

"Honey, I'm home," he whispered. Not loud enough that the vacuumer in the back bedroom could hear him, but for his own amusement.

Because it *was* home, his very first real apartment. Everything before was courtesy of a parent, a sibling, or a long-suffering friend, with Butch providing sporadic financial and structural support. Not that he ever harbored a desire to live in substandard housing, but when the back of the gas station had become too much Thong-and-Kasey territory, and when April's dad had threatened to throw her out if she didn't stop dating Butch, the path to this place was set. First, to get a Thong-and-Kasey-free space to share with April, he needed a steadier source of income than borrowing from Mom ('borrowing' not the correct term; 'extorting,' that's it) so he took a job as an orderly at the hospital. Second, after calculating his monthly take-home pay from the aforementioned job, he determined that his housing options were either a tent somewhere in the Barrens or an apartment in this complex. So he signed a contract, put down two months' rent (extorted from Mom), borrowed Cindy's boyfriend-of-the-moment's truck and headed over to April's (when her dad wasn't there) and escorted her and her suitcases up these stairs. They'd both stood on the landing and looked at each other.

"This is it," Butch said.

Boy, was it.

Typical slapped-together low-income apartment, carbon copy of Mom's with color scheme exceptions: green pile carpeting, sheetrock walls, three-burner electric stove and a half-sized refrigerator next to a stainless steel sink, a balcony overlooking the parking lot, no air conditioning, dubious heat, the ever-present smell of cabbage, and the constant serenade of doors slamming, cars peeling out, screams and other indications of very loud and bloody murder or very loud and violent dissolutions of marriages/cohabitations/whatever, always, always around midnight of every workday accompanied by various babies howling and the standard symphony of showering and urinating and defecating that three contiguous buildings offered. Not too much different from life at the Ellio's Pizza apartment except that this place was his. This was home.

Turned out to be more storage unit than home because they were never here. Ever. The moment they got off work, they rendezvoused at the front door, wolfed down whatever leftover Gino's stuff April had snagged on her way out of the restaurant and headed to the dojo so Butch could teach class and then train with Oak. They'd leave there about nine, usually giving Oak and his girlfriend-of-the-moment a ride to the girlfriend's apartment-of-the-moment, and then to a friend's house – alternating between April's friends and his – until about two or three in the morning, sometimes later, then back to the apartment stoned and/or drunk, make love with plenty of bellowing but absolutely no post-coitus crying, sleep for a couple of hours, then up and to work and start the whole process again.

It was heaven. For three months.

For three months, Butch had a life. An actual life. After twenty years or so of nightmare, he'd burst out of the jungle, tearing leeches and burrowing-worms off his face and stood before the gates of Avalon, songs and flowers raining down on him. This is what life was supposed to be: crazy and wild and dancing along the cliff's edge, the hand of the woman he loved keeping him from slipping off.

The woman he loved.

He listened to the rhythm of the vacuum cleaner removing all traces of him from the back bedroom. For three or four months April was the woman he loved. Then seven or eight weeks ago, she wasn't. "Well then," all the self-appointed love experts in history say as they shake admonishing fingers, "That wasn't love! You can't just turn it off and on like that."

Oh yes, you can.

Genuine love flares and ashes on a regular basis. That was a truth he'd learned from Dad. Probably the only truth. If there was one consistency in Dad's quite detailed love life, it was the speed with which a cherished wife or partner became a horrific witch, usually within minutes of cherished wife or partner discovering that she was not exclusive; indeed, that she was merely three of four or five. Should she have the temerity to object, Dad would, with screams and declarations of complete outrage, describe why and in what manner she had suddenly become witchlike. Butch almost admired the way Dad made it look like her fault. He was master at it. After all, he'd always made Butch feel like the world's troubles were Butch's doing.

It devastated him that Dad turned out accurate on the subject of love. If there was one person who shouldn't be right about any aspect of human relationships it was an evil, violent, disturbed crazy man who regarded his entire family as his personal plaything and punching bag. A man like that should be condemned across all categories, shunned and vilified, put in the stocks then drawn and quartered and never, ever credited with any sagacity. But Dad may be a prophet in his own country, and, despite the justified and well-earned opprobrium, spoke an occasional and uncomfortable truth. It could also be a chicken and egg argument: was Dad an evil, disturbed, crazy man because he discovered early on that love was a will-o'-the-wisp, or did evil crazy men turn love into something fleeting? Didn't matter. Having Dad as a source of wisdom on this was abhorrent.

Worse, Butch had emulated Dad by declaring April a witch within minutes of her special announcement ... well, that's not exactly true. She gradually became witchlike during the course of her post-announcement campaign to separate Butch from his friends and family and intents. And Butch, having no other example to fall back on, resorted to Dad-like behavior to counter the witchiness. Unlike Dad, though, Butch was justified: after working on Daddy April's chain gang all day for a shilling and a cup of gruel, to come home and find that April had bought several unnecessary pieces of furniture and enhanced her wardrobe and shoe collection thereby guaranteeing Butch's continued thralldom, then, like any reasonable human being, he lost it. Shoes flew across rooms, denting recently acquired furniture, which elicited shrieks of outrage and escalation and cops. At least three times, in each instance the cops moved to snap cuffs on Butch and haul him away, when April told them who her dad was and the cops looked at each other and unsnapped cuffs and advised Butch to go somewhere and cool off while they made a phone call and hoo boy, would he not hear it the next day? Yes, he did, but in the interim, go to Don's. Not Thong's. Kasey was too sympathetic to April's position, them being women and everything.

And Don's was where the plans got hatched.

He sighed.

So, not only is Dad right, but he's precedent. Except ... there's a huge difference between initiating the horror and being its victim.

If the monster comes after you, then screaming and physical attacks are self-defense. Whether the monster is a bruising dark-eyed crazy man with hulking shoulders and murder on his face, or a slip of a girl who couldn't muster enough of a slap to raise a welt, it was the monster's fault. Not his.

Let's go with that.

"Canna help?"

Startled, Butch woke up. A tall Korean man in blue overalls and carrying a portable vacuum cleaner stood in front of him.

"Oh, sorry," he said.

"You wanna rent apartment, airman?" the Korean man asked.

"You know I'm in the Air Force?"

Finally, someone who knew the uniform, and a furriner at that.

The man frowned.

"Uhm… well, dunno. I saw the door open and thought I'd check it out."

"You want?" No nonsense, this guy.

"I… how much?"

"450."

Butch started. Wow, a hundred dollars more than he'd paid.

"That's pretty steep."

"Is cheap. All rents goin' up. You want?"

Butch figured management was trying to recoup what April had stiffed them. "Not at that price."

The man turned away. "Then you go," he said, dismissing Butch and dropping the vacuum cleaner on the living room carpet.

Okay, okay.

He turned for the stairs then paused. "What happened to the last tenants?"

Sun Myung Moon looked over. "Some girl, she move out. No good." His eyes narrowed. "I know you?"

Butch hastily rolled down the stairs before Jae Chul Shin put two and two together. The guy was definitely smart. Not only knew uniform differences, he was also dead-on about April.

Chapter 10

Butch resumed a now half-hearted search for either Mason or April, taking a meandering, and rather pointless, cross-country course. He'd lost the urge to kneecap either of them so wasn't sure what he would do if, by some stroke of really bad luck, they crossed paths. Yell at them? Blow the horn and give a thumbs-up? Stupid. As was this driving around because all he had to do was head over to April's dad's office and ask where she was. 'Course her dad would run him over with a bulldozer so, no. He ended up parked on the shoulder somewhere on the road between Perkins and Mt. Holyoke across from some big farm. How he got here, no idea.

True for everything, wasn't it?

Amazing how many times he ended up in a place and circumstance of which he had no prior inkling. Strolling along minding his own business and, *bam*! On a Greyhound in the middle of winter heading to New Jersey. Get all settled in nice and comfy and *bam*! Living with some girl in an apartment one minute, running from drug dealers the next. Quick decisions made in the heat of the moment, no real idea of the consequences, just the need to resolve the situation right now, right now! And, then…

And then.

Visions of bloody sheets and April's tear-stained face merged and blurred and he shuddered and gasped, unable to breathe, spots before his eyes.

So this is what an asthma attack feels like.

Art suffered from it and Butch had spent many a day helping

little brother recover and so he knew what to do: *calmate, jefe, paz, paz*, repeat the mantra until Art calmed while Butch stroked Art's back and his air slowly returned so, *calmate, jefe*, and he stroked both sides of his face as he watched a distant tractor make what seemed like aimless circuits across a cornfield. Each pass, the corn rows lessened: a deliberate action with measurable results. Decisions in the micro were controllable. It's the macro where things got out of hand.

Like the decision to share an apartment with April, which, in the micro seemed a good idea, logical and appropriate but, Holy Hannah, the results. Ripples of unintended consequences spreading in all directions. The right thing turns out otherwise.

So what's the right thing, right now? Frank? Any suggestions?

He sighed and looked in the rearview mirror but Frank wasn't there.

Maybe that's best. Frank has no idea what's right anymore, heck, what's wrong, either.

Despite appearing older, Frank was fixed at ten years old, when one's sense of right or wrong was limited to one's sense of fairness. It's not fair that your dweeby little brother got a bigger slice of chocolate pie than you did. It's not fair that your best friend ran off with another kid to play hide-and-seek. It's not fair that your mother beats you to death with a baseball bat on the last day of school because you forgot your report card.

But life is unfairness writ large. Everything is unfair, at every turn, at every moment, and to peg fair treatment as one's measure of redress was silly. Simplistic. Childish. Maturity was the putting away of childish things. Not that Butch considered himself mature: sitting in an idling car PO'd at an ex-girlfriend was not exactly proof of adulthood. Saying the heck with her and heading out to the Lakes for a Dooby concert would be more in line, but this sense of outrage, this roiling in his stomach ...

Man, how do you adult out of that?

Outrage and roiled stomach were ever-present companions since he, too, was ten years old, but it shouldn't be the catalyst for momentous decisions. Doing something, anything, solely to relieve the roiling leads to even more regrettable decisions, like half-assed drug deals or joining the military. Frank, then, was not the best person ... ghost, figment, whatever ... to consult. Not that Frank didn't have a valid complaint: robbed of his life and condemned to wander the earth gave him special insight into life's general unfairness, a cord that binds and periodically caused Frank to shimmer into being ...

Hmm.

Funny he had not seen Frank since that insane summer of 1965. Funny he shows up today. You'd think that interim events like bloody sheets and midnight pool parties would have manifested the guy. If they were bound to each other by the unfairness of life, then those things should have lifted him from the grave. But nope, nary a peep, either poolside or on the bus to New Jersey, a strong indication that Frank was, as Butch firmly believed, mere figment. Of guilt, of fear, of… something other than reality. That Frank was no longer manifesting as a ten-year-old kid lent further evidence to his figment-status because a real ghost would stay ten forever. Victim forever. Filled with grievance, like Butch. Which was probably why Frank had re-conjured. Grievance begat a sense of being owed, and Frank was definitely owed something. Like a life. Butch had grievances roiling right alongside Frank's, so Butch was owed, too.

But who owed him? And what was owed?

Well, God. God owed him. God owed something to Frank and Cindy and Art and Mom and everyone else who had survived these last nine years or so of horror and misery. The comforting of the orphan, the wiping away of tears, that was God's job. Every preacher in every church said as much. The Bible said as much. Yet, Frank was still trying to put a cheekbone back in place; Cindy was in a different Piney car every week; Art was simply lost. And Butch… the tears perpetually coursed below the surface, contained only by his sense of shame. After all, he'd fallen asleep and missed his chance and, subsequently, was forced into a midnight pool party. Yet, no Benign Hand reached down from heaven with a Holy Kleenex to dab at Butch's eyes as some stentorian Voice comforted, "There, there…" And never would.

Because he was damned.

Damned and condemned for eternity. No argument there. Dad, grunting and sweating on top of a German housemaid, the two of them locked in dirty sewer-lust and what could come of that? He was the spoor of the damned. Begun with taint, shall end in taint. The sins of the fathers visited on the sons.

He was the rejected spawn of syphilitic urges, Esau, Ishmael, the lurker watching from hillsides. The pure and the clean bowed in holy light and received the blessings while he dwelled in salt and wastelands, eking a meal from the refuse thrown his way. The church doors did not open as Butch, trembling, mounted the steps. A hand on the knob and lightning raced from the sky and down the nave and blasted him off the portico. Holy water burned his skin; a cross made him hiss. God's disgust oozed from the white, summer-burnt skies, the Eyes red and angry, an Accusing Finger pointing, always pointing. Butch wore the Mark of Cain, but without the requisite protection.

And this was doubly unfair because he'd sought God.

He'd sought Him.

One of his first memories was lying on top of the storm cellar in the backyard in Oklahoma and watching the giant thunderheads form and soar in the white and red of the setting sun, their power so obvious, and he knew God was in them. He'd spoken to God right then, not in actual words, and felt an answer, also not in words but still and silent and filled with irresistible strength and kindness and knew that God was with him. It felt like a Special Hand lay across his shoulder. He'd gone to all the Sunday Schools in all the churches Mom regularly attended (and Dad sporadically so, mostly when he needed cover), absorbing the soft, mealy words of the Oklahoma Methodists and then the thundering condemnations of the Alabama Baptists and believed God was with him.

Until a rainy night by a pool.

Butch had joined the local Methodist church in Perkins almost right off the bus, attending religiously, so to speak, alongside Mom and his grandparents and cousins and uncles and aunts. He sang in the choir and volunteered to clean up and passed the plate and did whatever the youth groups were doing and even visited the nut cases at Buttonwood Hall, reading the Bible to them from some semen-stained alcove as they staggered by, gibbering. He did everything the Bible and the churchmen said he was supposed to do. And yet, every time he walked up the church steps, every time he pulled up a Sunday School chair or washed a dish or arranged Bibles on shelves, he felt Red Eyes on him. The pastor, an effete, pale, half-bald man who spoke aphorisms in a falsetto, stood behind the pulpit and warned against eternal damnation as his red eyes drifted across the congregation and rested on Butch.

Other eyes, judging, critical, offended ones, followed.

How did they know?

Butch examined himself for the Mark or, at least, to see if his fly was undone but could not spot what, apparently, everyone else did. Maybe the ability to see the condemned, the hopeless ones that God had already rejected, was a holy gift reserved for the blessed, His Accusing Finger stabbing repeatedly at cursed foreheads, so the blessed knew who to avoid. No matter how hard Butch prayed and agonized in closets and raged at the impure thoughts that seized him and left him prostrate with lust, he could not break the curse. God's Finger stabbed and stabbed. The eyes followed him everywhere.

After a while, Butch stopped going to church.

He fell among the craven, ran with the unwashed, and became a pulpit warning to others. Instead of the voice from a distant thundercloud, Butch now heard the whispered judgments of the righteous. And weren't they right? Was he not living in cast-off apartments eating cast-off food, alone and abandoned? Proof that God had cast him off.

And yet...

Butch still heard a far-off, indecipherable voice, somewhat tinged with irritation, like a friend yelling something important across the stadium but the game and the cheerleaders and the band drowned it out and the friend is annoyed because he really, really wants you to know something. It was important, critical, and Butch strained his ears but couldn't quite make it out. This Voice was at odds with what the pastors and the churches and youth groups taught, God as Hairy Thunderer baring His Teeth in Rage every time Butch pictured a girl naked (which was about five hundred times a minute), a God Weeping at Butch's sinfulness Who would Finger Flick Butch into the lowest circles of hell with nary a second's pause. So don't use bad words, don't drink, don't have sex unless you're married and for the sole purpose of bearing children, pray constantly, acknowledge God in everything from dinner to crossing the street, keep a head tilted heavenward and a beatific smile on your face ... or else. The voice Butch heard was impatient with all that. It wasn't Hairy Thunderer. It was the God Who Shrugged.

At goodness. At being good. God did not care if Butch was good. God was the essence of good and the last thing he needed was the poor, rickety facsimile that humans generated. He could get all the Good He wanted with a Finger Flick. He needed something else. He demanded something else:

He wanted Butch to be right.

The God Who Shrugged operated on the very simple premise that Butch and everyone else in the world knew what was right. And Butch did. He knew the right thing to do in every circumstance, in every situation. If he had never read a Bible or heard the teachings of holy men and society and the law, he would still know what was right. Because what was right was God, the God in him, the God in everyone. It was right to comfort Mom after Dad had beaten her; it was right to accompany her as she traveled the back roads of Alabama selling Tupperware to farmer's wives. It was right to feed the chickens and mow the lawn without being told so Dad would be in a good mood when he came home and consider Butch a dutiful, good (No! Not good. Right!) son and maybe, just maybe, not beat him. Not beat any of them.

If all that failed, it was right to shoot Dad in the head.

But he didn't shoot Dad in the head. He did not do what was right. And that pushed the first domino and the cascade followed and everything fell to ruin. He could not keep Cindy away from the Pineys and could not keep himself away from April, the ongoing cascade putting him in business with Jape and Truck and Pee Sea and the Air Force and now on the side of the road in an idling car, unsure what to do next. And none of this would have happened if he had made the right decision to shoot Dad in the head.

You have to do what's right all the time.

The God of Shrugs demands it. Otherwise, yours becomes a life of wrongs.

No wonder everything was so fucked up.

"Well, I didn't do anything wrong." Frank, from the back seat.

"Yes, you did," Butch said, glancing in the rearview. "You already said you did. You forgot your report card."

"The important word there is, 'forgot.'" Frank's eye, dangling on a thread from a socket, cast sardonic.

"But that's not what you said."

"You convinced me otherwise with that whole 'deserve it' argument."

Butch clucked that away. "Beside the point. Whether it's

omission or commission, it was still something you did wrong."

Popped the eye back in. "So I deserved to die because of a faulty memory?"

"No." Butch waved an impatient hand. "It's not a question of what you deserved or not, it's the consequence of the wrong action. If you had done the right thing, remembered the report card, you'd be driving your mom's car today on some backroad of Oklahoma, instead of riding in mine in New Jersey."

"Or not. She might have killed me just for the hell of it."

"Moms don't do that."

"Oh?"

Hmm.

Frank had a point. Moms gave you up, Moms abandoned you, so killing was not a stretch. And if a mom's predilection was to reach for a bat over something as innocuous as a forgotten report card, then Frank was a goner anyway. Some other triggering event would leave him jawless and eyeless; it was just a matter of when. So, fate in your own hands, or not? Need to ask a higher authority.

"What did God tell you?"

"He won't speak to me." Frank was playing with his unhinged jaw.

No doubt because Frank was still filled with grievance, which was an implied criticism of God's Functions. It's not like God *made* you forget the report card and your mom go nuts, Frank, so why the attitude? Asked and answered: Frank still seeks redress. Frank still thinks it's all unfair, like the ten-year-old he was forever to be, no matter what guise he assumed. Frank, man, fair or unfair doesn't mean crap. You were a good boy and what did it gain you? 'Good' is beside the point. It's *rightness* that spurs God's blessing and regard, not goodness. You still think He's the God of distant thunderheads, Frank, but He's actually the God Who Shrugs.

"You all right?"

Butch almost jumped through the top of the car. A gigantic police officer stood next to the driver's side window.

"Man!" Butch quasi-shrieked. "You scared me to death!"

"You didn't see me pull up behind you?" The cop leaned in, sniffing. "You high or something?"

Butch jerked away from the mirror sunglasses and Smokey the Bear hat and a big gold badge that said 'Perkins Boro Police' and five o'clock shadow and the smell and sound of ferociously chewed mint gum.

"No! I'm in the Air Force."

"Like that means anything," the cop snorted. "So what are you doing here?"

So the 'brothers-in-uniform' gambit wasn't going to work. Eff it, be straight-up.

"Trying to figure out where to go next."

"Where'd you go before?"

"My girlfriend's apartment." A pause. "She wasn't there."

"Hmm." The cop evaluated him. "Doesn't sound like she's your girlfriend anymore."

Butch blew out a breath. "I think you're right."

"Hmm." This time with sympathy. "License and registration."

Butch dug out his wallet while digging around the glove box. "This is my mom's car," he explained as he rummaged, "I'm home on leave." The cop said nothing, waited patiently until Butch located the documents and handed them over.

"I know you," the cop said, after a moment.

Butch scrutinized him. "I don't know you."

"Yeah, you do. From high school." And he tapped his gold name tag and Butch read 'Liston'.

"Sonny."

"Yep."

Yep. Butch knew him. Boy, did he. The guy was not exactly a friend. Sonny was a bully, one of the legions of black T-shirt types with long hair and big muscles who roamed the halls in packs, zeroing on the dweeby and nerdy and shoving them around. They were always in threes and fours, standing rudely at critical intersections and yelling "Wadda yew lookin' at?" at everyone maneuvering around them in an effort to get through without stepping on their feet or brushing their shoulders and subsequently getting slammed into lockers. They flexed and smirked and yelled incomprehensible things at each other and boasted loudly of sexual abilities that even a demon-gorged incubus would have difficulty performing. Three to four town slatterns accompanied them, tacitly giving proof of the boasted abilities, else why hang about with such louts?

Dunno.

The girls love the bad boys. Even when it's all talk. Sonny

and his pals had shoved dweeby Butch around quite regularly, especially during his churching, until the dweebiness turned into karate badassery.

"Didn't recognize you."

"You've changed a little bit, yourself."

"Um." Butch rubbed his skull. "Got a haircut."

Sonny chuckled. "Got a beer belly," and he slapped it.

"You became a cop."

"You joined the Air Force."

"Guess we're both surprised."

Sonny smiled and stood back and looked down the road and Butch wasn't really surprised at Sonny's chosen profession. Throwing weight around defined his high school life. A small-town cop job allowed him to continue to throw weight around, with the imprimatur of law enforcement.

"I was kind of a jerk in school," Sonny said.

Actually surprised, all Butch could do was raise eyebrows.

Sonny waved a hand. "S'kay, you can say it."

"I don't want to get arrested."

"For what, parking on the side of the road?" Sonny shrugged. "What do you think I do all day?"

Butch had no response.

Sonny did. "Anyways, I became a cop to make up for that."

And he looked at Butch expectantly.

"Is it working?"

"I guess." Sonny mused up the road. "I mean, I feel like I'm doing some good now."

Butch was about to launch into the difference between Hairy Thunderer and He Who Shrugs, rightness versus goodness, but figured it was a waste of speech.

"I joined the Air Force to get away from my girlfriend."

Sonny outright laughed at that and Butch chuckled in response and wondered why in the hell was he feeling friendly towards this jackass.

Man, things change.

"Listen." Sonny handed him back everything. "I've heard some things."

Uh oh.

Butch put on his innocent face.

"It might be a real good idea for you to get out of town."

Butch couldn't help himself.

"By sundown?"

"I'm serious, man." Sonny was serious. "Things are kinda dicey . You might want to make yourself very scarce. I mean, head out and don't come back. Ever." He leaned into the window. "And I mean, ever."

"Pee Sea," was all Butch said.

"Yeah, Pee Sea." Sonny gave him an exasperated look. "Why in the fuck did you get involved with that guy, man?"

"Seemed like a good idea at the time." He paused. "Why don't you guys arrest him?"

Sonny snorted. "C'mon, man. This is a small town."

Yes, yes it is.

Everyone knows everyone. Everyone knows whose wheels must be greased in what amounts to ensure lucrative activities continue to the advantage of key people, say, a chief of police or a mayor or something. Not that Butch had ever heard any specifics, and he was dying to ask Sonny exactly what he knew but Butch didn't want to risk an arrest he had, so far, avoided, so all he did was blink at him. Sonny smirked then suddenly turned his head and peered into the back seat. "Who's your friend?"

Startled, Butch looked in the rearview but Frank wasn't there.

"You can see him?"

Sonny's eyes narrowed and, suddenly, he went white. Jerking back from the window, his hand dropped to his gun as his jaw dropped open and his eyes blew wide.

Great, shot to death by a terrified cop. Thanks, Frank.

Sonny vibrated, unsure what to do, and then raced to his car.

Seconds later, the car door slammed and the cruiser U-turned off the shoulder almost on two wheels, throwing dust and gravel everywhere, and tore down the road.

Butch watched until Sonny disappeared.

"Thanks, Frank."

Chapter 11

Butch took off with the full intent of distancing himself from any and all other cops who might want to follow-up Sonny's no-doubt crazy radio call, hesitating when he got to Arney's Mount. A quick right and he'd be back in Perkins, but Sonny's warning still hung in his ear.

Press on.

He ended up in Perkins, anyway, but on the north side, far from the murder centers, and turned towards Ft. Dix to get even farther away and about a mile later…

Oh my my, look at this: Perkins Township High School, my ole alma mater.

The place looked as forlorn as only a school can during summer break, a few random cars here and there giving emphasis to its mass desertion and it's been a year since he last roamed these hallowed halls and ya know… sudden reflex, whip in, coast up the long drive…

And here I am, old girl.

Butch stared hungrily at the double doors. Talk about home ... God, he'd loved high school. Every morning of it, Butch hopped out of bed, wolfed down a plank of Ellio's or a bowl of Lucky Charms, grabbed his knapsack and practically ran all the way to the bus stop a mile off in Perkins, eager to get to it.

All the universes coalesced here, their various elements swirling and blending, then repelling and starting up somewhere else. His planets and comets shot from one end of the building to the other and, sometimes, he couldn't make class because of all the worlds he encountered. Don and he joined up outside homeroom and by lunchtime, they'd collected the Country Lakes boys, the PL girls, and the Braun's Mills gang, commandeering adjacent tables in the cafeteria. Right after lunch, Butch mixed with the bros and the jive-asses and the karateka and Mason and then back to the PL crowd and a good-bye to Don or ride with Mason and Don around Perkins or the county, or ride with Thong to the Archways' or to his parents' satellite CIA office in Country Lakes… or he simply rode the bus back to Perkins, quietly reading Herman Hesse and trying not to attract attention because Perkins belonged to Sonny and the rest of the hardguys and he didn't want to get into a fight, he just wanted to go home and eat Ellio's.

Despite these distractions, he did well: good grades, complete homework and class participation, not because the God Who Shrugs approved the rightness of it, but because school had always been his thing.

His *only* thing; in Alabama, the peanut farmer kids thought he was an alien and excluded him from their reindeer games and he took solace in academic excellence, alienating him even more, although the teachers loved it. He was still an alien when he arrived in Perkins, but the locals delighted in his oddness and adopted him and, next thing you know, Butch was groovin' and jivin' with the cool kids. Eventually, he became one of the cool kids. High school was the first place where Butch actually fitted in.

And it all came crashing down the day he graduated. Heck, the very moment the caps went into the air.

He'd had no idea that would happen. Yeah, sure, he was heading off to San Francisco, but the universes should have remained intact at least until he got on the plane. But, by ten o' clock that night, the universes had dissipated. Butch stood in the middle of the PL bandshell, right next to the lake, absolutely astonished because not a single person was around. Not one. Perkins Township had graduated an entire class of some 400 or more crazy teenagers mere hours before, many of them PL residents, and none of them was here. The place was a ghost town, and that wasn't right. There should be wall-to-wall greasers and hardguys and Pineys running from one end of the bandshell to the other, drinking and smoking and fighting and fucking. But, no. *Nadia*. It had made for a very frustrating night; instead of wall-to-wall partying from one universe to another, he'd ended up marooned on some distant, desolate planet.

The next day, he was gone. But the universes had beaten him to it.

Cindy had taken him to the airport and claimed sole ownership of Buggy and waved a cheerful hand out of the window and a "Don't forget to write, asshole!" and it wasn't until about a month later that he found out what happened: "We was looking for you, man, but you disappeared so we went to Groveville" Don wrote in a very short note (so short he didn't even mention marrying Sherry Baby). And Butch *had* disappeared: after tossing his cap, he'd hitched a ride from Thong back to the Archways' and then ran over to the apartment to get some Ellio's and grabbed Buggy and headed out to Oak's in Willingboro and stayed there working out until early evening and went back to the apartment and packed a suitcase for San Francisco and laid his ticket on top of it then back to Buggy and began a Flying Dutchman search for the universes ending up in the empty bandshell wondering where the hell everyone had gotten to.

So, okay, start a new universe. And the San Francisco one had been rollicking and insane and completely foreign. It was more a parallel existence than an actual universe, where the physical laws were slightly off, as were the residents. He lived in the back of Dale's townhouse right off the beach, and Butch sat on the sand, stoned out of his mind watching the sun set, which was wrong, all wrong. You sit on a beach to watch the sun *rise* and he would never, ever fit in here. It was too far from anything he considered normal, his night orderly job overseeing a bunch of Haight lunatics the final proof.

He returned in December to reconstituted universes, at least, until the end of April (in both senses) but, even then, things were not the same. Buggy was gone. The Piney-of-the-week had wrapped it around some pine somewhere in the Barrens and left it there to rot. Oak was in the throes of the romantic trauma that led to his recent disappearance. Butch started his own romantic trauma that altered the Thong and Archway and Don universes and now, here he was, about to flee into the American hinterlands. The threads of the remaining universes dissolved, efforts to tie them back together doomed because there was nothing left to tie. Forced associations became unforced.

Because the friends from high school were the friends of circumstance.

His worlds were artificial, a result of the geography and peer-grouping that brought these planets together, a mere function of physics. At a certain place and at a certain time mandated by law, persons of high school age met in a designated building for purposes of social and educational training. From these people he picked his associates, galaxies forming from the material available, an association forcing compatibility as gravity crunched dust and rocks into planets and stars. But when the gravity was gone, everything devolved to its constituent parts, like a supernova blasting space to atoms. The caps thrown in the air was the explosion.

At that point, the universes loosed because every person in them was now free to make choices. Law and tradition had kept them all together, a lot of them against their will, and the release of caps meant they were no longer beholden. They could, and did, scatter to the four winds. A lot of them were off to colleges in distant states, some in distant lands, and an argument might be made that this was, still, forced association in an educational setting except these places were chosen, so everyone who attended did so because they wanted to, not because they had to. The same was true for those who joined the military, those who took jobs, those who simply took off: where they ended up and who they ended up with, was a choice. The undying vows of high school friendships died, blood brothers and sisters, best friends forever and ever stay in touch, stay in touch, man, and we don't. We don't.

Because we're not blood brothers anymore. We got replaced.

Share foxholes in far-off jungles, share internships in far-off cities, get hired in the same company on the same day; from this pool, your lifelong pals emerged. They became each other's best men, watched each other's children, compared snapshots of grandkids. They helped you move, spent their summer vacations at your lake house, came to your funeral. This is the way of it. This is normal life.

Butch, though, did not have a normal life

He'd lost far too much in too short a time. The bulwarks of normality – family, parents, community – had been usurped. He didn't even have a mother, at least one filled with concern about his well-being. The only family he had were surrogates expansive enough to add him. But, even then, he remained an outlier, the orphan with a nose pressed against the glass, adrift and tossed by waves so when a spar hove to, he clung to it. The universes had been entire rafts and rescue boats and he pulled himself up and over their keels, dropping exhausted and grateful in their bottoms while their crewmen joked and laughed and tossed him an oar and said here, join us.

Join us.

Which was why he needed to find Don. Restore at least one universe. Today. But first, let's take a little trip through time.

Butch got out of the car and walked through the double doors, taking in a huge breath just as he cleared the threshold. Ah, there, the perfume of pending school: a blend of chalk and chlorine and that red sawdust which every janitor in every school in America threw on the floor every August. By the second week of September, it was a perfume blended with vomit and gym shoes and square pizza but now it was freshness. He chuckled, remembering how the old janitor at the Yoman school varnished the wooden floors during the summer break. School opened back up the last week of August, when it was one hundred degrees in the shade, and the halls were carpeted with abandoned shoes stuck fast to the floor, abandoned socks a few steps farther on.

Hilarious.

Butch peered through the glass windows that lined the office on his left but no one was in there. He stepped around the corner and peered at the guidance counselor offices but they were empty, too. Ditto the hallways. All was still, all awaited Labor Day.

Begin the walk down memory lane: here, Mr. Years's classroom, where Thong and he sat in the back cutting up until Mr. Years's seal-like face rose from behind his desk and blinked giant eyelashes at them and chided, "Gentlemen?" Mrs. Jonas's English class, where he and Don argued with her about Shakespeare and Frost and Charges of Light Brigades while the jocks and greasers rolled their eyes and made fart noises with their armpits.

Philistines.

Here, history, with Mr. Malanza, Butch's first avowed Communist; over here, the dreaded math classes, Algebra I with Mr. Audi, a small nerdy guy who had an unlimited intellect and the driest sense of humor on earth.

LOOKING FOR DON

Ah, there, German class, Mr. Rollo, one of the most popular teachers in the school because he was funny and open and constantly playing jokes on everybody. Butch took German with great enthusiasm because, 'Hey, I'm German, this should be easy.' Three years later, Butch's skill was limited to asking the location of the nearest post office. Just. Didn't. Get it.

S'kay, doubt I'll ever need to ask some Kraut where to buy stamps.

Butch finished the tour at the gym, stepping through the heavy doors, which clanked to a close behind him. Dust-laden sunbeams flowed through the ceiling windows, making the entire room almost ethereal. Mats hung on the walls between the pull-out bleachers; seven or eight basketball goals circled the floor from one end to the other, all canted at a forty-five-degree angle like a guard of honor presenting arms. His footsteps echoed as he walked to the middle.

Man, loud.

School dances held inside this acoustically terrible enclosure, assaulted by bands that substituted amp volume for talent, destroyed more eardrums than did one J. Geils concert. 'Course, one rather memorable J. Geils concert t at the Spectrum left him deaf for weeks. And blitzed.

Good times, good times.

This is where the Don universe formed, during the first gym class of sophomore year. Don and he had been sitting in adjacent lines as Coach Hardass, er, Hardaway, yelled that they were all worthless and weak. Butch was telling the guy behind him, Nick Something-or-other, a dirty joke and Don laughed and leaned over and told another dirty joke and it became a dirty joke festival up and down both lines in between Hardass's invective. Turns out Don and he had an almost identical schedule: both were in the previously mentioned English class and in Social Studies and the best-forgotten geometry, where Don and he teamed up with another prisoner of the education system, the appropriately named John Kool, a crazed far-right nutcase classmate who was absolutely one of the coolest people Butch had ever met and who would disappear over the following summer because his Dad got arrested by the FBI or something. For reasons never articulated, John loathed the brand-new math teacher... what was her name, Miss Apple? Something like that... and made it his life's mission to have her commit suicide. John instigated everything, including a class-wide paper airplane war. Hundreds of paper airplanes blizzarded the room every single time Miss Apple turned to the board, all of them landing the exact moment she turned back to see what all the fuss was about. That included an airplane John folded out of a New York Times into an aerodynamically perfect baby dragon that floated across the room blocking out the sun and always, always, slipped under a desk when she flipped about as the class dissolved in hysterics. John was a diabolical genius, a Bond villain. Too bad he left. Would have made a wonderful addition to the Three Musketeers, turning them into The Four Horsemen of the Apocalypse.

The tyranny of high school scheduling had unintentionally lumped Don and Butch alphabetically together, not realizing they shared identical senses of humor and anarchy and musical taste. Alliance became inevitable during the four to six hours a day they spent in each other's company, Don turning into the brother that Art should have been, especially after Butch accepted an invitation to Don's home and met his parents and saw Don's life. Butch wanted that life. So he joined the family.

Don's universe assumed a higher ranking than all the others, even Oak's, although Butch did everything possible to mesh the two, even getting Don to join the karate club, two long-haired white boys among the 'fro'd brothers, which meant they spent even more time together. Became even more family.

Family.

Butch stood quietly and let those days wash over him. Everything was possible then: a normal world, achievable with the right friends, the right circumstances, and by doing the right things. But he hadn't done the right things. He ignored the God of Shrugs. Okay, so, been there, done that, lessons learned and now he knew, and God is omnipotent and omnipresent and knew that Butch now knew, so what about a do-over?

I will it, God Who Shrugs, that You Who Knows That I Now Know should grant me this boon: open a wormhole or a vortex and make it sophomore year again and this time, this time, I will avoid the acts that created this present.

Butch would not go to San Francisco or Alabama or move in with April and find himself in such desperate straits that he caused everything else to happen.

Everything else to happen.

He waited, braced and ready, wondering if he would remember enough of the circumstances and events of 1971 that he could pass muster and not betray his time-traveler status to the newly-met Don and the yelling Hardass and…

What was that joke he told Nick Something-or-other, what was it?

He felt nothing, no tingling and disorientation and nausea that every decent sci-fi novel said accompanied time travel and he opened his eyes and, dang, still in the ethereal beam-striped gym of the present day, still in a brand spanking new Air Force uniform and still mere days away from leaving. Forever.

"Can I help you?"

Butch turned. A guy in a green work uniform and carrying a gigantic broom had popped out of the back hallway that led to the dressing rooms and stared at Butch suspiciously.

"Can you time travel?" Butch asked.

Green Jeans gaped and then his face cleared and his suspicion softened. "No. And neither can you."

Butch saluted the wisdom, turned and walked through the noisy doors, down the hall back towards the office, hesitated, and then slid down the main hall, passing a few more corridors until he got to the senior wing and beelined straight for his locker without having to think twice. He giggled. Imprinted memory.

Now, did I imprint my combination?

Not that it would work: hasn't been his locker for a year and they changed it after every graduation. Right? Besides, the most recent resident, whoever that was, should have removed any lingering traces, physical and psychic, of previous occupants. So, if by some miracle you can open this, what do you expect to find? He had no idea but ghosts leave traces (right, Frank?) and maybe this locker was like the wardrobe to Narnia and all he need do was chant or invoke and presto change-o! A re-do.

Let's see, let's see…

Holding his breath, he spun the three numbers from imprinted memory, and, Holy Hannah, felt the latch click.

Oh, my God. My God Who Shrugs. Take me back. Please. And pulled it open.

Empty, of course.

He waved a hand inside to see if that triggered any energies but all that did was dislodge a piece of paper that flapped its way off the top shelf and into the air. Probably some forgotten class note from the previous resident but could be the incantation he sought and he seized it mid-flap. A green piece of construction paper with something on the back.

Please, please, incant…

He turned it over.

It was a picture of Don standing on the football field, a picture out of the yearbook. Don's head had been removed and pasted onto his stomach, with ink lines running down it like blood. Printed underneath it were the words, "You're next."

Chapter 12

Butch drummed his fingers on the steering wheel.

That's it. Enough of this crap. Come on, Pee Sea, let's finish this.

He fixed on the rearview mirror, tensed and ready. Any moment now, the El Camino roars around the corner of the school, fishtailing and bearing down on him, Pee hunched over the wheel, wild murder in his eyes…

Okay. Fine. Let's go. Let's do it.

Pee Sea probably had a gun, his earlier finger-point so indicating. All right. Don't give him a chance to pull it. Plan A: drop the Pontiac into reverse and stomp the pedal and drive the trunk right into Pee Sea's grill, then leap out, drag the stunned Pee out of his car and beat him and beat him and beat him until either Pee Sea was Jello or the police pulled him off.

Plan B: run like hell.

Butch weighed both plans and concluded B was the more logical and doable, especially since he had a built-in escape route all the way to Illinois. But Butch was way too pissed off to listen to anything like logic so, Plan A. By God, Plan A.

Come at me, you hillbilly Piney-ass two-bit thug.

Butch savoured the idea of smashing Pee's skull into Jello. The arriving cops would take one look at the mess, sing "Ding, dong Pee Sea is dead!", hoist Butch onto their shoulders and parade him about town before giving him a medal. That is, if they ignored all the prior doings leading up to this. Sonny indicated they were so willing.

Prior doings leading up to this ...

The Archway's New Year's Eve party, of course. Two seemingly unrelated events occurred there: his meeting of April, and Jape and Truck whispering, "Hey, man, you interested in making some money?" Stage set. Roll tape.

Right after he and April shacked up in January, Butch snagged the pretty cool hospital orderly job. Righteous. The hospital was close enough that he walked to work every morning or hitchhiked in bad weather (April's shift started after, and ended before, his, so she needed the car). He ran from one floor to another all day long picking up patients and wheeling them to surgery and then wheeling them back. The surgeons let him watch, which was fascinating. Not so fascinating: cleaning the suites afterwards. Ick.

Ick or no, it filled him with a righteous resolve: I will be a medical man. Of some kind. There was a nobility in this hospital work, even in his lowly carting of the sick from one place to another. To be a medical man was to serve mankind, and not in that old Twilight Zone episode sense. It was purpose. It was direction.

It was redemption.

Righteous pay, too. Well, righteous enough he didn't have to opt for the tent in the Barrens. It covered the rent and the electricity and gas for April's Coronet. She bought their food and incidentals, and that's about all because she didn't make all that much but she supplemented by bringing home Gino's throwaways at least three nights a week, saving them bucks, and who ever got tired of Gino Giants and apple pies? Certainly not him. Life was great.

More than great: he had a place and food and a main squeeze and even a car. April was cool with everything, just like I said, Don, and seemed to enjoy his universes as much as Butch did. Seemed to.

"You sure 'bout this girl?" Oak asked him one night when he'd gone to the dojo alone and they were in the office sprawled around couches and chairs, ghi's open, trying to cool down after having kicked a bunch of red belts' asses.

Butch, startled by the question, answered, "Yeah!" on reflex. Then, after a moment, got curious. "Why?"

Oak shook his head. "I dunno, man. She's got an agenda."

"What are you talking about?"

"You'll see."

That was the last week of January. By the first week of February, he knew what Oak meant: she wanted to take him over. Body and soul.

It started with Don. "Do we HAVE to go to Presidential Lakes?" she whined one snowy Friday night as Butch negotiated a slide down the Perkins/Mt Holyoke Road on the Coronet's nearly bald tires.

"Don't worry, babe," he said with great smugness, one arm around her and only three fingers on the bottom of the wheel, "I got this."

"No!" She squirmed away, almost causing him to no longer have this as the Coronet fishtailed. "Let's go somewhere else."

"But!" Butch spluttered, "Dooby's coming over with Loretta," – his squeeze of the week – "and we're heading to Ralph's" – to smoke doobies and play head games like 'Woodstock' until well past dawn and then a snowy drive back to the apartment and make love and then sleep for about twelve hours, wash, rinse, repeat – "for a while. You like Loretta. And Ralph."

"I want to go to my dad's."

Butch almost put the car into a 360. "What? I thought you two weren't talking!"

After all, he'd thrown her out a mere handful of weeks ago. Well, more accurately, she belatedly walked out sometime after Daddy's "You're not dating that idiot" declaration and Butch's subsequent urging of her to shack up with him, but it amounted to the same thing. Daddy swore she was no longer his daughter, tore his clothes all Tevya-like (Butch supposed), the very same routine he'd followed for his other wayward daughters ... who were no longer wayward.

Hmm.

"We made up."

"You did?" Incredulity flooded him. And then anger. "When?"

"A few days ago. What does it matter? I wanna go there now. My sisters are all going to be there."

"What?" Butch, dumbfounded. "This some kind of family reunion?"

She crossed her arms, face satanic in the dashboard lights. "It's my car."

It was. They turned around as Butch fumed over the sudden

change of venue, completely missing the far more sinister implications of this unexpected reconciliation. At the house, Butch pointedly stayed in the background as her dad pointedly ignored him while April and her sisters and her mom gushed over each other like ... long-lost family. One or two blurry sons-in-law silently butlered dad and the girls, fetching this or that per respective spouse's command.

Double hmm.

Butch spent subsequent weekends at either April's dad's house or office, instead of with Don or Oak or even with Mom at Ridge's, which wasn't a loss so much as a replacement: he'd traded one glowering overweight middle-aged Korean war veteran for another. Except this one, like his daughter, was also intent on taking over Butch, body and soul. "What are you doing?" he'd growl at Butch from behind his beat-up metal desk in his trailer office on the worksite of the moment as April skipped off with a couple of the sisters who worked there, butlered by blurry sons-in-law who also worked there, ever since becoming sons-in-law.

Hmm, hmm, and hmm.

"Nothing," Butch said, guarded, and checked his hands to make sure he wasn't fooling with a valuable whatzit or whoozit or something that might blow up.

"Damn right, nothing. Working in a hospital as a janitor," he sneered.

"Orderly."

"Whatever." Glower. "You need a real job, one with a future. Come work for me and I'll get you on the big machines."

"Pardon?"

And Mr. April dragged him outside and threw him into the cab of a steam shovel or whatever the hell it was and started it up and let him drive it around a bit and Butch threw the shovel at something and dug up something and carried something over to a pile of crap, grinning by the end of it. "Cool," he said.

"So, when you startin'?" Mr. April stood next to the treads as the shovel idled, arms crossed, and grinned back, the grin ending well below his eyes.

"Uh, thanks, but this isn't what I want to do."

"It's not?" Mr. April was astonished. Who wouldn't want to do this? He cocked an inquiring eye at this obviously crazy kid, demanding an explanation.

"I want to be a nurse anesthesiologist."

And he did. Butch's medical resolve had been narrowed by the two nurse anesthesiologists working the surgical suites, both very cool middle-aged women who made boatloads of money, worked about three or four hours a day, and didn't have to go to medical school for their jobs. What a great life. Yeah, sure, Butch would have to go to nursing school and anesthetic school or whatever they'd called it and there were internships and about five years more of school after that with about five years of residency before he got the cool job but, hey, worth it. Barring that, he wanted to be an X-Ray technician or lab tech or some other kind of medical man, not run a steam shovel, no matter how cool that, also, was. And especially not for Mr. April.

"A nurse?" The contempt dripped off him like cobra's venom.

"A nurse?" April's mom, with the same level of venom, spat in a heavy Japanese accent at the dining room table on one of the increasingly successive nights of dinner with the parents and the sisters, who all looked at each other and laughed.

Butch considered breaking the table in half with an axe kick, thereby re-establishing his manhood but, wow, really? Did he really have to do something like that? Who are you people?

"A nurse?" April, at night, in bed, repeated her parents and sisters' sneers instead of making love and Butch wondered who she was. It was becoming clearer, in tandem with the escalating family visits, that she was nothing that he thought she was, or was exactly who she was all along and had done an excellent job concealing it until Butch was right where she wanted. Butch suspected a family-wide plot to get her married so that dad could have another son-in-law to bully.

By the last week of February, Butch knew they were over.

By the following weeks of March, Butch was prepared to slip out the back, Jack, make a little plan, Sam… say, that might make a good song. He'd already floated the idea of taking a corner of the garage in Thong's newly purchased house, just for a while, Thong, you know, until I get things sorted out, maybe snag a surgical orderly job at that Heart Hospital in the middle of Braun's Mills, which was a walk and not a hitchhike away, and made subsequent adjustments to things like buying food and getting to Oak's without the Coronet, lost in plans and self-debate as he strolled up the apartment's stairs and stopped dead on the landing.

April and her dad and her mom lined the couch glaring at him. Well, the parents glared. April cried.

"I'm pregnant," she said between sobs.

"You're going to marry her," Mom said.

"You're going to come work for me," Dad said.

"Bwa?" was all Butch could muster.

What he'd meant to say was: there is no way in hell I am marrying your daughter. There is no way in hell I am ever working for you. But all he could manage was a single-syllable *meep* because of a single inconvenient fact: he, himself, was the product of illicit lust.

So how could he do that to his own kid?

Butch felt his entire life fall away like an elevator with its cable cut. He looked at April, the tears puffing her eyes into ugliness, and wondered if the pregnancy was true, or deliberate, but that didn't matter, didn't matter at all because any refusal to marry her and raise his child meant he was standing by a pool during a rainy midnight supervising the results.

He was Dad.

Not quite, at least, not all the way. He wasn't ready to kill his child. He was, though, very willing to do what Dad did in an earlier situation: give the child up for adoption.

Of course, Dad was the one doing the adopting. Of yours truly.

As a result, Butch spent his life at Dad's mercy, culminating in the pool party because, well, Dad wasn't going to go through THAT again! Especially with a kid who was not only his child but his grandchild.

But this wouldn't be like that; this would be a true adoption: give the kid up to a good family. Maybe Don's. Don's mom would love to have another baby to raise and, while Don's dad would grouse, he'd go along because he loved his wife and this meant Butch's son would be raised by good people in a good environment and Butch could visit him every day while also running around with Don and Dooby and Oak. Watcha say, April?

One look at her and Butch knew it was a no-go.

"Okay," he said.

Butch was working for Mr. April by the end of the week, but not running the steam shovel or something else cool like that, oh no. He was piling broken pieces of concrete onto hills of other broken crap while slope-headed Pineys and incomprehensible Mexicans laughed at him and pulled pranks like stealing his lunch and leaving sharp pieces of steel in the middle of the broken concrete or flattening his wheelbarrow tires. Mr. April came out of his trailer once an hour to scream something unintelligible at him and then went back inside shaking his head while the slope-heads roared their mirth. By the third day, Butch had lost fifty IQ points.

April made a miraculous recovery from the panic and tears of their come-to-Jesus meeting and spent her free time running around with her mother and sisters making arrangements for churches and receptions and dresses. Butch pointed out that a white wedding dress was out of the question, given present circumstances. Big mistake, because a variety of female relatives screamed outrage at him over the following seventy-two hours, making it sound as if Butch forced himself on her, that she was an unwilling participant in the untoward acts leading to the aforementioned present circumstance.

Coulda fooled me. But, then, maybe she had.

So there was no way he was going to point out the expense of churches and receptions and dresses in comparison with twenty-five dollars and a short trip to the mayor, a point made more cogent now that April had reduced her hours. Running around making wedding arrangements was time-intensive, ya know. Butch's day labor became their only source of income, which, okay, fine, it paid a couple dollars per hour more but hardly represented a shift in tax brackets. And yeah, okay, he was working three or four more hours per day so bringing home more bacon, but it was allocated to far more things than before. Like bacon. No more free Gino's food supplements because April now left work before the nightly throwaways. The rest of the bacon went to the mounting wedding expenses. And unnecessary pieces of furniture. And wardrobe enhancements. And shoes. Debts he had not personally incurred mounted and geez, April what the hell are you doing to me and Butch conjured Dad and accused her of witchery and things were thrown and things were kicked and tossed out windows and cops showed up.

He did not tell Mom about any of this. He did not tell Oak, either, because the guy tried to warn him. He did tell Don.

"Dude," Don said, "You have got to get the hell out of there."

Yes, he did.

So he and Don discussed the options, and all of them led to the conclusion that Butch needed a sudden influx of cash, not to cover wedding expenses, but to disappear without a trace for at least six to eight months or whenever the baby was born and delivered to a loving family, possibly Don's. Don had not been cold to the idea, merely shrugged and confirmed what Butch previously thought: "Mom'd love that." And hope sprang deep in Butch's heart because the things he wanted were confirmed by a like-minded pal.

To reinforce that, they brought in Dooby, always a level-headed guy, and he listened and nodded and said yes, skedaddle until faits have been accompli'd and, yes, that will require a sudden and very large influx of funds, and then concluded, "You gotta do a drug deal."

And Butch immediately re-heard Jape and Truck's whisper from that fated New Year's Eve.

And everything blew up.

He watched in the rearview mirror for a moment and then unfolded the green paper and looked at the picture.

So what are you telling me, Pee? That you've killed Don? That you intend to kill Don?

The "You're next" was more evidence of the former than latter. But they'd found *Jape's* headless body on Deep Hollow, not Don's, so this must mean Don's the next target, but then why put it in Butch's locker? Did Pee think he'd deliver it to Don going, "Dude, you're next!"? That's stupid. Didn't make any sense. Unless it was Pee Sea's way of rattling him.

I'm not rattled, Pee. I'm furious. You wouldn't like me when I'm furious.

Like most cowards, Butch was willing to take a lot more abuse than normal people. He'd been taught by Dad that defending himself, even reflexively raising fists, was a great way to get killed, so he kept his hands down and set his face and took it. One of his motives for studying karate was the desperate attempt to break his passivity in the face of aggression, and was somewhat successful in that he gained a rep. Not that he was very good, although he could hold his own, but his karate brothers spread rumors of Butch's badassery, more for their own amusement than anything. People who were inclined to harass him left him alone.

Mostly.

There's always a few yahoos who want to see how fast the new sheriff is, and three said yahoos took it on themselves to test Butch, saying smack in the halls, insults during gym, the usual. Butch took it, unable to shake Dad's conditioning, but all that did was encourage the three and others looked at him wonderingly because, karate boy, why haven't you gone all Bruce Lee on these guys yet?

Because, he already had at least one broken knee to his credit, and he didn't want to add any more.

So he ran away and hid in classrooms and otherwise avoided those three as much as he could until one day the idiots trapped him in the locker room and demanded he give them his lunch money. He said he didn't have any lunch money and the biggest of the three grabbed Butch's shirt lapel and yanked him up and spat in his face and warmth mushroomed in Butch's spine and flooded his brain and his vision altered until all was grey and red and he became filled with a terrible resolve.

Let's just say those three never, ever bothered him again. After they got out of the hospital.

So what chance do you think you stand, Pee?

Apparently, a good one.

Butch frowned. Yes, Pee did.

He'd already gotten Jape, may have gotten Don or was planning to do so, and had hired some muscle to deal with other hired muscle. Maybe Dooby was right. He should head over to the Philly airport right now, leave the car in long-term parking and call Mom and tell her where to find it and get on the first thing smoking to Illinois and go to the airport USO and hide until he boarded the first bus smoking for Chanute. And stay in the barracks for the rest of his life.

But he had to find Don first. Now, more than ever.

That, though, was a bigger problem than anticipated. It was clear that Pee Sea was on Butch's ass, following him around, else how would he have known that Butch was at the high school, especially since it was a spur-of-the-moment decision? For that matter, how did he know Butch would open his old locker but, hey, when you visit your old high school, some things you do automatically.

Do you?

Do people make regular visits back to their high schools and beeline straight for their old lockers? Wasn't something that had ever come to his attention and, frankly, sounded a bit implausible. For the sake of argument, let's say Butch had ignorantly stumbled into a tradition, but, the lock combinations got changed every year ... okay, so they missed a couple here and there and one of them happened to be his but how could Pee count on that? Unless he paid somebody to ensure the locker remained unchanged and simply waited for Butch to observe a tradition he'd never heard about.

That didn't make any sense at all.

He frowned at the paper. Maybe I've got this all wrong, but I can't afford to think that. So, take this at face value and conclude that looking for Don is a dangerous task. Don was more than likely right now in PL somewhere, maybe even at home. But if Butch went there, he'd get cornered and beheaded, Don right alongside him. Best to hide out for a while longer until Dooby showed up at the band shell. There, Butch'd have the protection of the crowd and his few remaining allies like Dooby and the band and Don because it was a sure bet that Don'd be there, so he didn't have to risk it right now. Okay. Good. In the meantime, where to?

The shore.

Chapter 13

It took Butch only an hour to reach Seaside. Now, how had he managed that? Bumper-to-bumper nightmare traffic caused by badly-timed lights through Toms River was standard fare any random day in August and included games of dodge car with Philly drivers who stopped in the middle of the road for no apparent reason or made left-hand turns from the far-right lane and could not negotiate a traffic circle even with big signs telling them what to do. Yield to the people already inside, idiots.

Every single traffic accident in New Jersey involved someone from Philadelphia.

But despite the odds here he was, sitting on a side street in the village and worriedly scanning the parking signs for time limits or tow-away zones or other obscure and rather expensive restrictions. Seaside was notorious for those. He also scanned for a notorious purple El Camino. Nothing.

Bit strange. No Pee Sea anywhere along the route, even on the lonely stretch from Country Lakes to Route 70. That was the best place for Pee to make a move. But no move made. Maybe Pee thought the stretch was *too* lonely and couldn't make an approach without Butch making him. Why, though, should he care? Little chance anyone would interrupt. Perhaps Butch's killer karate rep made Pee hesitate, but that seemed wishful thinking. More likely, Pee planned on doing something unexpected, such as walking up and shooting Butch in the head as he peered at street signs.

Butch jerked away from the window, half-convinced a pistol was already pointing at him, and felt a little foolish when no bullet grazed his head. Pee's not going to shoot you here, man. Too many witnesses. He's a decapitate-you-in-the-woods kind of guy, so relax. Until you get to the woods.

Satisfied he wasn't offending the Seaside parking Gestapo, Butch slipped out of the car and stood and stretched full in the sun and took in a full breath of sea air.

Ah man, the beach.

Soul renewing, mind-clearing, and a great place to hide from Piney thugs bent on taking your head.

He looked down at his uniform. But not like this.

Stroll the boardwalk all 1505-d and he'd be thrown off a building in about three seconds flat, or trussed up like a rodeo calf, dropped in the water and left for the Coast Guard to fish out. No thanks. A few seconds later, the blouse was off and hanging on the headrest of the passenger seat, the cunt cap on the seat itself. He stepped back and examined his reflection in the car windows: a crazy skinhead prison guard in plain white T and khaki pants stared back.

Good.

Butch cast about and spotted the two-story Howdy Doody statue and headed that way. Moments later, he walked up the Howdy Doody ramp and stood on the Casino Pier.

Magic Land.

The place was in full swing. Hordes of people clumped by in both directions like Viking warbands, the smell of cotton candy and cheesesteaks and raw clams trailing them. Shirtless boys, freak flags flying, pulled at muttonchops and beards and surreptitiously passed joints to girls in skimpy bathing-suit tops and short shorts or beach towels wrapped about like dresses, flipping their Joni Mitchell or Farrah Fawcett hair. A couple of little kids bumped along bewildered by the Jupiter-trip psychedelia of games and lights and rides, grasped firmly about the elbows by moms still sporting the beehives and hair-sprayed curls of their youth while fat-armed and tattooed dads, their beer bellies busting through unbuttoned shirts, groused alongside and sneered at all the damn kids, look at 'em, Martha! Yeah, Martha. Look at this wild-in-the-streets teenage wasteland, this hippie paradise. Madman drummers, bummers, and Indians in the summers.

The sun blasted and beat and raged and he was blinded by the light and the pressure cooker of all summer in a day, the boardwalk resin and the Coppertone and the girls walking by making his head swim. Warband boom boxes dueled as they flowed past each other battling the speakers from the side-by-side games of water balloon and basketball throw and knock-the-pins-down screaming everybody was kung-fu fighting the night Chicago died sweet home Alabama clap for the Wolfman and nothin' from nothin' means nothin' at maximum volumes. The sirens and the joeys yelling "Yo Yo Yo, take a spin, everyone's a winner!", the shrieks of girls on the Star Jet and Swiss Bob and the Ferris wheel, all of it whirling and weaving and clapping Butch's ears in a vise of party bass and treble. It was the Woodstock beach boardwalk festival of summer and freedom and he threw his head back and crowed and wished he had a joint.

A couple of hardguys hard-eyed him, tossed their cigarettes in the universal sign of kicking his ass and Butch hard-eyed them back with skinhead psychopath-eyes go ahead, try, and walk on walk on and girls giggled at the skinhead's silly T-shirt but their eyes shone because he had psychopath's eyes and was dangerous and *eew* they loved the bad boys and Butch smirked because he *was* dangerous and a danger here in August...

So walk on, girlie.

This was everything and nothing, a moment and forever and Butch clasped it in his hands and squeezed it down and tattooed it on his forehead so he could, years from now, look in a mirror and open a perfect summer day.

Brownsville Station was playing somewhere to his right and Butch's ears pricked like a dog's following a chittering squirrel and...

Ah, man, the arcade!

...and he floated along with summer and the hardguys and the girls through the entrance where it was dark and dusty and the boards creaked under his steps. The air turned cool and dry and the boardwalk heavy metal assault segued into bells and chimes as machines twirled and sang and dropped the claw on the prize and the pinballs fell and jingled and the shooter games killed ducks and Gran Trak cars revved and wooden balls flew up ramps clacking into holes and Butch grinned.

Skeeball!

He skirted the carousel smack dab in the arcade's middle,

thousands of kids astride wild-eyed plaster horses and squinting dragons spinning just past his face screaming and grabbing at him like he was a free ride ring or something and Butch good-naturedly played dodge-nose until he spotted a change machine and bought tokens, then commandeered an empty Skeeball lane and dropped the first of many.

Man, he loved Skeeball. He wasn't that good at it, but it was the perfect boardwalk game: lots of noise and action for very little money, low-tech and low-skilled and timeless happy moments of watching the ball loft at the end and beeline for the one hundred points and, invariably, miss. He went at it for about thirty minutes, racking up about 300 tickets. He tore them off and turned to a ten-year-old kid playing two alleys down.

"Here you go."

The kid goggled at the ticket strip, snatched them out of his hand and said, "Gee, thanks, mister!" and then ran towards a couple of other kids farther down, "Look what I got, look what I got!"

Butch chortled as the kid tried to attribute the sudden wealth to his own prowess and waved and headed back around the carousel. He stopped and watched someone playing *Pong* then noticed a game called *Panzer Attack* next to it and threw in a token and spent about twenty minutes blowing up tanks and airplanes until he was broke, so he watched some guys playing a new game called *Wild West* where a cowboy on a TV screen tried to outdraw you. Looked like fun but Butch didn't want to get any more tokens. Instead, he slid around the floor for a while watching kids grab harmonicas with the claw and other kids attempting the swinging bars game that was supposed to knock coins into a chute.

Can't be done, kids. It's a rip-off.

He walked outside.

Could have sworn he was in there for three or four hours but the sun hadn't moved a bit. Of course. The boardwalk was a parenthesis in the space-time continuum. He ambled down one of the alleys, careening from one side to the other, looking from one game booth to another, finding a spinner clock with just four numbers, another spinner with fifty numbers, the ever-present basketball game, a throw-the-rings-over-the-bottle game, each joey yelling at him to come over and try his luck, how easy is this, man, c'mon, you can do it, wassamadder, you a little girl? Butch laughed and waved and kept walking until he got to the balloon race game and, okay, slapped down a dollar and took a position and the bell rang and right away knew he'd lost because it took him more than two seconds to get the stream of water in the clown face and, sure enough, some kid three stools down busted first.

All is fine, all okay, and let's stroll, let's stroll.

Butch stood.

"Hey, sailor."

Butch spun. A girl stood behind him, an elf, barely coming up to his armpits, tight tank top and short shorts painting a gorgeous body accentuated by waist-long light brown hair falling down either side of her head, framing blue eyes drenched in too much eyeliner and eyebrow brush and an almost non-existent nose but the most ravishing smile, tiny teeth, individually separated with wires here and there and opening and closing in rhythm with the Wrigley's she was popping, which made it all the more endearing.

"Hi."

"Lost, huh?" she said, eye gesturing at the balloon race.

"Usually do."

"Poor baby," she said and patted him affectionately on the arm, throwing flirty eyes right into his face.

Oh good Lord, did lightning just strike him across the gonads? He canted his knees to cover the rising flagstaff.

"Yep, poor me. What's your name?"

"Bobby."

Butch head gestured at the balloons. "Wanna go?"

"Yeah!" She smacked a smile at him and put a very shapely bottom on a stool and Butch took the one next to her and lost two out of the next three games to her, both of them losing the third to some kid.

She leaned into him every time to throw off his aim so he didn't mind losing. Not at all. "You cheated," he observed and she smacked another smile.

"You liked it."

That he needed to shift and twist to try to contain a now fully installed flagstaff proved her words. She smiled at his antics, like he was fooling her or something, and hopped backwards off the stool. "Let's go ride something," she said and headed through an alley to the Ferris-wheel side.

"Star Jet," Butch called while making a mental suggestion about what else could be ridden but let's not go all crude this soon and caught up and they ran to the ramp and Butch threw money at the joey and they turnstiled and squeezed into a car together and the chain pulled them up and Butch laughed aloud because the Star Jet was the best roller coaster in the world, it just was, and here, now, look at this cute girl riding with him and have to say, going to the beach was a great idea.

The car pitched over and Bobby screamed and Butch did, too, as the car swayed over the ocean like it always did, always threatening to hurl off the track and fling them into the water and then it careened back, shaking and bucking and it was going to come apart this time he knew it just knew it and they were dropping and turning and flying and slowing down and over.

"Again!" Butch demanded and they rode three more times, Bobby grabbing her stomach and gasping for air going, "Ohmigod! Ohmigod" and holding on to him each trip.

"Swiss Bob!" she said and they headed for it, joey and turnstile and locking into the car along with a thousand other screaming people and the cars lurched and stopped and lurched and they dipped and rose, dipped and rose, and the joey started his, "Yi yi yi yi yi yi! Do you want to go faster?" and everyone screamed "Yeah!" and they did and then jerked to a stop and it ran backwards and did they want to go faster, yes they did, and oh man oh man.

They got off and sprinted, hand in hand, to the Matterhorn which was pretty much the same thing as the Swiss Bob so Butch wasn't all that excited. In fact, he felt a little sick at the end of the last go.

"Wassamadder?" Bobby teased, "Can't hang?"

"Let's go to the Silliwalk," was his only answer and he did not let go of her hand and she did not try to break it loose and they paid and went in and acted the fool in front of the mirrors, first like monkeys scratching their underarms and the tops of their heads and then jive-ass pimp walkers and then hoedown hillbillies and finally came to the end and Bobby turned and kissed him hard, with tongue, stepping back after a moment and taking his breath with her.

"Let's go on the beach," she said, lips parted, her eyes sparkling.

They got on the Sky Ride and, as it slowly lifted, Butch keyed on the sun. So, time does pass, parenthesis or no, but not in a noticeable manner; it simply reaches a farther point and that's when you spot it, a reminder that this too shall pass and you shall pass but isn't this a fine day and aren't you having a good time? Butch squinted past his joy and calculated okay, a couple of hours until sunset and heading back to PL and the bandshell and finding Don…

But this girl, this girl.

He looked at her, all cinnamon and incense and humming some toneless tune with a small smile on her face and an occasional flash of flirty eyes at him. Don would understand…

I'll catch up with you tomorrow, man, because, this girl.

Hey, dude, aren't you in a big mess because of some girl?

Yeah, but not *this* girl…

"They're all the same, man," Don's bitter voice in his ear. "They're all whores."

"Dude," was Butch's incredulous response as Don turned the Batmobile onto Deep Hollow and accelerated up and over the bridge – yee hah! – bottoming out on the other side and racing for the turn at Springfield and the dirt road beyond. "That's a bit harsh."

"Ain't harsh enough," he growled as they sped past the turn and the Impala bounced on the first hummock. "Ready?"

Butch seized the hang strap. "Do it!"

Don whipped the wheel to the left and stomped it, the back end flipping around and the tires *shurr*ing through the dirt and gravel. Immediately, he whipped it to the right and stomped it some more and they fishtailed from side to side, the big fins barely clearing the berms, the dust thrown up like an artillery barrage behind them. Yee ha!

They ended up with the front of the car wedged against a pine tree brake as the dust cloud swarmed them and settled, turning the pinkish car brownish. If some ranger happened to spot it, he'd call in a fire warning.

"Whew," Butch said, waving the air clear in front of him. "That's a good one. So why are all women whores now?"

Don threw the Batmobile into reverse and cracked it out of the brake. "JoAnn." Not to be confused with Butch's Joan. Pale and nebbish Joan, tearful and frightened and afraid, so afraid. No, not in any way my Joan. JoAnn was hot and willing, not cold and resentful.

"What about her?"

"She's been fuckin' some Piney."

"No shit?"

"No shit."

They backed down the road at about sixty miles per hour and Don dropped it into first and floored it and they tore and swayed and spun up the road to the same spot. This time they ended in a 180, facing the way back to PL, the two of them giggling and high-fiving each other.

"How do you know?" Butch asked.

"She told me."

Butch shook his head. "Dude."

"Yeah," he said and stomped it and they did the same thing the other way and ended in another 180 so, of course, a repeat in the opposite direction. By that time, the engine was making a funny sound and they stopped and opened the hood but neither of them knew what they were doing. Dooby did but Dooby was not here and he'd always warned them not to touch crap they didn't understand. The engine was still running – that was good, right? – so they decided to heed Dooby's advice and leave well enough alone. Don reached into the trunk and pulled out a couple of warm and very shook-up beers. They churchkeyed them and had a foam fight, leaving barely enough beer to actually drink and sat on the berm in the shade, although it was October and the air was already cool. "So who's the Piney?"

"Dunno." Don stretched out. "Didn't ask."

"We could go beat him up."

"Could, but, ya know?" He folded arms behind his head after flinging the bottle back over his head into the woods and settled. "I don't give a shit."

"Don't litter, man," Butch warned as he pitched his own bottle through the Batmobile's back window. "Why don't you give a shit?"

"'Cause it's all the same crap. Angie before JoAnn, Andrea before her… done, man."

"Maybe it's your tiny little dick."

"Fuck you," Don growled as Butch giggled and fished a joint out of his top pocket. He lit it and inhaled and held and held and the world sang in colours and he passed the joint to Don. "So what do you mean you're done?"

"With women."

"Shit," Butch coughed, "You gonna become a monk or something?"

"Nah, man," Don wheezed. "I'm still gonna fuck 'em. Just ain't gonna have a girlfriend."

"Gotta have a girlfriend before you can fuck 'em, dude."

"You'd know, wouldn't you?"

"Fuck you, man," Butch said, stung, because that stung. Butch's girlfriend after Joan was Patty, another church girl with whom he'd struggled for months to get past her bra and never even got a real tongue kiss before she called him an animal and broke it off. The dating, that is, not his dick. That was still quite operational, thanks to Mason's little forays. Maybe it was for the best, then, because if he had ever gotten that bra off, there would have been bellowing and roaring and crying and hate and more and more of the good girls, true girlfriend material, regarding him with horror up and down the hall as more and more stories circulated. At least with Mason's harem he retained a measure of anonymity. He bellowed and cried within a discreet population. Mostly.

He inhaled about half the joint and felt a symphony tuning in his veins and realized the solution to Don's problem. "So does this mean you'll spend more time with Mason and me?"

"Don't bogart that, man," Don said and grabbed the wet joint from Butch, finishing it off. "Nah. Don't like black girls."

"Huh?" That surprised him. "What's not to like? They love giving head." Especially when they didn't want to. All you had to say was that you were going to say all up and down the halls that they didn't and, boy, did they became enthusiastic.

"Maybe." Don choked back the last bit of smoke. "But it's like fuckin an ape."

Knocked back. Butch was. "Oh, wow," he choked, not sure he'd heard right. "Oh, wow, did you just say that? Really? I can't believe you just said that."

Don shrugged. "It's what it is."

"You say something like that to Mason, he'll tear your head off."

"Whatever."

Butch laughed, his usual reaction when incredulous. "Can't believe you're a racist, man."

"I'm not a racist. I think everybody should own one or two."

Butch lost it, fell down laughing with the aid of the full orchestra playing his entire body and Don joined in and they slapped each other's shoulders and did the silly, helpless, meaningless, apocalyptic laugh of the stoned for about three or four hours, or three or four minutes.

"So I've been thinking about whores," Don gasped.

"Yes." Butch wiped tears away. "I believe we've already discussed your whore girlfriends. And your tiny little dick."

"Are you that fascinated by my dick?"

"I'm just wondering how you pee."

"Got a string tied to it."

Which caused another round of slap-happy laughter for the next four or five hours/minutes and Don wheezed and spluttered and finally found his air. "But, seriously, man. Whores."

"What about them?"

"I think they're the way to go."

"As you've discovered."

"No, no, asshole, not them. Real whores."

"Real whores?"

"Yeah, the ones over there by the Palmyra bridge."

Butch blinked out of his slap-happiness. "Are you crazy?"

"No. Think about it. It's perfect. You pay for what you want. You get what you want. You get some fine-lookin' woman to fuck your brains out and then they… Go. Away." He smacked his palm on each of the last two words. "No muss. No fuss. No dating. No drama."

"They don't exactly go away," Butch said, picking at a pine needle and enjoying the texture. Felt like paper and leather at the same time. "They leave you with crabs and VD."

"Eh." Don dismissed that. "Nothing a good dose of penicillin won't fix. All upside, man."

Butch sighed and watched his sigh spin away, away. "Be awful damn lonely, man." And, Don, you don't want that, you really don't, because if there's something I know, it's loneliness. It's a glacier, man, cold and forbidding and blue and grinding, always grinding. The constant, quiet thrum of grinding solitude was Butch's true symphony, the strings played and plucked and sawed and sang to him, man, sang, like his blood did right now but as background, not as chemical alteration. It's the sense of being slightly apart from everyone, dude, even from your best friends, out of step, out of synch, and, Don, man, listen, there's no relief. Ever.

From birth to whatever type of death awaited, Butch walked alone, always would, and he was desperate not to. He wanted people he loved and trusted around him and sharing his life all the time, but he was walled off by how he was born and how he'd been raised and midnight pools and genealogy.

And, Don, you're not. You've got options.

Apparently Don knew that because he was the first one married.

The cold distant thrum of loneliness made Don as desperate as Butch and he made a disastrous choice and no doubt Don was, right now, sore and hurting and swearing off women again and promoting whoredom but…

Don, dude, you can still beat the loneliness. You can find the right girl. I can't.

Butch could not marry.

Look what happened when I got close; it blew up due to walls and genealogy and, actually, thank God, because wow, I did not want to end up driving a steam shovel but, Don, the best I can do, all I can do is pretend and lookee lookee, Don, here I am in the Sky Ride with this girl, an obvious whore, repeating a behavior that had put me in the middle of this current mess and here I'm about to start another big mess because, Don, the cold thrum of the glacier.

Don't be me, Don.

He pulled Bobby closer to him and she giggled and snuggled and her hand drifted to his upper thigh, dangerous and close and Butch nearly suffocated because he could not breathe. There was fire in his veins, not ice, and he heard a distant bellow gathering as the Sky Ride descended. "Do you have a place to go?" he breathed.

"Yeah," she whispered back and smiled knowingly as the car bumped to a halt and the joey more or less flung them off. "Follow me."

She headed off the boardwalk and passed the beach gate and stopped there looking at Butch as he dug into his wallet and bought day passes which seemed unfair because it was getting late so why did he have to pay for the whole day but was he really going to start an argument with the gate guy as Bobby stood there, hands in her short shorts teasing at them like she wanted them off right now, her eyes half-lidded and promising?

They walked down the stairs to the beach and the sand was in the shade and cooler and Butch took off his low quarters and socks and dug his toes through it and Bobby slipped her flip-flops off and did the same and they held hands and ran along the piers, staying in shadow and laughing and it was like something out of a movie. They slowed down and Bobby turned and kissed him again and head-jerked towards the piers.

Took Butch a minute. "You mean, in there?" he said, taking in the columns and cross latches of the boardwalk's understructure.

"There's a song about it, ya know," she said and winked and took his hand and led him underneath and Butch looked back to see who was watching and a couple of people out towards the beach smirked at him and…

Oh, boy, I don't know about this

…but then he looked at that fine, winking ass dancing him through the piles and he ducked along.

Who cares who cares oh boy this is actually happening…

…and they were suddenly in a wide spot of sand and darkness, wide enough to lie down on and spread around and do whatever he wanted. A bellow reached the launching pad.

She stood for a moment, hands folded in front of her, chin down, eyes up and fluttering, a small smile on her face. Butch dropped his shoes. She stepped back.

Four guys stepped up.

"See ya, sailor," Bobby said and skipped away.

Chapter 14

Butch did a quick 360. Boxed in, a guy at each diagonal, so no matter what angle Butch made for, two would instantly be on him. If he broke for the empty space between guys, they'd collapse it. If he went straight at them, he'd be running at a wall because, Holy Hannah, these guys were big. Biker big.

Big bikers.

Right out of central casting: mile-wide shoulders, cascades of hair, cascades of chains. They wore the regulation jean jackets, except for the guy to Butch's right front, who wore only a brown leather vest open to his belt, revealing a waterfall of tattoos from the neck down to a proudly displayed navel: "Born to Ride," "His Satanic Majesty," "US Army Vietnam," in sequence, a walking art poster. Butch ordinarily would have admired all that work except it was a fairly strong indicator that this guy was effin' crazy. 'Course, most bikers were.

Three of them sported beards and moustaches and hair that had not been cut or washed in about seven or eight years. The biker to his right rear had tied his up in a bun that looked like a Brillo pad glued to the back of his head, while the guy to Butch's left front had a ponytail quite reminiscent of a macramé project. The left-rear guy was shaved into a cue ball, which was more terrifying than the sasquatches. Vest Boy was different. He had hip-length straight brown hair suspiciously like Bobby's and a dangling Fu Manchu, all carefully tended. Butch examined the vest but it was bare, although Butch could see some stitching on the shoulders indicating colours sewn to the back. The others wore the standard "1%" and "13" patches here and there, along with some angel wings ranging from white to red. Butch wondered what those meant. He couldn't tell what gang colors they flew, but they were probably Pagans. This was their territory. And Bobby was one of their babes.

Idiot.

Butch was not all that read-up on biker lore, but knew enough to realize he was in deep shit. Bikers were peripheral to south Jersey, seen at a distance, heard roaring along back trails on the few occasions Butch was out in the Barrens hanging with Pineys. Pineys gave them a wide berth which was an object lesson because Pineys were the scariest people Butch knew. Generations of inbreeding and lawlessness turned Pineys into mutants, murderous ones at that. Whenever the New York mob needed someone to disappear, they gave them to Pineys. Pineys knew how to make someone vanish.

Mostly.

Every autumn, some hapless deer hunter back around Egg Harbor put his boots into the rotted chest of a vanished, who could not be identified because teeth and fingers and whatnot had all been removed. Butch heard tales of finger bones lining certain Piney back porches and how much tooth enamel stiffened newly poured parking lots from here to Wilmington. Butch played with Pineys out at the Train Wreck and the Carranza Memorial from time to time but only because of Cindy, who hung out with a lot of the dangerous ones. Butch made it a point to never be in their presence without Cindy nearby. A few of those times, Butch spotted some crazy-eyed Piney lumberjack staring at him across a bonfire near one of the blue holes, as if Butch was a tasty steak. He'd scoot a little closer to Cindy and her Piney of the moment and came away uneaten.

Bikers, though, were a whole different species. Butch didn't know any, that's how rare, or clannish, they were. No Pineys were bikers, although plenty of Pineys sported the look and rode the Harleys. Pineys were businessmen and ran the smuggling and burying routes through the Barrens in the business-like manner that the New York boys favoured. Yes, Pineys were crazy, but they were so for a reason. Bikers were simply crazy. Maybe that's why the Pineys avoided them. Purposeless crazy was unprofitable.

Bikers spent their time in the cities. The Pagans were the

biggest gang, centered in Delaware and in charge of the meth trade in the tri-state area. They ran the strip clubs and the after-hours bars and were constantly at war with the Breed and the Iron Horsemen and the occasional Hells Angel foolish enough to fly colours around here. Bikers were like mosquitos: annoying, but to be endured whenever Butch ventured into the great urban jungles, like sometimes when he was crossing the Tacony-Palmyra Bridge and a pod of Breed blasted around Buggy while jeering at him. Simply the way it was, world without end, amen.

The biker gangs mostly stayed out of the Barrens, an occasional ride to Atlantic City taking them through the backways, hence the occasional distant roar. Butch heard references to some event in the middle sixties when bikers, probably the Iron Horsemen, made an encroachment to which the New York boys and the Pineys took umbrage and, well, after all the smoke cleared, bikers avoided Pineys and vice-versa. Guess there was plenty of mutual damage.

But it appears things were changing. The Stilt brothers, most Piney of them all, hired Pagans. And Pee Sea hired Breed. Missile silos slid open; rocket engines roared.

Time to duck and cover.

He measured the distance to the guys in front. Couple of side kicks should double them over.

Should.

They'd have to be very fast side kicks and he wasn't wearing his shoes so they would be less effective but should create an opening.

Should.

He looked at the shaggy biker to Vest Boy's right, a guy with absolutely insane black eyes. He was set, ready to receive anything Butch offered, so no-go. Besides, even if this worked, he'd end up deeper under the boardwalk and even more cut off. His only chance was breaking towards the beach behind him.

Before we do something suicidal, though, let's conduct a more in-depth evaluation.

He looked over his shoulder. The guy on his left rear was not only a cue ball but about nine feet tall and nine feet wide, the sleeve of his jacket torn out so that Butch saw the cannonballs where his biceps should be. The guy's eyes were so sunk into his head that Butch couldn't really see them and he was grinning with very few teeth, the ones remaining covered in silver.

Nice look.

The other Cro Magnon to the right rear had all his teeth. And a baseball bat.

Hmm.

This was going to be tougher than he thought. But, dude, what choice do you have?

Okay, here's the play: back kicks at the rear guard, which would give him momentum in that direction and maybe a half-second head start towards the beach and daylight and safety before Vest Boy and Crazy Eyes reacted. Scoop up his shoes on the run and throw them in the horde's faces, thereby gaining a few more half-seconds. Better throw the best back kicks ever, devastating ones, perfectly balanced Bruce-Lee-level at a nine-foot-tall guy with arms like bulldozer pistons standing next to a guy with a baseball bat.

Face it, you're dead.

"Hi," Vest Boy said.

It was such a soft, disarming voice that it took Butch by surprise, interrupting his preparation for the suicidal kicks. Butch goggled at him as Vest raised a mild eyebrow. "You're about to do something really stupid, aren't you?"

Man, am I that obvious?

"I wouldn't," Vest continued, "We call that guy" – Vest pointed at cannonball arms – "Boulder, and that guy," point at bat boy, "Home Run, which should give you an inkling of their capabilities. This guy," a thumb at Crazy Eyes, "is Charley Manson. Metaphorically, that is." A pause and a smile, a dead-eyed one. "As for me, the boys call me Professor. See, I'm very well educated, speak three languages, including Latin. Know this one?" Professor widened the dead smile. "*Vivere militare est.*"

Butch blinked in confusion. What the hell is this?

Professor cocked his head. "No? It means 'to live is to fight.' It's from Seneca. You know Seneca?"

Butch found his voice. "Uh… no."

Professor shook his head in mock sorrow. "Kids these days," he said to the others, all of whom chuckled, "So you've never read Dante or Chaucer, then."

"Uh..."

"Well, let me assist your very poor education. Seneca was a

Stoic philosopher and advisor to Nero. Forced to commit suicide, because you play with the devil, you get burned." Professor lost the smile. "You gettin' all this?"

"Uh… yeah."

"Good!" Professor beamed at him, clapped him on the shoulder. "Saves lots of time." And he looked at Butch expectantly.

Butch wavered. "Look, I've got about a hundred bucks, that's it." He pulled out his wallet. "Take it. Just leave me my ID card and license."

"Well, we don't really want your money but thanks, anyway," Professor said and stripped the wallet out of Butch's hand and the cash out of that, dropping the wallet on the sand. He waved the cash around. "This all Uncle Sam paying these days?"

Uh oh.

These guys knew he was in the military. Must be the low-quarters in the sand next to him.

"'Cause Uncle paid us more than this, right boys?" Professor held the cash up to the others, all of whom joined in a chorus of, "Fuckin A" "Got that right" and related slogans. "Overseas pay, ya know. 'Nam."

Great. Bad enough they were crazy bikers, they were crazy vets, too. Like Butch hadn't figured that out from the tats.

Which gave him an idea. "They'll probably send me to Nam," he said, hopefully, brothers in arms and all that.

All four of them bust out laughing, genuinely amused belly laughs, and fell to slapping each other's backs and maybe this would be a good chance to beat feet, or side kick or something, but all four of them kept their distance and spacing while expressing their comedic appreciation and the moment was lost when Home Run slapped his palm with the bat and snorted, "Don't think so, creampuff. They only send men there."

"That's right," Professor said, "so you should have joined the Marines, Butch, not the Air Force."

An iceberg slalomed up Butch's stomach and over his throat and encased him from jaw to brain.

Oh. No. They know who I am. Which means they are not Pagans. They're Breed. Pee Sea's boys.

Which means I'm dead.

So this was the unexpected move. Hand to hand it to Pee, it

was a good one. Butch wondered how they'd do it. Pee Sea was partial to beheadings, but that seemed messy and loud and might attract some interest, so they would probably just shoot him, also loud and messy but quick, affording them the chance to melt away before somebody got curious enough to see about the noise. Or, better yet, stab him. All of the disadvantages of guns and beheadings eliminated by putting a six-inch switchblade into his liver. Be days before anyone found him.

All that karate training flew away on the breeze. He was completely paralyzed, Dad in front of him swinging a belt and Butch could do nothing. Not even raise his hands. The thought of a sharp blade plunging in and out of his stomach terrified him. Beat him up, break a leg, hit him with the bat, shoot him but, God, please, don't stab him.

"So, Butch, let's get down to business."

Please don't pee your pants, please don't pee your pants, please don't…

"Wait, wait," Butch managed to stammer.

Professor raised eyebrows and stepped back a bit. "Wait? Why, you need toilet paper or something? Because it looks like you're about to shit yourself." Which brought another round of guffaws from the monsters.

"I… I can get the money."

"You can?" Professor rolled an exaggerated look around the circle of chuckling beasts.

"Yes… yes." Take a breath, get control. "I can. I can get it."

"How much?"

Butch furrowed his brow. They didn't know? Of course not, Pee Sea didn't send them here to collect but to kill. "Ten thousand."

Professor whistled appreciatively and the others nudged each other and nodded. "That is certainly a lot of moolah. A lot more than this." He waggled the cash. "Now where on earth are you going to get that amount of money?"

"I… can borrow it."

Professor said nothing, just gestured 'go on.' Butch hesitated. As much as it would delight him to have fifty or so bikers show up at Ridge's house, Mom would be in the way. "I just can."

"Then why haven't you done so before now?"

Good question.

One Butch could not answer without getting killed. Because the truth was, he didn't think he owed Pee Sea anything. He didn't arrange the deal. He didn't substitute oregano and catnip for the marijuana. That was Jape. And Jape had already paid. And Ridge wouldn't give him the money anyway, no matter how much Mom begged him. Because it would delight Ridge for years to come that fifty or so bikers had beaten Butch to death.

Professor waved a finger at Butch's silence and said, "*Tsk, tsk.* You shouldn't tell lies. It makes my associates and I quite irritated. Home Run, show him how irritated we are."

Wham!

A sledgehammer drove into Butch's right kidney, driving him to the sand and all the air out his body. His entire back burst into flame and he melted into a quivering mass of frightened Jello. This was it. He couldn't fight back if he wanted to, even if he wasn't in full-blown passive Dad mode. The raging pain encased him like a straitjacket. It was like getting kicked in the balls, but just higher and to the right.

"And that was just a love tap," Professor noted, then reached down, grabbed Butch by the T-shirt, and hauled him up, nose to nose. "Here's what you're going to do. First, you're going to bring us the ten thousand. Right here. Next Friday, same time. See, I'm nice that way, giving you time to 'borrow' the money…"

"Uh, ba."

Butch needed to interrupt right here but this was about all he could muster.

"What?" Professor shook him. "You trying to say something?"

"I can't pay you both," Butch gasped.

"Both? Don't know what you mean but not my problem. Next Friday. Here. Or we're going to pay your sister a visit." The monsters sniggered at that.

"Second," Professor continued, "and the reason for this little tete-a-tete—"

"Titty?" Boulder queried.

"No, you fuckin' moron!" Professor screamed at Boulder, which spoke volumes of just what kind of badass the guy currently shaking Butch to death was that he could intimidate a nine-foot-tall-brick-built-baldheaded crazy guy into silence. "Read a fuckin' book! As for you." His forehead smacked into Butch's. "You tell

Pee Sea to keep his fuckin' people out of our business."

Wait.

"What?"

Professor's eyes went wide and bloodshot red and he picked Butch up higher, if that was possible, and slammed him down on the sand.

"Am I not speaking English, motherfucker? Well, let me try another language!" And he screamed at Butch in German, kicking him in the shin with each guttural, evil-sounding grunt that passed for a language.

Butch rolled in the sand groaning, clutching at his leg, which he was sure was broken.

"Get me now?" Professor screamed.

"But you work for Pee Sea," Butch managed to say.

That genuinely surprised Professor, who stopped trying to shatter Butch's leg bone and regarded him. "What?"

"Aren't you Breed?"

There was a pause, just long enough for Butch to realize he'd made a very serious mistake. "Breed?" It was as though Butch had called Professor a dick sucker or something because his entire face went black with rage as he ripped off his vest and flourished the back of it where Butch could see the colors there. It was some kind of skinny bird with a woman's face and a banner across the top. No need for Butch to make it out because Professor roared it right in his face.

"We're Warlocks, motherfucker! Warlocks!"

All four of them, this time.

Chapter 15

Butch tried to open his eyes. No luck. Oh no. I'm blind. The bastards ripped my eyeballs out. When did that happen?

Sometime after they'd beaten him into a coma. You'd think eyeball ripping would've jolted him to full consciousness but no. Didn't feel it.

'Course, he couldn't really feel much of anything right now except head-to-toe pulsing numbness, wave upon wave of it, far more painful than numbness by definition should be, so eye-ripping may simply have not registered. Or no eye-ripping occurred and there were other reasons he couldn't see, like they'd buried him alive in the sand.

But I'm still breathing so that's unlikely. Let's check for other possibilities. Carefully, slowly, he probed his eye sockets.

Ouch, but ah. Not empty. Blood crusted.

A couple of hours picking at the scabs freed his eyes to the point he could halfway open them and then, Holy Hannah, I *am* blind! But no, it's dark. Getting dark, that is.

The boards over his head were murky and shadowed but he saw sunlight beyond the piers.

Wonder what time it is? Wonder what day it is?

Let's find out.

Or not, because that involved moving, which was the last thing he wanted to do because he was a bruise, one solid bruise, from his hair to his toes. Heck, even his hair was bruised. No doubt things like skull and ribs and kidneys were broken, so he was also dead, or would be in a few minutes. No one can feel this bad without approaching death. Or wishing for it.

Never call a Warlock a Breed. They tend to get upset.

"I'll remember that for later," he whispered and began a very slow examination of his body to see what was no longer connected to what. Immediately, his hands fell on some lump in the middle of his chest.

Oh no, they've cut me open and laid my heart and intestines on top, just like surgeons do when they needed a clearer look inside some schlub.

How the scalpel jocks got everything back in place without killing said schlub Butch couldn't figure, but it required expertise that Professor and his gang probably lacked so, yeah, Butch was dead, kaput, finito... but, hey, shouldn't he already be? Suspicious, he squeezed the lump, which was soft and yielding just as he imagined a heart would feel but that was silly. Dead people can't squeeze their own hearts.

Right?

The lump came off his chest and in his hand and slowly, as the bruises allowed, he pulled it to his face. Not his heart, his wallet. Empty, of course, but his license and ID card were still there.

"Thanks, guys," he whispered. A piece of paper fell out and he pawed it off his chest and up to his eyes and squinted at the rather elegant handwriting: *Next Friday, asshole. Oderint dum metuant.*

What did that mean?

Not something good, he was sure. He continued the wound check and found most things intact, except for a couple of suspect ribs, and no additional holes and tears other than those along his hairline. Which explained the blood: a couple of rather intense karate matches had taught Butch that heads tore easily and bled like a river, a case of mountain out of molehill, because head cuts were a minor thing unless the skull got parted. As far as he could tell, his wasn't. Mighty nice of Home Run to restrict his skills to the softer parts of his body.

He pressed the wallet into his chest and using it as a leverage point, rolled a slow sit up then butt-walked backwards until he got his legs under him and pushed his back up the pier while stifling screams.

Wouldn't do to attract attention.

He reached a shaky standing position and stopped, leaning

against the pier for support.

Oh, God, did he hurt. Slowly, painfully, he put the wallet back in his pocket and was surprised to find Mom's car keys still there. Thinking about it, though, no self-respecting Warlock would be caught dead in a Pontiac.

He took a tentative step then another, proof that his legs weren't broken, the roaring baseball-sized aches in his hips and back proof that experts who knew how to hurt someone without leaving compound fractures had worked him over. Cool sand sifted between his toes and he looked at his bare feet, then around until he spotted one of his low quarters. Shuffling over, he reached down and grabbed it, again stifling screams –wouldn't do to attract attention – then spotted the other one almost buried under the sand a few feet away and repeated the shuffle and stifle.

Only one sock, though. Fine.

Clutching the shoes, he inched through the sand towards the light, each full step accompanied by a groan. Felt like an hour before he made it past the pier and onto the beach. There were still a lot of people out here but it was noticeably cooler and the light had developed the sharp quality of near sunset.

"Mister, you all right?"

Butch turned his head. Painfully. A couple of boys in bathing suits stood off to the side, one holding a pail filled with sand gaped at him in astonishment. Did he look that bad? Well, yeah: half-dressed, drenched in blood and sand,what do you think?. He watched a drop of blood fall past his nose and blossom on his T-shirt. Gingerly he explored the front of his head and came away with fresh blood on his fingers.

Lovely.

Kids must think he was straight out of a vampire movie.

"Yeah, I'm fine," he lied, "I bumped my head." He flipped the bloody finger back at the piers. "Under there."

"Do you want me to get a lifeguard?" the first boy asked. He was about ten years old and the one standing next to him about eight, both of them bearing enough resemblance that Butch concluded they were brothers. Which meant a parent hovered nearby and as soon as mom and dad saw their precious wee ones conversing with a bloody monster, whistles blow and authorities appear and while that would have been nice at the beginning of this episode, now it would be a major inconvenience.

"No," Butch waved a bloody hand. "I'll be fine. Would you tell me where a bathroom is, though?"

Both boys pointed behind him and Butch slowly pivoted on his heels, trying not to scream, and shuffled towards a crappy garage-looking green cement building plopped between the piers and the stairs. He risked a look back and saw the boys racing excitedly towards a lump of towels and coolers and umbrellas near the water and in moments platoons of lifeguards, whistles blowing, would descend on him.

He gritted his teeth and picked up the pace, keeping as close to the piers as he could. He caught the metal banister at the end of the garage ramp and used it to whip onto the pad, barging into a gaggle of teenyboppers who gasped in utter horror and then giggled and veered away, amazed and pointing.

The beach is cool, ain't it?

He cleared the ramp without further encounters and slipped into the men's bathroom. An older guy at the urinals jumped when he turned and saw Butch then hastened outside but didn't say anything and didn't start yelling for the cops, either, so that was good. Boardwalkers asked no questions. Butch commandeered a sink, grimacing at the crap on the floor. He didn't want to think about what he was walking on.

Man, did he look bad. Half his face was dried blood and sand and black and blue. The other half was just swollen. He looked like False Face. Why those two kids hadn't screamed bloody murder when he emerged from the piers he couldn't figure. He would have. He marveled that his cheekbones weren't pulverized and his jaw unhinged, because a baseball bat to the face did a lot of damage.

Right, Frank?

Slowly he took off the T-shirt and examined himself from the waist up. He was turning black and blue and even red all over, which reminded him of a corny joke involving nuns falling down stairs, but, as far as he could tell, his suspect ribs – and clavicles and sternum and fingers – were intact. Further proof of the expertise required to work someone over without leaving compound fractures

So why didn't they leave compound fractures?

Four big bruisers with lots of experience beating people into bloody piles, with or without a baseball bat, had at him, yet he was fairly okay. Fairly. He could walk, he could talk, he was still breathing, which meant he could still drive over to Ridge's and borrow ten thousand dollars and show up here next Friday and hand it over. Now, should he fail to do so…

Consider your present condition a down payment.

Frowning, Butch dabbed at the blood-covered side of his face with the now useless T-shirt, rinsing it and re-dabbing to cut through all the clotting and restore himself to recognizable humanity. Given the situation, they'd gone easy on him. It could, and should, have been a lot worse. A wave of relief and gratitude flooded through him…

…and he stared at his battered face and whispered, "What's wrong with you?"

What kind of a wussy-ass poofter actually felt some measure of kindness towards four jackass thugs who'd beaten the hell out of him? Butch wasn't into chains and leather and a red ball strapped into his mouth (although there were a couple of girls with whom he wouldn't mind the experiment), so it wasn't enjoyment of the pain. Sure, there was precedent: Butch felt some measure of kindness towards persons who had royally and painfully whipped his ass in various karate tournaments, but that was a warrior's respect for the superior fighter. He was actually quite proud of the wounds they'd left him, the two or three dislocated fingers that no longer lay right and the scar on the left side of his head where that Philly guy with the great legs wheel-kicked him, opening up a gusher of blood that soaked the ring and the head judge and teaching Butch the bloody nature of minor head cuts. This was none of that; this was a criminal act, full-on aggravated assault, and shouldn't prompt feelings of gratitude.

Should it?

Had he ever felt grateful as Dad belt-stroked and stroked and stroked? No. Terrified, ashamed, confused, yes. But never grateful, even when it was his fault, even when the beating was deserved…

Deserved.

Sometimes, the stroke of belt and whip and Dad's fists were the proper and necessary response to something incredibly stupid that Butch had done, like forgetting to water the chickens or turn lights off, things that had dire economic impact. How else would he learn? He'd think twice the next time he decided that reading a book was more important than livestock. The problem lay in Dad's blurring of the lines between deserved punishment and downright cruelty. Letting chickens die of thirst deserved a beating; spending ten extra minutes finishing a chapter before heading out to water said chickens didn't. Dad couldn't see the difference because frequent arbitrary discipline of offspring served his other interests, but it left Butch confused over what constituted a legitimate beating. Did he deserve this Warlock beat-down or not?

Have to apply criteria.

The last time he'd suffered a legitimately deserved beat-up was three years ago, by Pepsi, over a prank. Butch liked to waste time after school messing around in the Perkins library and one afternoon he found a special effects record filled with sounds like clanking chains and ghostly moans and screams and, it being the middle of October, immediately saw the possibilities. Sneaking it under his jacket, he took it back to the apartment and moved the dresser drawer in Mom's bedroom and put the record player back there and briefed Cindy. This was during a period when Mom was making a show of concern and spent at least one night at the apartment and it was one of those nights. About a half-hour before Mom was due to show up, he squeezed behind the dresser, record in hand.

As Butch scrunched down, he heard Mom key the apartment door (cheap construction. Waddya expect?) and Cindy giggled and flopped over in bed and pretended to be asleep. Butch heard Mom shuffle in, muttering to herself and bumping into things getting undressed in the dark because she didn't want to wake Cindy and after some moments, she settled. Butch waited about two minutes, turned on the record player, and dropped the needle.

"OOOOoOOOooo AAAAAAHHHHHHH EEEEEEEEEE!" filled the air.

Mom popped right up. "What's going on? What's going on?" Butch immediately removed the needle and, suppressing his laughter, waited. After a moment, Mom muttered something and then lay back down. Two minutes later, "AAAAHHHEEEEEEIIII!" followed by "What's going on?" and Mom getting up and heading towards the dresser and Butch standing up and going "Rah!"

Mom was so terrified she couldn't even scream, just dropped to her knees and duck walked back to the bed as Butch and Cindy fell about the place roaring with laughter. After Mom regained her senses, she accused both of them of trying to kill her but had to admit, good one.

So good that they decided to expand their victim base. They recruited Cindy's idiot boyfriend-of-the-moment, some 25-year-old draft dodger, to make a cassette tape of the album and then took Pepsi into their confidence because Pepsi's brother, C-Note, made an excellent target. As did Art, who was back in the apartment in between Alabama forays and was more annoying than ever and needed to be pranked. Idiot boyfriend took the tape and a portable cassette player out to a little shack in the woods behind the apartments as Cindy and Pepsi innocently proposed an afternoon dope-smoking session out there. Hapless victims enthusiastically agreed and, when they approached, "OOOOoOOOooo AAAAAAHHHHHHH EEEEEEEEEE!" bellowed from the dark door of the shack, bringing all of them up short. Pepsi bravely proclaimed he would go see what that was and idiot boyfriend, wearing a devil mask, jumped on him and dragged a screaming Pepsi inside.

Zoom! Art and C-Note broke land-speed records back to the apartments. Cindy and Butch fell on the ground laughing…

Until every police car in the surrounding five counties showed up.

After they all got out of jail (except idiot boyfriend. He got sent to basic training) with stern warnings about pranking people, Pepsi decided that Butch should have stopped Art and C-Note before they alerted the police. Pepsi trapped him against one of the apartment walls and beat him up. Butch more or less let him because he was in Dad-attack mode and could not defend himself.

And because he deserved it.

When he reviewed the events, he concluded Pepsi was right and he should have stopped C-Note and Art before they burst into the apartment parking lot shrieking incoherently of monsters and murder, prompting the resident drunks and junkies to place numerous calls for police assistance. Why the onus fell on him was debatable but he was willing to accept the blame. Besides, all he got from Pepsi's efforts was a bloody lip and a good story, which was an excellent tradeoff.

The criteria, then, for a deserved beating involved missing a properly timed intervention that circumvented or prevented an adverse consequence. In this case, intercepting C-Note and Art before they alerted the authorities would have kept them all out of the hoosegaw and idiot boyfriend from getting killed in some forgotten Pleiku firefight. Neglect of a required intervention necessitated a retaliatory beating, for nothing more than the principle of the thing.

But this wasn't that. Not even close. Pepsi and Butch remained friends afterwards and loved regaling others with the story because this was something they had done together, willingly and with malice and joy aforethought. Butch and Professor were not friends, not now, nor would they ever be. And Butch didn't deserve this because Butch didn't cause this, forces out of his control did; Butch the hapless sailor caught by Charybdis. In cruder words, this was a shit situation not of your doing, dude, and Butch, you've really, really got to stop feeling like everything's your fault, man.

Even though it was.

Crap.

All right, let's pull it together. Professor and company emphasized two points: don't call us Breed, and get us the money. Or we will do much worse to you.

And to my sister.

Butch's spine iced over, adding to his hurts.

How the hell did Professor know Cindy?

How the hell did he know Butch, for that matter? It was obvious that Professor and Pee Sea weren't pals. Too bad he'd assumed otherwise because he had doubled his debt and owed it to two separately insane people. You know what happens when you assume.

"Idiot!" he snarled at himself in the blood-speckled mirror. If he had not pussied out and tried to negotiate with Professor, they wouldn't know about the money.

Would they?

Butch frowned.

Not so sure about that.

They'd sent the fetching Bobby out to lure him, that bitch. They knew he knew Pee Sea. And they knew Cindy. A lot of people Butch did not know sure knew a lot about him.

What to do?

Go to Philly, get on the plane and go to Illinois. Right now.

He examined himself in the mirror. Other than the very obvious cut along his scalp line, the bruised face and wincing every time he took a step, he could pass muster at the Chanute gate. No doubt some crusty chief would yell at him for falling down the stairs or off a roller coaster or whatever excuse he planned to use because the military took the unique view that any damage to his body not involving a war or some other mandated mayhem was considered abuse of government property and could lead to a court-martial.

Sheesh.

Going to jail because someone else beat him up. But it wouldn't come to that.

Would it?

He sighed.

Who knows?

His limited exposure to the Air Farce convinced him at least 75% of its population had sticks up their butts. The vast majority of those were at training bases like Chanute because sticks-up-butts were needed to gently shepherd goobers like Butch into steely-eyed killers. After a couple of years of sticks-up-butts treatment, Butch would be ready to commit genocide, so it seemed a valid system. It's possible some crusty chief will, indeed, send him off to Leavenworth for excessive bruising, so let's not test it. Need to hang around here until injuries are less apparent, which will take until well past this Friday and dangerously close to the end of his authorized leave. Not that it would matter; he would be dead sometime Friday evening anyway. As would Cindy.

Need to get the money.

How?

No idea.

Have to warn Cindy.

Well, at least that was one task he could accomplish right now. He finished cleaning his face and scrutinized his reflection in between the specks and cracks and figured he could walk to the car without drawing undue attention. Not that a shirtless and heavily bruised skinhead wasn't noticeable, but this was Seaside . and freaks were everywhere.

He tossed the T-shirt into the trash and struggled to put on his low quarters, gasping the whole time, especially when negotiating the one without a sock. If he ignored the gritty molasses crap now coating the inside of his shoes, he'd be all right. He limped out of the building using the rail as a cane, his back and hips now frozen into blocks of cement, and dragged onto the sand. Tough going through the irregular contours and every bob and weave caused spasms of pain. He headed away from the boys and the teenyboppers frolicking in the water because he didn't want to be recognized and, in about ten painful minutes, got to the exit. He pulled himself up the stairs by the metal pipe-railing as about fourteen hundred moms and dads overloaded with kids and blow-up Donald Ducks irritably pushed past him.

Kinda late to be heading for the water, kids ...

Or was it?

He took a moment at the top of the stairs to gaze at the sun. Puzzling. It hadn't moved a whole heckuva lot since he and Bobby took the Sky Ride. Speaking of the bitch... he looked around angrily but she was nowhere in sight. Too bad, he'd like to have a word with her. If anything, she owed him a blowjob. So what's the deal here? Well, the beach *was* a time vortex, and time flew when you were having fun, so the inverse should be true, if he remembered his geometry proofs correctly. Combine the two and Butch was surprised it wasn't yesterday and he was squaring away his locker in the barracks and collecting his orders in preparation for catching this morning's plane to Philly. That means he should live this day over again, right?

No thanks.

Butch stepped through the alley between a series of game booths and a cotton-candy vendor and reached the main drag and stopped to get his bearings. He spotted Howdy Dowdy's hat off to the right and hobbled that way.

The going was just as rough as the beach because he was dragging his feet and kept catching them on the uneven boards which made him stumble and gasp as his tortured back and hips spasmed. Lots of people stared at him as they walked past, giving him plenty of room and Butch exaggerated his jerky movements to convince them he suffered from some neurological condition and leave me alone, please.

That worked fine until a couple of Seaside cops came by and Butch was sure they were going to stop him and demand ID, discover he was military and out of uniform and club him to the ground, because cops knew stuff like the Uniform Code of

Military Justice and being out of uniform in public was a Violation of Article Stick-Up-Your-Butt subparagraph Kiss My Ass and hand him over to the SPs and he would spend the rest of his life in Leavenworth.

At least I'd be safe.

But the cops merely gave him a wry look and pressed on and Butch sighed and pressed on and about seven or eight hours later, he groaned his way down the stairs and onto the sidewalk and nine hours after that, reached the car.

Now let's warn Cindy.

How?

He stood keys in hand, indecisive at a moment when a decision was imperative because, once warned, Cindy would leap into action, grab idiot boyfriend and go hide somewhere in the Barrens. Better yet, get idiot boyfriend to drop her at the apartment, Butch swings by and she jumps into the Pontiac and they head out to Illinois together. Or Canada. Anyplace where bikers and Pineys and pissed-off drug dealers couldn't find them. Or Mom. Or Dad.

Or anything.

Was it too late? They had, in the past five years, lived forty years each, two entire lifetimes of affliction and grief. Cram that much trauma into such a short amount of time and it was like the waters piling up behind a dam, breaking it and devastating whole villages and intents and wishes, leaving behind a desert, a void that will take generations to mend. He lost sight of her as the deluge carried them both towards the falls, suffered his own plunge knowing she was already smashed somewhere on the rocks below, and that they were done. They were done.

So what's the point?

Because it was all his fault and he still owed her.

All right. Get in the car and go find her… where? No idea.

She didn't work, at least, as far as he knew, and, extrapolating from her earlier appearance, was at the moment careening around south Jersey in a green Challenger. That shouldn't be hard to find but he needed to narrow down the search area. Where would idiot boyfriend most likely spin doughnuts to impress his friends? Who knows? He didn't know the idiot boyfriend's name, much less his friends. All right, call someone, but who? How 'bout Cindy's best girlfriend what's-her-name, you know, the girl from Jobstown, the one with the smashed-looking mouth like she wanted a harelip or something or had gotten one repaired, the one who was always, always hanging out with Cindy no matter where she went… what's-her-name. Butch shook his head. Good Lord, bud, if you can't even remember the name of *that* girl, how are you going to find Cindy?

Call Mom.

As much as he didn't want to, he saw no other solution. Mom would have a good idea where Cindy was right now. At the very least, she could tell him what's-her-name's name and number. Have to risk Mom fretting and whining about where he was and when was he bringing the car back and I haven't even seen you since you got home and I never get to see you.

Jeez.

He needed two things, a dime and a phone. He checked his wallet but already knew he had no change in it. Even if he'd had a penny or two, Professor would have taken it along with the cash. He unlocked the Pontiac and rummaged around the ashtray and, bingo, a quarter and two dimes. He pocketed them and stood for a moment considering then reached in and grabbed the blouse and, gingerly, with much groaning, put it on. He didn't know if it made him any less conspicuous, but at least he was warding sunburn and it might have a positive effect on any other Seaside cops happening by. He grabbed the cunt cap and put it on, too. Go for the full effect. Besides, he was already out of uniform with one sock and no T-shirt, so might as well not aggravate things.

He headed back towards the boardwalk, actually walking a little faster and straighter. Must be the uniform. He spotted a bank of phone booths lined up near the Howdy Doody entrance, a couple of bums hanging around them. He glared one away from the booth at the end and slipped inside. He dropped a dime, heard the tone change, and dialed Mom's number. After about seven rings pegged to his growing annoyance, Ridge answered. "Hello?"

God, the guy always sounded mad.

"Hey, Ridge, this is Butch. Is Mom there?"

"Who?"

"Mom."

"Who's this?"

Jesus, the guy was dense.

"Butch. Is Mom there?"

"Did you wreck the car or something?"

"No, Ridge, the car is fine. Filled with gas and washed and waxed." That should get him off the car. "Is Mom there?"

No such luck.

"When you bringing it back?"

Butch steamed. "In a few minutes, but I need to speak to Mom first."

"Why?"

"Grocery list."

"Okay, get some milk. The two percent kind, not the regular milk, we can't drink that anymore because your Mom has that hiatal hernia. And some hamburger. Two packs. Some mayonnaise, the light stuff because your Mom, she can't have the regular stuff because of that hiatal hernia. Not mayonnaise. Miracle Whip. And some beer."

Butch pulled the phone away from his head and looked at it, incredulous.

"Anything else?" in his most sarcastic voice.

"Naw, that'll do it." And he hung up.

Took Butch a moment to realize that and then he cursed and yelled and actually thought about ripping the phone off its pedestal. One of the bums walked up and stared at him curiously and Butch waved him off then grabbed another dime and shoved it in and redialed and, again, seven rings later, Ridge: "Hello?"

"Don't hang up, Ridge. Don't. I don't have another dime and I really need to talk to Mom."

"Why? I gave you the list."

"I need to talk to her about something else."

"Did you write it down?"

"Pardon?"

What, did he want me to send Mom a letter or something?

"The list."

"Did I write down your grocery list, is that what you're asking me?"

"Did you?"

Butch actually counted to ten. "I need to talk to Mom right now, Ridge. Right. Now."

"She's taking a nap."

"Then wake her up."

"I ain't going to do that unless you tell me what it's about."

"It's between her and me, Ridge."

"Well, I ain't gonna wake her up then."

Butch contemplated finding Professor and telling him that Ridge had the ten thousand dollars in his truck right now and had said terrible things about Professor's mom. And, oh yes, had called them Breed.

"Then get me Cindy's phone number."

"Don't you have it?"

No jury in America would convict Butch because no man this stupid should be allowed to live.

"No, Ridge, that's why I'm asking you."

"It's the same number it's always been."

"I don't happen to have my address book with me, Ridge. It's inside the duffel bag I left at your place this morning."

"Well, why don't you come by and get it?"

"Because I need to talk to Cindy right now, not later."

"I thought you wanted to talk to your Mom?"

At this point, Butch was sputtering.

"Ridge, I was calling Mom to get the number. Since you won't wake her up so I can get the number from her, then you can get me the number."

"I don't have it."

"Then it's in Mom's address book."

"That's in the bedroom with your Mom."

Butch took in a deep breath and held it because if he unleashed on Ridge right now, he'd hang up and Butch would have to hit the bums up for a dime to call him back and have another futile conversation but maybe a constantly ringing phone would wake Mom up, and then he heard a woman's voice in the background.

"Is that Mom?" he asked.

"No. It's Cindy."

"Augh! Put her on! Put her on now!"

Butch was sure that Ridge would hang up but instead Butch heard him say, "Here, it's your brother," and then there were phone fumble sounds and then Cindy.

"Hey, bro, what's shaking?"

…and then the operator…"Please deposit another ten cents."

"Wait. What?" to the operator at the same time he shouted, "Don't hang up! Don't hang up!" to Cindy. Back to the operator,

"But I'm still on the first... er. Second... oh, never mind, dime, operator!"

"But this is a long-distance call, sir."

"Dammit," Butch muttered and fished around for the quarter and panicked when he couldn't find it and ah! There! He dropped the quarter inside the slot.

"Thank you, sir," the operator said with a hint of sarcasm and Butch immediately, "Cindy, Cindy! You still there?"

"Yeah, I'm here. Don't have to yell, ya know."

"Oh, thank God. Man, what an ordeal."

She laughed. "Yeah. Saw you earlier out by the apartments. What were you doing, visiting your old people friends across the street?"

"Yeah, I was."

"So were you there when it happened?"

"When what happened?"

"The old man. He got killed...

"Stop!" Butch ordered. "Just stop right now."

"What?"

"Just stop. I don't want to know. I just don't want to know."

"What?" Incredulity. "What do you mean you don't want to know?"

"I don't want to hear it."

"Huh? He was responding to a fire call when he got plowed into right at the intersection—"

"Stop. Talking. Now!" Butch in his coldest, most dangerous voice. "Right now! Not another word about it!"

Confused silence, a baffled snort or two then, "Well, Oookay!"

Butch's chest heaved and his world spun and no, no more of this. No more.

She read his distress over the phone. "Where are you?" asked with concern.

"Uh." He shook himself out of it. "Seaside."

"Oh yeah?" A sudden brightening, antidote to the previous tone. "Wacha doing? Skeeball?"

"Among other things."

"Oh yeah?" Her voice got lewd. "What's her name?"

"Bobby."

There was a pause.

"Bobby?"

"I think you know her."

"You get away from that girl as fast as you can."

"Too late."

"What happened?"

"I met Professor. And Boulder. And Home Run. And some other guy who does an excellent Charlie Manson imitation. Metaphorically, that is."

"Fishkill."

"That's his name or hobby?"

"He likes to fillet people."

"Oh."

He considered the cleverness.

"How do you know these guys?"

"I know a lot of people. Are you all right?"

"No."

There were a few moments of silence.

"I really fucked up, Cindy."

"I'll say."

"Professor wants me to bring him ten thousand dollars next Friday or… he's going to pay you a visit."

She snorted and then broke into laughter.

"I'm serious, Cindy. This is some serious shit!"

"Isn't that how much you owe Pee Sea?"

"As you know."

After all, she'd tried to get him out of it. Tried.

"So now I owe the same to them. And, man, don't let Ridge hear you!"

"Ridge is in the living room watching a ball game."

"So how do you know these guys—"

"Look." Cindy dropped into her all-business voice. "Don't worry about Professor. I'll take care of it."

"What?"

"I'll take care of it. You need to stay away from Pee Sea. You need to get out of here."

"I… know. Guy's been getting close. But, I gotta see Don first."

"I wouldn't."

"What do you mean?"

"I wouldn't. Stay out of PL. Come get your shit and get out of

New Jersey and never, ever come back."

"Cindy," his voice a plaint, a tear.

"Do you hear me?"

"Cindy… I'm… so sorry." Pause. "It's all my fault."

"What is?"

And he was about to say "everything," when the operator busted in, "Ten more cents, please."

Butch hung up.

He stood, swaying with heat and apocalypse. Everything was lost. These were his last hours. The punishment and horrid death he deserved was spiraling down on his location, like a bomb dropped eight miles high and accelerating. If he got out of here, did exactly what Cindy said, it would miss him.

But he had to see Don. Had to.

He stepped out of the phone booth, waved the bums away, and headed for the car.

Chapter 16

Butch and approximately 100,000 other beachgoers decided to head back home at the same time but, just like the earlier drive, the traffic was unusually smooth. A collective spirit of cooperation and fraternity descended on the roads, drivers displaying rare politeness and regard for others. Even the Philly drivers showed courtesy. That never happens, especially at this point in late summer.

What the heck's going on?

Butch couldn't help feeling it was a divine effort to hasten his fate. The bomb canted over as God ushered him to ground zero.

So it was still too early by the time PL hove in to sight, the sun in exactly the same position as when he left Seaside, God allowing Pee Sea more daylight to destroy his enemies. Butch wondered why Pee Sea enjoyed such divine favour. Whatever the theological implications, Butch was too exposed and if he turned onto Washington and cruised back down to Don's house, he'd be dead before he made the driveway. He hadn't spotted the El Camino but that meant nothing. Pee Sea knew where he was heading. Everybody knew where he was heading. Stupid to go back.

But he had to see Don. He had to fix things. Just not right now. Later, under cover of darkness and Merlin concert. It was the most likely place Don would show. It was also the most likely place for Pee Sea and his Breed pals to catch Don and Butch simultaneously (or, if the note in his locker were to be believed, just Butch). Dooby and Merlin would have their backs when things broke but no offense, guys, you're not going to do well against hardened bikers. Maybe he should call Wayne and ask him and a couple of others to attend. Hardened bikers would then get handed a big surprise but that meant dragging other people he loved into a mess of his own making.

At this point, best to limit the damage to the people at fault. Like me…

When it became acutely clear that the only way out of this mess was the sudden infusion of cash Don had mentioned months (years) ago, something only possible (as Dooby had concluded months, years, ago) through illicit transfers of controlled substances, Butch called Jape and met him at the White Dotte.

"You remember back on New Year's Eve when you asked if I was interested in making money?"

"Yeah?"

"I'm interested."

A slow grin broke on Jape's Scottish freckled face.

"Good!" and he sketched the situation: Truck's cousin had a line on some excellent Jamaican out of New York City. Maybe even some Thai stick. The cousin was antsy to move it. Quickly. And was willing to cut them a premium for the assistance. All Butch needed to do was hook them up with someone who could move quantity, say ten pounds.

"Ten pounds?" Butch goggled. "You mean, ten pounds?"

"Of the best Jamaican. Mon." He smirked.

Butch sat back.

"That's, what, $2000?"

"Three."

Butch stared at him and laughed. "I don't have $2000, much less three."

"You don't have to pay anything."

"Why not?"

"It's fronted."

"By who?"

Jape smiled and cocked his head and wagged a finger. "Ah, now, c'mon, that would be telling. Let's just say Truck has some good friends up there."

"You mean the cousin."

"No. The cousin's just the point man. It's some other New York pals of Truck's."

"I thought he was from Passaic."

Jape waggled a hand. "Close enough."

Odd, but plausible.

"All right."

Butch drummed fingers on the table while sipping his milkshake. Ah man, White Dotte shakes, the best in America.

Imagine how much better if he were stoned. Imagine how much better stoned he'd be on Jamaican. Or Thai stick.

"Why don't you guys do it yourself?"

"We don't know anybody with that kind of money."

Butch snorted. "You think I do?"

"You know Mason."

Butch shook his head. "No way. Mason's a straight shooter."

"You know everybody."

Which was true. His universes wheeled and collided at so many points and intersections that Butch traversed whole populations containing likely candidates. And immediately he thought of one.

Pee Sea.

Everyone knew Pee Sea, including Jape and Truck, but very few people could approach him because Pee Sea was insane. Literally, figuratively, in whatever way to term it, the guy was nuts. He once stabbed an assistant principal in the leg with a fork. He'd burned down his stepfather's mom's house because she wouldn't let him keep a pistol there. He blew up a Braun's Mills police car with a couple of M80s twisted together and shoved into the gas tank. With the cops still inside. All of this before Pee Sea was sixteen.

After his stints in juvy, Pee Sea took over all merchandising of stolen property that passed through the Barrens. Quite an accomplishment because the Barrens had been a center of smuggling and dubious transfers of ownership for about three hundred years and at present under the control of various New York and Philadelphia crime families. That Pee Sea operated with near impunity under the protection of proven killers spoke volumes about the respect – or fear – in which those families held him.

By the time he was eighteen, Pee Sea had made hundreds of thousands of illegal dollars, but you would never know it. He wore the same lumberjack plaid jacket and corduroy shirt and ten-year-old pants he'd been wearing since he stabbed the principal, drove the same POS El Camino he'd stolen a day out of juvy, and lived in what amounted to a tar-paper shack on the other side of Chatsworth; that is, when he wasn't hiding out with one or another of the ten or fifteen Piney girlfriends he kept throughout the area. Pee wasn't in it for the money; he was in it for the thrill.

Pee Sea had no friends, only associates, and those ever-shifted as whatever demons driving him changed intents. He'd once been pals with the notorious Stilt brothers, the main guys with whom the Philly mob contracted to make select people vanish, until some hunter stepped through their rotted chests. And now he was not, for reasons that were not clear. That may have something to do with one of the Stilt cousins showing up one morning on the porch of the Stilt homestead, minus a head. Yet Pee drove and walked around with impunity and fearlessness, even in the face of a continuous Stilt threat.

No one talked to him. No one approached him. You had to go through intermediaries, such as the Bowers or the Haneys or one of the other Piney smuggling families whose business interests crossed all lines. Unless Pee liked you.

He liked Butch.

No one knew Pee Sea liked them until he made it clear. In Butch's case, Pee Sea made it clear when he sold him Buggy's FM converter. He'd done so because of Cindy. Pee Sea was an associate of Cindy's boyfriend at the time and somehow she had mentioned in Pee's presence Butch's love of FM. Apparently Pee Sea was a big fan of FM, too, and saw Butch as a fellow traveler and one day, pulled up behind Buggy in the parking lot at Perkins High, walked up to the open window and said, "Give me ten dollars."

Which Butch did without question because he thought he was being robbed and it was simply not wise to resist Pee Sea.

"Here," and Pee tossed the converter, still in the box, onto his lap and drove away.

Ever since, Pee would give him a wave when passing by, raise a glass to him at a party they happened to both attend, sell him a joint when he was light. But Butch remained scared to death of him – as was most of the population of south Jersey, because no one never knew when Pee would suddenly decide he no longer liked them, at which point friendly waves turned into removed heads left on a porch somewhere.

But on that day with Jape at the White Dotte, Pee Sea and Butch were still on good terms. And there was a business proposition on the table that was right up Pee's alley. And Butch needed the money. Because he had to get the hell out of Dodge.

A week later, Jape came to the apartment when April was, fortuitously, out doing something and handed Butch a small envelope of the most potent-smelling weed Butch had ever encountered. Of course, they had to roll one and Butch almost lost his life when April came home unexpectedly and instantly bowled over by the powerful reek of excellent weed and the sight of Jape and Butch boneless and stuporous on the couch with half the week's groceries emptied on the coffee table. Cops almost came that time, too, but, thank God, she calmed down enough to realize sending her fiancée to jail for twenty years would disrupt her plans.

A couple of days after, Butch finally returned to this reality and headed out to the Do Drop Inn, a Piney bar off Meerschaum Road, and sat down while indigent bikers and lumberjacks discussed which of them would bunghole him to death. Five minutes later, Pee slipped onto the stool next to him. Butch handed him the envelope and left, bunghole intact.

The next day, Pee ran him off the road and pulled Butch out of Buggy and threw him into the Camino and sped down some Barrens road and pulled over and pulled out a .45 and held it to Butch's head.

At that point, Butch figured they were no longer on good terms.

"Where'd you get it?"

"Jape."

"That little fuck? Where'd he get it?"

"Truck."

"How much?"

"Ten pounds?"

"How much?"

"Five?"

At this point, Butch braced for the bullet. But it didn't come. "I'll take twenty pounds."

Pause.

"And this is on you."

The pistol went away and they careened back and Pee threw Butch out of the Camino without stopping and Butch rolled right into Buggy's bumper and thanked God he was alive because this was how Pee treated the people he liked.

'This is on you.' If everything went right, well and good. But if it didn't…

A week later, behind a Farmer's Market warehouse reeking of backed-up sewer, Truck and Jape tossed an old duffel bag reeking of old moldy dope, not sharp and fresh as a Jamaican sunrise, from the open back of Truck's Gremlin and onto the broken pavement. "Here you go, man!" Jape said and pushed it over to Butch as the two idiots fell to giggling and slapping each other silly.

"Been sampling, I see," Butch said while grabbing at the duffel's handle.

"Oh no, man, no way," Truck said, leaning back on his duct-taped taillight. "I'm on prob."

"So what's so funny, then?"

"Oh, nothing," he said with an air of feigned innocence and he and Jape exchanged glances and fell to giggling again.

Danger, Will Robinson.

Butch straightened and looked at them hard.

"You guys better not be fucking around here." He gave the duffel a significant glance.

"Take it easy, man, it's all right," Jape assured. "We're just excited."

Which Butch could understand. With the 2000 of his cut, he could hightail it to Alabama and live for a few months in one of Dad's trailers… well, not Dad's, his wife's or girlfriend or whatever she was of the moment… and lay low until too much time had passed for April and her dad to do anything about it and then Butch would see. Maybe come back, maybe stay in Alabama, maybe go to Oklahoma and see if Frank was still living in the schoolyard. Whatever, out of sight was out of mind and Butch planned on staying out of sight until enough of the guilt was out of his mind that he could live with himself and start over. Somewhere.

Dad would be proud.

"Let's go, then." Butch yanked the duffel off the lot and headed towards Buggy, one eye out for random staties cruising by looking for dope dealers. He glanced back. Neither of them had moved. He raised a querying eyebrow.

"Ah, man," Jape waved him away, "I can't go with you."

"What?"

"Pee hates me, man. He'll kill me on sight."

Butch looked at Truck, who held up 'oh well' hands.

"Same thing, man."

What the fuck?

Butch shook the duffel. "He's expecting this tonight."

"No problem. You handle it," Jape said.

All Butch could do was stare at him.

"Yeah," Truck said, "you're a karate guy. You'll be fine." And he made Edwin Starr karate moves that got both of them giggling again.

At this point, the robot should have rushed up waving its arms and screaming, "Danger, Will Robinson!" That is, if Butch was a little more discerning. F'rinstance, the sudden reluctance of Jape and Truck to accompany him with $10k of product, of which they were on the hook. Maybe that was a sign of how much they trusted Butch, but wasn't lack of trust a staple among big-time drug dealers? Not that these two nimrods were big-time anything except nimrods, but there was a principle involved: if you wanted to *be* something, then you *act* like that something. Act classy if you want to be classy; act tough if you want to be tough. These two weren't playing the part. And, really, if he'd thought about it, Jape first broached the idea of money-making several weeks ago, and if Truck's cousin was so antsy to move this product, why hadn't he before now?

But none of that popped into his head. He was overwhelmed by other interests, such as the getting out of Dodge. Without another word or backwards glance, Butch, threw the duffel into Buggy's trunk and drove to the apartment. He sat there and considered how many ways this could go wrong, then went upstairs and dialed the phone.

"Don," he said, "I need your help."

He'd then driven to PL and sat in Don's living room with Mom and Dad and a very suspicious older brother until Don and he could extricate themselves and then they headed towards Lakehurst. It was well after dark by this time and Butch almost missed the turnoff.

"We're late." His voice was tight.

"Relax, man, we'll be okay." Don pulled a bowie knife out of his jacket.

Butch almost drove Buggy off the road. "Throw it out! Throw it out!"

"What?" Don looked at him like he was crazy. "This is my favorite knife!"

"Throw. It. OUT!" Butch yelled and grabbed at Don's window, careening Buggy all over the sand road.

"Okay, Jesus! Don't wreck the damn car!" he said as he tossed the knife through the window.

Butch regained control and let out a huge breath. "You trying to get us killed? This is Pee Sea."

Don looked at him, paled a bit, and then turned forward. "You owe me a knife."

"You're late," Pee said, arms folded, flanked by two sasquatches just out of Buggy's headlight range, hulks in shadow that looked as if they wanted to eat him. Pee's Camino was off to the side.

"I know," Butch said, standing in front of the headlights, "I suck driving at night."

"Hmm." Pee actually chuckled at that. "Who's with you?" Pee chin-pointed at the passenger side of Buggy.

"It's Don."

"Bring his knife?"

Butch almost crapped his pants right then.

"Uh… I made him throw it out."

"Hmm. Where's Jape and Fucknuts?"

"They're too scared of you."

"You're not?"

"Pee, I'm shittin' bricks."

Apparently, that was the right answer because the sasquatches and Pee laughed and Butch opened the trunk and took out the duffel. Pee pointed at the ground in front of him and Butch placed it there. One of the sasquatches picked it up and moved behind the Camino.

"Twenty-one," he grunted, a few moments later.

Pee cocked an eye at him. "You gave me an extra pound?"

Oh crap.

"Must be the duffel."

"It's not."

Oh crap.

Butch made a mental note to kill Jape when he got back. "Think of it as a baker's dozen."

Apparently, another good answer because Pee smirked and jerked his head and a sasquatch walked forward and dropped a satchel. No one moved, least of all Butch.

"I don't know what I'm supposed to do next," he said.

"Leave," Pee said.

Butch obediently turned and made for Buggy. "With this, idjit," Pee said, highly amused.

Butch turned and Pee's foot was on the satchel. "Oh," he said and walked back, feeling like a complete idjit. He reached for the handle but Pee did not move his foot.

"Wanna count it?"

Butch stood straight. "No."

"Do I need to check the dope?"

"No."

They all stood straight, still, ready, and Butch was sure this was it and wished Don still had the knife, when Pee smiled, deadly and empty, moved his foot and gestured for him to go on. Butch grabbed the satchel and spun on his heels, expecting the rip of bullets any second, got in Buggy, backed up about six times making a complete mess of his getaway, Pee and the sasquatches standing there, arms folded, in and out of the headlights and watching with great amusement until he gunned it back down the road.

Butch did not breathe until he reached Route 70.

"Dude," Don said and Butch looked over at the open satchel and all the cash in there. He breathed better.

"Thanks, man, thanks for doing this," he said. "Take some for your trouble."

Don snapped it closed. "You need it more than me."

Jape and Truck did a happy dance in Truck's apartment when they opened the satchel, throwing the cash up and around and screaming "WaHOO!" at the top of their voices and laughing and slapping each other's backs and Butch and Don exchanged glances. All decks, battle stations.

"You guys wanna calm down?" Butch said.

"Nah man, nah man, this is great, it's great." Truck was

hyperventilating. He scooped up some wads and handed them to Butch. "Here's your cut, man."

Butch looked at the wad, bigger than he expected, then counted it. "This is thirty-five hundred. You gave me too much."

"No, that's yours. We split more or less into thirds," said Jape.

Butch was puzzled.

"How's that? You need to pay six for the load, don't you?"

It was the math, all along, that should have spurred an earlier appearance of the arm-waving robot. They'd promised Butch two, which only left them two to split between them which was a very small profit margin for two big-time drug dealers but a good one for Butch who simply needed to get out of Dodge and did not care whether Truck and Jape made a measly 25% each to Butch's 50%.

If they were that stupid, they were that stupid.

Unless they had done something really stupid.

"Relax, man," Truck said. "It's all cool. Spend it in good health."

"What did you do?"

"Nothin', man." But Truck's eyes slipped sideways.

"What did you do?"

"Look, it's cool," said Jape, on a bench sorting the bills. "It wasn't exactly Jamaican. It's some shit we grew in the back over by the shed. Along with some catnip."

Butch's jaw dropped. "But," he spluttered, "the sample!"

"Oh, THAT was Jamaican," and he grinned at Butch.

Butch hit him so hard he was sure he had broken his knuckles, but it was actually Jape's teeth caving in.

"Hey!" Truck came off the couch and Butch side kicked him across the room.

Oak would have been proud.

"Move!" he shouted to Don and they were out of the door and into Buggy and screaming towards Groveville and Dooby's…

In retrospect, he should have completed the beating half to death of both idiots, gathered up all the cash, threw that and the two idiots into Buggy's trunk, headed right back to Pee Sea and begged for his mercy. In the name of their friendship, watcha say, Pee? Butch probably would have lost a finger or two, maybe required to help with the idiots' decapitation, but it would have turned out okay. He wouldn't have spent the next couple of weeks running from one hiding spot to another, sending Cindy out to plead Don's innocence and Butch's lack of concern for April so, yes, trash the apartment (which Pee did) and trash April, too, while you're at it, possibly solving Butch's other problem, which Pee didn't, and finally ending up in the Air Farce recruiter's door.

Water under the bridge.

Speaking of which…

He saw the bridge. In a moment, he'd be at the point of no return.

What to do? If he followed God's plan and went to Don's, game over. Perhaps he should go see someone else, but who? Everyone he knew was either dead or now an enemy. Perhaps he should simply drive around aimlessly for a few hours, visit the scenes of his teenage life, the one of wheeling universes and high hilarity before it all became ash and evil. He glanced at the fuel gauge: less than a quarter tank and no more money, thanks to Professor, so it would be a short trip.

Go home? Not the apartment but to Ridge's? Possible.

Maybe he could punch Ridge in the mouth for costing him an extra precious dime.

Whatever, make a decision.

On reflex, he cut a hard left onto Reeves, causing an 18-wheeler to blare at him long past the point of being rude and, ya know, screw you, man, had to turn. He slowed as he reached Woodmansie and stopped. He looked at the sky. Few more hours to go. Decision made.

Moon Crater.

He sped up and headed down the road.

Chapter 17

He'd been to the Moon Crater once about two, three years ago, crammed into the back seat of a 1956 Opel Rekord alongside Pepsi and Truck and Cindy's girlfriend, the one whose name he couldn't remember. Cindy's Piney boyfriend-of-the-moment drove the Rekord, Cindy in the middle of the front bench seat wrapped around Piney boyfriend, with Piney boyfriend's slope-headed cousin sitting shotgun ... Rebar, yeah, that was the cousin's name.

Why did he remember slope-head's name but not Cindy's girlfriend? And what had this motley collection of people been doing in the back of an unregistered and probably stolen Opel careening through the Barrens?

Simple. While sitting around the apartment rolling and toking, Butch had mentioned to the gathered group that Thong and he had made a hasty reconnaissance of the Barrens a couple of weeks ago in a futile attempt to find the Crater. The Piney grinned and said, "You really want to see it?"

He did. The place was legendary, party central 24/7 replete with beach, and Thong and he had gone out to chase down the rumors and got chased out by a large group of Pineys who took dim views of non-Piney incursions. Needed a Piney to get in and here was one, courtesy of Cindy, on the couch getting stoned on Butch's dope. Next thing you know, piled into the Rekord with a bunch of stoned hangers-on and careening through the wasted tracks, wasted

Butch saw very little of the approach because he had a very limited view out of the Opel's windows, crushed as he was against

Truck in a desperate effort to avoid physical contact with Cindy's girlfriend (what the HELL was her name?) because, no thanks, and the whole interior was a fog bank of dope smoke anyway, so his chances of finding the place now were nil, even though he was going in the right direction. That's because there was no other direction. Once he'd dumped off 70, he was in the Barrens. Roads led in. Nothing led out. And everything looked exactly the same.

Need a Piney to show the way.

He chuckled and briefly considered heading over to Tabernacle to pick one up. His luck, it'd be one of Pee Sea's henchmen who'd direct him to some lonely house out past Chatsworth and Butch'd never be seen again unless some hunter stepped through his rotted chest.

No, gonna have to figure this out on my own. Okay. How? Don't remember the route; don't remember much of anything else, for that matter. Except the near death experience.

They'd arrived after dark, the fog bank in the Rekord matched by the fog rising from the woods, the world outside and the one in his head grey and invisible. The Piney yelled, "Here we go!" and the next thing Butch knew, the Rekord went over the edge of a fog-bound crater and plunged down a sheer 90-degree angle of sand and crap aiming for a fog-draped bottom of rocks and crap, the Piney stomping the accelerator to hasten their destruction. Everyone, including Butch, screamed as they fell/drove, the Piney and Rebar in sheer joy, everyone else in terror.

Somehow they didn't pancake into metal and blood but, instead, raced across the bottom and up the far side, fishtailing the whole climb while throwing rivers of sand behind them and then vaulted over the edge and onto the plain.

Dune-buggying, Piney style.

The Moon Crater wasn't an actual crater. It was the remains of an old quarry, the far side given over to blue water and cliffs. Woods backed the wide lip all around it, with an actual grey sand beach running down to the blue hole. The crater side was bare and dusty like the moon, hence the name, and had been converted by prior Piney generations into the insane sheer-drop dune-buggy course already experienced. And experienced, and experienced. They dune buggied at least six or seven more times before smoke poured out of the hood and a horrific grinding noise from underneath the floor forced them to stop. Once they all fell out and checked for injuries and discovered they were merely bruised and battered and not suffering from compound fractures, Piney and Rebar worked on the Opel as the rest of them built a bonfire and danced all night and ran into the blue hole in their underwear and got into a stone mud fight. Spirits in the night.

Wouldn't mind doing that again. If I can find the place.

He peered at the skinny asphalt road. Sandy trails intersected it every twenty yards or so, the land between covered with the skinny pine trees that gave the place its name. Bogs and quicksand and pestilent creeks ran right up to the asphalt and out the other side, thousand-year courses through woods and gullies and brakes and an impenetrable darkness that humans had yet to fully explore. No wonder this was a favored Mafia dumping ground. The place was too eerie and bland and maze-like for all but those most experienced with its ways, like the hunters. Like the Pineys, who understood it, who loved it, a place haunted by legendary beasts, demons, and unsolved murder.

It was New Jersey's soul.

Stirring the trees and muttering down the sand roads, an unheard voice fraught with peril urging the unwary into Mordor, dark and bleak but star-filled, glints in bog and hummock and that was God, no, that was gods, the old ones of moor and peat, lost and banished and sullen, rearing back on eldritch haunches and howling ancient griefs and their worshipers, the shadow people, the Pineys and the hunters and the murderers heard and crowed a barbaric "Yawp!" in response.

So different from Alabama, which was horror and sin and unpaid consequences. Different from Oklahoma, with its ghosts of murdered children playing on dust-ridden swing sets and forgotten Apache women mournfully singing in lost cemeteries. He'd felt that difference the moment he'd stepped off the Greyhound, freezing and bleary-eyed and shocked and heard the distant yawp, the call from cedar creeks and marshes. The world is different here. Come find out.

And he had. Midnight runs to beach and boardwalk, huddled by the pier as fireworks arced overhead and the chill sea air braced and he shivered and pulled some girl closer. Sitting by Mirror Lake with seven or eight citizens of other universes as the fog rolled in and they hushed their stoned babble while the witchery spun mist and cloud and enclosed them and what if the world has ended and we are the only ones left and out in the fog someone calls, "Help us, help us!" and they all leaned forward breathless and listening and for a moment it's real and true and the horror freezes them and man are we stoned! We're so stoned! and they laugh and laugh. Or midnight in these sorcery woods Thong and he searching for the Leeds's house and the Jersey Devil and swear something ran across the road just in front just there did you see it and they screamed their ecstasy and some Kinks song and you can be seventeen now and years from now and the beach road and the swamp road and lakes road goes on forever.

I want to be seventeen forever.

Come be seventeen forever out here, sing and party and ride motocross or swim the blue holes unrestrained, as close to a witch's orgy with attendant human sacrifice as could happen these days. Partiers ran giggling into side brakes and were never seen again; motorcycles hit inexplicable vines that tossed them down ravines, and the blue holes turned into bottomless death traps for the drunk and stoned and otherwise careless. It's okay, okay, the attendant cost of being seventeen forever, raise a beer can and salute the lost brothers and sisters. The elder gods smile.

The Pineys know. The Pineys worship here. This is their church, and they whoop and call across sand and cedar waters, kneel by a blue hole and listen to the stillness as the bonfire climbs ever higher, drink and sing dirty songs and throw golden crowns and axes into bottomless waters. Yawp. The boundaries thin, the answers here to questions that shouldn't be asked but foolish mortals ask them and deep in black cedars a god with antlers as wide as the heavens snorts and glares and grins and stomps inexorably towards the petitioner.

Butch petitioned as he drove: how do I get out of this mess, how do I get Don and Dooby and Mom and even Ridge out of this mess? What should Butch do next, that is, if he somehow managed to get out of this mess? Elder gods, answer me.

But first, he had to find them.

He studied the passing woods. Everything looked the same. It was like fifty identical doors encircling the arena and he must pick the right one, the tiger or the princess. But how? He wasn't a Piney with a genetic ability to discern the secret ways. The Piney boyfriend drove easily and confidently straight to the Moon Crater, laughing and drinking Pabst the whole time and running his hand up and down Cindy's leg and Butch was resentful, wondering if he was now required to kick Piney's ass but no, he'd get left on some cedar berm trussed and ready for horned gods to feast upon. He had no totem, no golden crown ready for throwing in deep waters to appease, and the Barrens regarded him with ill intent.

And then it didn't.

A jolt of recognition, like walking down a street and realizing the guy approaching was an old pal. There was something about this particular curve of asphalt combined with the cancerous trees and angled sand that was instantly familiar and he coasted into a left-hand turn slipping and spraying and in danger of getting stuck in the berm but he regained control and set the wheels into older tire racks heading deeper into the brake, which closed up behind him, snickering. The road snaked right and left, hiding the straightaways but this was right, this was the way.

As if to prove it, two Enduros suddenly burst out of the woods, the two riders helmeted and goggled and face-masked and fishtailed alongside his front bumper staring back at him, exchanging looks and then wheeling back into the trees. Angels of the Barrens. Butch paralleled them on the road, curving in and out of view but they remained the same distance and pace on a hidden track through the pines. There was a dip then a sharp rise that Butch topped and the land opened.

And here he was.

The Enduros raced along the moon side and then cut up the far bank, momentarily lost to sight in the woods and then emerged on the beach side. People milled around three or four pickup trucks parked there and, as the Enduros slid up to the trucks, their riders pointed at Butch. The people all turned.

He didn't hesitate.

Gunning it, Butch spun the back tires and careened all over the trail, straightening out at the last minute as the front of the car plunged over the crater's edge, Butch screaming but not in terror this time. Joy, the joy! I'm seventeen! Fighting the wheel, he kept the Pontiac straight, jerking it here and there to avoid first a boulder and then a rusted out car that didn't make the run, bouncing hard and drifting too far in one direction and threatening to flip over, the bottom of the crater rushing up and then *bam*! The angle still odd enough that he didn't plow straight into the ground but bounced up and he gassed it and the tires caught and spun and threw up dirt and sand like a WW2 smoke barrage and he was rushing across the floor, dodging boulders and *bam*! Ramped up the opposite wall as he floored it and tossed the car right and left and right and left to gain traction and a path and he screamed and screamed as the front of the Pontiac cleared the lip and launched onto the beach side.

Seventeen! Seventeen!

He was still screaming with absolute cowboy joy as hippies and Pineys all rushed him cheering and roaring the great yawp and pounding the hood and ripping the door open and peeling him out and carrying him like a conquering hero to their campfire. "Oh, man!" "Out freakin' standing!" "That was great!" "Thought you were going to lose it there a couple of times!" and dropped him into a camp chair, a beer thrown in his hand as people slapped him on the back.

Dune-buggying, Barrens style.

"Shit, you got one set of guavas on you!" shouted a hippie Piney wearing a tank top and jean shorts and shoulder-length hair and an even longer moustache who dropped onto a stump opposite him.

Butch was about to ask what a guava was when the hippie, still laughing asked, "Is that your car?"

"My mom's."

Everyone roared with laughter: the two Enduro racers who turned out to be fourteen-year-old blond twins, boy and a girl; hippie Piney; his old lady – the way she draped over HP Butch assumed it was his old lady – a long-haired Joan Baez type; a very skinny hippie kid with Pete Townsend looks; a gigantic-shouldered Viking-looking Piney who had to be a lumberjack; and a couple of other girls and a couple of other boys and they were all shadow people, living in the haunted forest. These were the elves and sprites dancing in the moonlight, seventeen forever.

"Well, Mom's gonna be shaking sand out of that thing for weeks!" HP concluded jovially and slapped Butch on the knee and gave him another beer. "Were you scared?"

"Out of my mind."

More roars and someone gave him a grinder off the campfire and someone cranked up a boom box and it was Wishbone Ash and there were distant cheers and Butch peered around the Dodge

Ram behind him to see bathing-suited figures at the beach all jumping up and down and giving thumbs-up. Butch raised his beer to them and they cheered more and the bonfire behind them suddenly leaped and music too distant for him to quite make out wafted from the trees and the bathing-suit people fell into a chant and dance. Dithyramb, pan pipes and goat-people bleating. Yawp.

"Did you get banged up on the climb?" HP asked, leaning forward, a look of concern on his face.

Butch cocked an eye, puzzled. "No, why?"

"You look beat-up."

"Oh." Butch gingerly touched his sore head. "No. That's from something else."

HP sat back, satisfied by that answer, and popped himself another beer. Pete Townsend snagged his own beer, no doubt a misdemeanor, drinking-age violation, and gazed at Butch curiously. "So what you doing out here, soldier?"

"Airman. Just had to do it one last time before heading out."

"Orders, huh?" HP nodded. "I get that."

"You were in?"

"196th, baby." And he slapped a tattoo on his shoulder that Butch could not quite make out. "Me and my brother here." He nodded at the Viking, who nodded back, and Butch was about to ask if they were real brothers or Army brothers but decided it was irrelevant. "At Da Nang, eighteen months. Left there in '71." He spread expansive hands. "Been here ever since."

"I guess they'll send me to Vietnam," Butch mused.

"Nah." HP popped another beer and handed it to Butch. "It's all over except the crying."

Butch supposed that was true. Getting sent to Vietnam was a background terror he'd harbored ever since joining but it seemed more boogeyman than actuality. The real boogeymen were a lot closer, on the other side of the Barrens waiting for him to show up. Besides, they didn't need weathermen in Vietnam. It was hot and rainy all the time.

"Ain't this the best?" HP said as he curled back on his stump and closed his eyes and nodded to the music and downed his beer and then another one and offered Butch another but he waved it away. "No thanks, I'm driving."

They all chuckled at that. "The way you came across, thought you were drunk already," HP noted.

"Probably would have been easier."

"So, get drunk and try it again."

"No. Pushing my luck, I think."

"I hear that." HP went back to tune nodding. "So when you shipping out?"

"Maybe tomorrow."

HP raised an eyebrow. "Maybe?"

"I got some stuff to do tonight. If it doesn't work out…"

"You leave?"

Butch nodded.

"Ah, man." HP was sympathetic. "That sounds like a sad story needing to be told." He waved the beer around. "We are a receptive bunch."

Butch let out a long breath.

"Things just don't work out the way you think."

HP and Viking and Joan Baez murmured agreement and hand slapped all the way around and they all settled in and the fire crackled and the shadows lengthened and it was ten thousand years ago and the tribe had gathered to tell of fallen kings and broken swords and jealous gods.

Butch felt a thousand years old, not seventeen.

"I fucked everything up. And I don't think there's a way to fix it."

The fire cracked.

"I didn't do what I was supposed to do. I didn't protect my people. I was too scared. So they got hurt. All these people got hurt because of me. I think my best friend got hurt." He paused, suddenly worried. Please be at the clamshell, Don, please. "I was a coward and ran and I'm still running. Still. I mean, that's why I'm wearing this monkey suit." He flourished hands down his uniform. "Because I ran… I ran," he whispered. "I should have manned up. Should have. I caused all this. I caused… bodies."

"I think you're a little too hard on yourself," Frank said.

Butch blinked. Frank was squatting by the fire, toasting a hot dog on a stick. The fire was bright because everything else had gone dark and shadowed. The pickup trucks and Enduros were still there, but HP and Viking and the twins were gone. The music was distant and unrecognizable now.

"I don't think I'm being hard enough."

"Hmm." Frank tested the hot dog and then put it back in the fire."You're right. You should have killed your dad like any self-respecting thirteen-year-old kid would have done. Without even thinking about it. I mean it's not like it's your dad's fault for acting like a jerk, it's yours for not understanding the situation. You should have known months before, heck, years before, that your dad was doing terrible things and you should have taken action when you were six or seven. I guess that means this is my fault, too." And he pulled his jaw off his face, waggled it at Butch, then snapped it back in place.

Butch threw out palms. "All right, all right." He watched Frank reconnect jaw hinges. "It's not all my fault, at least with Dad. And Cindy. But all this with April. Man, I should have seen that coming."

"Yeah." Frank nodded. "Because when people say they love you, they must mean it. Like mothers and sons." He frowned at the hot dog and set it back in the flames.

"All right, fine, so it was a setup. Her or her dad or both of them, I don't know. But I should have known."

"Yeah, 'cause a guy desperate for someone to love him knows all the signs."

Butch regarded him.

"Is that what I am?"

Frank snorted. "Please. You're downright embarrassing."

Butch looked at the beer and shook it and there were a couple of drops in it and he poured them out.

"So what do I do?"

"Go save Don. Because that *is* your fault." And he pointed the hot dog stick at him accusingly.

"So Don's alive?"

"I dunno." Frank pulled the hot dog off the stick and juggled it between his hands. "Ow ow ow!"

"So that means he is, right? 'Cause all you dead people would know. Right?"

"You think we hold conventions or something?"

Butch *tsk*ed. "You know, you've got a real gift for sarcasm."

"Comes from following you around." Frank pulled his jaw to his chest, stuffed the hot dog inside the lower part, and then put it back and worked it with his hands to chew. Pieces kept falling through the hole in his cheek and he shoved them back inside.

Butch watched, fascinated. "Frank, why are you still here?"

"Wanted a hot dog," he said, between chews.

"No, I mean, why haven't you moved on?"

"Followed the light? Gone up to the clouds? Shed this mortal coil? That?"

"Well, yeah."

"Do you know how far it is?"

"Uh… no."

"No, you don't." Frank eyed him. "How big is the universe?"

"Pretty big."

"You betcha pretty big." Frank threw the stick onto the fire. "Billions and billions and billions of light-years. That's just the universe itself. Getting to the *end* of the universe…" Frank made a 'whew' sound.

"Well, it's not like you have to walk." Butch blinked. "Do you?"

Frank made a wry face. "No one's gotten there yet."

"What?"

"No one. It's all physics, see. You can only travel at the speed of light. That's the universal constant for physical beings."

"But you're not a physical being."

"I was born, wasn't I? Anyways, that's your top speed. And that's only six trillion miles or so a year. The universe is billions and billions and TRILLIONS of light-years across. So the first human, let's call him Adam, say he died 35,000 years ago. So he's been travelling six trillion miles a year for 35,000 years. Do the math."

"I… can't."

"Let me summarize, then. Adam, the first guy to take a crack at heaven, is only a fraction of a fraction of a fraction of the way there."

"But—"

"And that," Frank raised an emphatic finger, "is only if he's heading in the right direction. Easy to get turned around out there."

"But…" and Butch paused for an expected interruption. None. "But, that makes no sense. You die, you go to heaven or hell."

"If you're willing to make the trip." Frank settled back near the fire.

"And… you're not."

Frank looked at him.

"You're not planning on sleeping here tonight, are ya?" HP asked.

Startled, confused, Butch looked around but Frank was not there and everyone else was. It was full-on dark now, the fire as the only source of light, the sparks flying upwards and casting shadows and brightness over the angels and their chariots. "What time is it?"

"Nighttime," HP said and stirred the fire. "If you wanna stay, it's cool. We're going skinny dipping at midnight." And he winked broadly as Joan Baez slapped him playfully on the arm.

"No, thanks, but… I gotta be somewhere pretty soon."

"How much leave you got?"

Butch furrowed a brow. "A couple of weeks, but that's not it. Didn't we already have this conversation?"

"No. Unless you were dreaming it. You passed out pretty quick after the third beer."

Butch sighed.

"Never could hold my liquor. Essentially, when I go and where I go depends on how the night goes."

HP smiled and spread arms at the darkness outside the fire.

"Could go well. We've got food and beer and smoke. And music." He nodded at one of the trucks.

A boombox balanced on the bed, ELP blasting from it. Welcome back my friends, indeed. This show never ends.

Butch considered. What would be wrong with staying? No one knew he was here. Pee Sea couldn't find him, neither could Professor. In the morning, he could drop off the Pontiac, wheedle a ride from Mom or Cindy or whoever to McGuire to pick up the airport shuttle and be gone. If he left everything alone, it would resolve itself. If he never came back, things would simply progress along their natural lines and life and time would go on, the show that never ends. And it wasn't like this was the first time he had, with no prior notice or inkling, completely changed his life and locale, losing everything he loved and all of his friends, and things had worked out pretty well. He gained universes he did not have before. He could acquire new ones.

"Your friend can stay, too," HP said as he threw another log on the fire.

"My friend?"

"Yeah. The guy sure loves hot dogs." He chuckled at Joan Baez. "Hope we brought enough."

A chill ran up Butch's spine.

"Where'd he go?"

The blonde twin pointed at the dark. "The woods. Guess he had to take a crap."

They all laughed at that.

"What happened to his face?" Blond twin asked.

Butch stood.

"I gotta go."

"Ah man, seriously?"

HP looked genuinely hurt, which warmed Butch.

"Yeah. I'd like to stay." Probably was in his best interest to stay. "But I really gotta go do something."

"Okay." HP shrugged. "You're going to miss a helluva party."

"Actually." Butch re-tucked his blouse. "I'm going to a helluva party. Real killer."

"Yeah?" Joan Baez was interested. "Where?"

"Clamshell. Merlin is playing."

"Ah, man!" HP jumped up excited. "I love those guys!"

"Come on by, then."

Butch headed towards the Pontiac.

"You dune-buggying out?" Viking asked as Butch started the car.

"No," Butch said out the window. "I need to stay alive for the next couple of hours."

"What about your pal?"

Butch paused, glanced at the tree line. "He'll catch up." And drove away.

Chapter 18

Butch coasted along the beach road frowning at all the activity around the clamshell. Merlin wasn't there yet but anticipation ran high, evidenced by lots of people running around lots of vehicles parked half in the road at off angles, Piney disregard for orderly traffic flow. The smarter fans had seized the outer perimeter, forcing the later arrivals, like Butchie boy, to park next to the shell. Not a good idea; once the crowd wound up, beer cans and kegs and people went flying, sometimes right through windshields. Worse, he'd be made, Pee Sea and his horde of bikers converging on him within seconds. That wouldn't do: avoiding Pee Sea until Butch (a) located Don and (b) acquired allies was task one.

So where to go? He could park farther up the road towards Washington Street, but same problem: everyone heading to the concert came down that way and he'd be spotted and dimed out and dead.

Leave the car at Don's?

Yeah, right. A skinhead wearing an incomplete set of 1505s, cunt cap set at a jaunty angle strolling through PL wouldn't attract much attention, would I? The hardguys would kill him on sight, with or without Pee Sea's concurrence.

Leave it at the store.

Seemed the best solution. The store was set against the beach, out of the way and out of sight, but close enough to the clamshell to serve as secondary parking for those attendees who didn't want kegs crashing through their windshields. The store was closed by now, dark and dreary, and no one would notice a nondescript Pontiac sitting way over there next to the steps. The woods bordering the store's lot ran all the way to the back of the clamshell so he could slip through unnoticed, except by the guys scattered here and there among the trees smoking dope and/or screwing their girlfriends. The screwers would merely grouse at him and get back to what they were doing. The dopers, though, would take one look at his uniform, think he was a deputy and either shoot him or run. Someone was actually shooting deputies these days, so this was a risk, but, of all the risks he faced, it was the most acceptable.

He drove past the clamshell, hoping no one noticed him, and slid in and out of the short curves and came to the driveway and turned left…

…into a brightly lit store and parking lot.

What the hell?

He mentally smacked himself.

Of course.

The angry couple who ran the store wouldn't pass up a chance to make some extra dough. And a bunch of Pineys and stoners suffering from the munchies before, and after, a Merlin concert were a guarantee of profit. Which meant a lot of foot and car traffic through the lot. About the only saving grace, most of them would be too stoned to see him.

He hoped.

Shaking his head, Butch crawled to the far end of the way-too-big lot and parked at the last slot right before the beach, next to a rusted out Fairlane. Probably the angry couple's car. At least he was out of the light and out of the way and could use the Fairlane as camouflage while cutting through the lot to the woods. Longer walk, but still safe. He could stand a Pepsi, though, and he half-heartedly dug around in the ashtray and armrest for change, not expecting any but lookee-lookee, a few more quarters and nickels.

Sheesh, why didn't I find those when looking for phone change? Concussion makes you stupid, I suppose. Let's go see what we can get.

He slid out of the car, stood for a moment looking around, and then hastily ran for the steps and up them and inside.

The angry couple was on duty, both staring at him

suspiciously from the cashier island to the left of the entrance. Any moment now, they'd yell at Butch, just like they yelled at all the kids whenever they came inside to buy a coke and a Tastykake and then sit on the steps to eat and grabass. It was a time-honoured PL tradition, accentuated by the yelling. Rumour was the couple used a long stick with a hook on it to snare shoplifters before they cleared the doors, but Butch had never seen that done. Not that anyone he knew ever tried to shoplift here because the two of them looked like they'd beat a kid half to death for merely thinking about it. The man was short, about 5'8" tall and wide, with a requisite old-guy beer belly made of iron. He had grey crew-cut hair, a bullet head, pig eyes and a permanent frown. His wife looked exactly the same, with the exception of long white stringy witch hair falling to her shoulders.

"Wacha wan?" they shouted simultaneously.

They always shouted. And simultaneously. In classic Piney patois.

"Uh, soda," Butch said and headed back to the coolers.

"Dey inda back!" yelled simultaneously and Butch shook his head because, Man, didn't you see me headed that way?

Butch grabbed a Pepsi and returned to the cash register.

"Fifty cents!" they yelled and Butch reeled under the onslaught, recovered, and handed over two quarters.

The old man's eyes narrowed, if that was possible. "Wacha doin'?"

Butch looked at his Pepsi and then around, stalling for the time necessary to figure out what in the bejesus this guy was askin'. Possibly what he, a uniformed member of the military services, was doing in his store? Worth a stab.

"I just joined a few months ago," he explained. "Used to come in here a lot."

With a terminal case of the munchies, he did not add. Hoping they didn't recognize him and call the SPs and provide background information regarding previous activities contributing to said munchies, which would make his signature on certain recruitment documents perjurious.

"Wacha doin'?" the old lady, this time.

What the devil?

Butch furrowed a brow and puzzled on it and… Ah. She's merely tag-teaming her husband, furthering this line of inquiry.

"I just got back. Visiting some friends."

"Hmm," from the two of them and they crossed their arms simultaneously so he must have passed muster. And non-recognition. The man nose-pointed towards the clamshell.

"Stay oudda dat."

Butch puzzled some more but then it came clear.

"Oh. Right. Don't worry, I'm heading home."

And he raised the can in salute and hastily backed out the door. They both yelled something that sounded almost like, "See you later!" as he cleared the steps. He looked back. They were still watching him…

Drat. Can't make for the clamshell.

…that was in their line of sight. Instead, he ran to the Pontiac and slid inside.

All right, let's give it a few moments.

He drummed fingers on the wheel and wondered how long before angry couple's short term memory emptied and he could resume his stealthy approach to the concert. Several minutes, at least, so might as well listen to the radio. He turned the key and clicked it on.

Paul Anka sang joyously about someone having his baby.

Oh, come on!

Butch groaned and switched the key off.

The passenger door ripped open.

"Oh, no, leave it on!" April said as she slid into the seat.

Butch, paralyzed by horror, could only stare at her.

"I said, leave it on!" and she twisted the key so ferociously that Butch was sure it would break in the ignition. Paul Anka re-gushed.

"Hear that?" she smirked. "He's happy she's having his baby. He says it shows how much she loves him, that she's willing to bear his bratty kid!"

And she slapped him. And then slapped him again.

Butch was too gripped by the horror to react. She slapped him over and over. It felt like Professor and friends were in the car touching up their earlier work.

"What the HELL!"

Butch finally snapped out of it and grabbed her wrist and would have twisted it to the point of breaking but she collapsed against his chest, crying with great animal gulps of air and rage.

Paralyzed him again. This time with guilt And worse, empathy.

His greatest enemy.

Why anyone thought empathy a good thing, Butch could not reckon. Soft pudding people thought it wonderful to experience someone else's feelings and thoughts and life, but Butch found it debilitating. Take Mom. Watching her suffer under Dad's rule racked him with guilt and sorrow and sparked in him an urge to ease her pain. So he went to church with her, rode shotgun on the Tupperware trips, to the Piggly Wiggly and to the doctor's, whenever he could for whatever she wanted or needed so she wouldn't feel alone. He lost time, lost sleep, got called Momma's Boy by Dad and Art, even Cindy, but that didn't sway him.

Because he could only ease his pain by stopping hers.

It was balm on his own wounds, the only way to cure them, because her pain was his fault. He consoled her after the beatings, sitting with her and holding her hand and uttered soothing words and she seemed to respond, seemed to, and she increasingly took those moments as *her* balm, a shared healing. Until something finally broke within her and she exposed him to Art in the car and then ran away from him altogether to be with Ridge ...

And he did not blame her. Because of empathy.

Imagine what it was like for her. She'd married Dad, this charming, handsome, devil-may-care soldier, fresh from defeating Hitler, and they moved in with Grampop as fresh-faced bride and groom bent on making their fortunes and Devil-may-care opened a photography studio in the basement and then bought a gas station and life promised wonder. The future was bright. And then Devil-may-care became the devil, spreading his seed among all her friends and relatives, most of them of age, and he lost the studio and the gas station so went back in the Army and became a devil-may-care pilot with worldwide range and spread his seed worldwide, foisting this mewling, troublesome kid from another woman on her. And she knew it was not the kid's fault but each time she saw him, each time the kid did something annoying, she could not help remembering this was a child too far, a child she did not owe, a reminder of her broken heart. Not fair, yes, she knew, but she could not bring herself to love or favour this child, no matter how empathic the kid was to her suffering.

He concluded, after much observation, that empathy was a twofold problem: it made him do things he did not want to actually do, and it was not reciprocated. He didn't want to spend his nights sitting at kitchen tables in strangers' homes doing his homework while Mom conducted Tupperware parties. If he stayed home, though, she had to make these trips by herself, afraid and abandoned. But when *he* felt lost and alone and orphaned and directionless, Mom did not hold him, did not utter consoling words. He was on his own.

And now, here was April, collapsed against his chest with grief-stricken cries of sheer pain and it was his fault, entirely his fault that she now felt lost and alone and orphaned and directionless and he had to do something to make her feel better. He had to marry her and go to work for her dad and make her life better.

No and no and no.

He grabbed her shoulders and pushed her back against the passenger seat.

"What the hell are you doing?"

"I'm seeing you. Isn't that what you wanted?" she sobbed.

"What?"

"You went by Gino's looking for me."

Ach. Of course, May would convey that message.

"I wasn't looking for you. I was looking for Mason."

"So you *are* jealous!" she sneered.

"No, compassionate."

She furrowed brows.

"I want to warn him."

Her furrowed brows darkened, a real trick in the half-light. "God, you're an asshole."

"I'm an asshole? Who just committed assault and battery? And how did you find me, anyway?"

"You deserved it." She sat back, facing the window, her eyes suddenly dry of tears – imagine that – arms folded across her wonderful breasts, if memory served, and her wonderfully flat and sexy stomach…

Huh?

"Shouldn't you be showing by now?"

She turned her head slowly, a Linda Blair smile on her face. "Showing what?"

Butch made a helpless gesture at her profile.

"How far along you are. Or doesn't that happen yet?"

Butch didn't know. Maybe girls didn't swell up until about a week before delivery.

"Doesn't happen if you're not pregnant."

A couple of heartbeats passed before Butch saw red.

"So you made it up? You made it the fuck up? You made all this shit up to trap me?"

His hand twitched. He really, really wanted to punch her face in.

"No, you jerkoff!" she screamed. "I had an abortion!"

And she slapped him again, hard, and then again and again. But that was secondary to the knife she'd driven hilt-deep into his chest.

He could not breathe, could not lift his hands to stop the ongoing slaps. All he could see were bloody sheets and a poolside and shovels and open graves and his sister, his beloved sister, broken, destroyed, altered forever.

Congratulations. You are now, officially, Dad.

"Stop," he whispered.

The slaps continued. "Please stop," he said and she did but not because of anything he said, because she was spent. She fell over, sobbing, into his lap.

He was numb. Not from the face slaps, although his cheeks were completely without feeling now (wonder if that's how Frank felt). His heart was gone, his soul, everything. He caused this. He did this. He destroyed her just as Dad destroyed Cindy. He could not escape what he had done, could not escape what he would do. Blood will tell.

Please, God, help me.

"You just… disappeared. You were gone. No one knew where you went. I couldn't find Don or Dooby, either, so I thought all of you just took off back to California or something. I thought you abandoned me and then I came home one day and somebody tore up the apartment and I couldn't live there anymore and so I had to go back home and Dad…" her voice trailed off.

"Your dad did this?"

She nodded.

"Dads do that," he said, tonelessly.

She turned to him, tears flowing down her face. "Why did you leave me?"

"I…" and he had no words.

"You just left." She gestured at his uniform. "You joined the Army?"

"Air Force."

She said nothing, just looked at him, mouth agape, stunned. "You hate me that much?"

"I don't hate you."

"But you don't love me."

He said nothing.

"I knew it. Just used me to fuck and drive my car. Dad was right."

"Your dad isn't right."

"Yeah?" And she turned, hostile and violent, full on him. "He's not? You know what Dad said? Said you were gonna run!"

And she slapped him and slapped him and slapped him.

He felt nothing. He saw nothing.

When he finally did, the passenger car door was wide open, the interior light on and he saw April stumbling across the parking lot towards a big yellow Continental, top up. Its lights came on and it drove away.

Butch reached over and shut the passenger door, leaned his head on the steering wheel, and cried.

Chapter 19

The last time Butch cried, really cried (not counting the after-sex wailing and tearing of robes) was right after the fight with Pepsi, or, more accurately, the half-hearted beating at Pepsi's hands. The last time before *that* was at Mom's friend's house when he was listening to the Roger Miller album. Years between tears.

Hmm, that made a pretty good song title.

When he'd finally tired of punching Butch in the stomach, Pepsi walked away yelling something incomprehensible and Butch slunk into the apartment and sat on the couch quietly for a moment and then, without any ceremony, launched a full-tilt, chest-ripping bawl, huge animal tears of grief and humiliation. Mom was there for some reason, probably dropping off a bag of Ellio's, and was suitably alarmed.

"What's wrong?" she clucked and came over and sat down next to him and tried to take him in her arms but he pushed her away.

He knew how much that hurt her and how helpless she felt – damn empathy – but he kept her at bay, shrank into himself and cried harder, if that was possible, while refusing to speak. Why?

Guess he was due.

Given everything over the past ten years, he should have experienced many such crying jags. After all, he was a big wimp; might as well carry a purse. But no, he could count the jags on one hand. He'd met the long-term onslaught of pain and loss mostly stiff-upper-lipped and dry-eyed. Mostly. Repressed it, he did, into ulcer or aneurysm and heart attack reserved for some unspecified future point. That's what a man did. That's why a man died. But Butch wasn't a man and it wasn't John Wayne stoicism that kept his helpless, girlish weeping to a minimum:

There was simply no point.

No one heard him. Everyone else had bigger tears, larger pains, and his crying was an insult to their greater need. Who was he to weep and wail over a silly pummeling when there were things like betrayal and murder and abandonment? Yeah, he suffered those, too, but he caused most of it, so what right did he have?

What right?

Sometimes, though, the magma pushed a little too hard and cracked the top off the volcano and he was absolutely helpless, a village overwhelmed by hot ash, and could not stop the tears raining down. Like when Pepsi walked away. Like when Roger Miller sang to him.

Like now.

He killed April. He killed his own child. He screwed up everything and there was nothing he could do to fix it. It would never get better. It would never be healed. He'd dug his own small grave by a pool at midnight.

He cried for about five minutes, his usual duration because, any longer, and he was vulnerable to attack. Someone would hear, like Dad, and descend on him with belt and fists and the illogical "Wanna cry? I'll give you something to cry about!" But the agony swelled past the usual cutoff point, the razors inside cut and cut and he remained head down and stuck to the wheel because he did not want to look up, did not want to see himself in the rearview mirror because he would see Dad, and not the Dad of raised belt and incomprehensible reasoning: he would see himself *as* Dad. Everyone said he looked like Dad anyway, something that had always puzzled him when he was a kid because didn't these people know he was adopted? But then he found out the truth and it made sense. People saw him better than he could.

Did they see the Beast in me, too?

The sins of the fathers were visited on the sons, down to the third generation. When Butch first found that Biblical passage, he thought it grossly unfair because who asked to be born in the line of a man so sinful that his grandchildren paid for it? Talk about behind the eight ball. Butch eventually realized this generational punishment wasn't an act of commission by an unjust God but merely an observation of trends. Born with these chromosomes, taught by the sinful father, take the examples to heart, and predilection became emulation. Not always on purpose, with malice towards all, but simply because there was no counterforce. In other words, he didn't know any better. And while Butch firmly believed that everyone had an inherent knowledge of right and wrong, the borders became fuzzy when bad acts were repeatedly executed with no consequence. Lightning didn't strike Dad, so his actions must be okay.

Or, at least, unimportant.

In this three-generation curse thing, then, where did he stand? Second? Third?

Third. Pawpaw Deats started all this crap because boy, oh boy, what a jerk. Dad, chip off the old block, outdid Pawpaw for jerkiness which, by process of deduction, meant Butch was third, unless great-grampaw was in the mix. Butch had no idea about that. No one ever mentioned him, which might be a clue.

Given the absence of information, have to go with what we know, which meant Butch was the end of the line and the curse died with April. If he could manage to avoid any future pregnancies, that would be that unless Dad's worldwide sprinkling of other bastard children counted. But that wasn't his problem. It was God's.

How much does a vasectomy cost?

The idea of a scalpel hovering about his boys made him squirm, however, so no thanks. Celibacy was cheaper and less painful, but he doubted he could maintain it. After all, he was his father's son, curse him. Perhaps he should become a master masturbator.

That made him chuckle and he sat up and wiped his eyes and decided to go home.

Let's just go home.

Where, exactly, was that?

The apartment, but probably not for much longer, now that he was in the Air Farce and Cindy was more and more lost in the Barrens and Art was… God knows where and Ridge didn't want Mom to spend the money maintaining the place anymore (translation: Ridge wanted Mom's money) and since when is an apartment a home? It's just a place to keep your stuff.

Oklahoma.

What a home is supposed to be, a place of magic and dreams and sandlot baseball and all-night hide-and-seek and bike rides up and down a mystic street that went on forever and ever. But nothing lasts, especially magic, and who knew what kind of neighborhood it was now, maybe cars on blocks in front of every house, overgrown lawns, and surly residents who eyed each other suspiciously.

Alabama.

He stilled. Alabama was home. It was. Not because of magic or mystical streets but because, everything waited there, like a gothic mansion brooding on the edge of swamps with things inside shuffling from room to room and peering out of broken windows, yearning for rescue. Someone had to go there and shoulder-open warped doors and let things out. Let them out.

Let's go to Alabama and let them out.

He actually turned the key, shutting off that nauseating Righteous Brothers song about rock n' roll Heaven, almost engaged the engine, almost, but then realized there were some impediments: this was Mom's car. He was in the Air Force. Dad still lived there. And he had to find Don.

Fine. Go to Alabama when the impediments are cleared.

Butch opened the door and stepped out. He spun the keys for a moment to listen to the jingle then pocketed them. He noticed his cunt cap on the floor all wrinkled and smooshed because, April.

Going to get in trouble for that but, what the hell.

Groaning with the multiple bruises and hematomas and might-as-well-be-broken bones he'd acquired in the last three or four hours, he dug the cap out of the car and put it on. No doubt he was well below 35-10 standards but no one at the clamshell would know that, just that he looked like a slovenly member of some kind of armed force and therefore needed the crap kicked out of him.

Go to your death proudly.

He stepped into the woods and beelined to his 10 o'clock but, boy, this was hard going, especially when every part of him ached. He didn't remember it being this overgrown. No wonder the dopers and lovers used it. Even if someone spotted their untoward behaviour, who would want to come in here and make them stop?

The underbrush made stealth impossible. He kicked up a helluva lot of noise but that's fine: gave the lovers and dopers plenty of notice he was coming. Gave anyone looking for him the same but, hey.

Go to your death proudly.

More like stupidly, because he made so many diversions through the crap that he actually got lost. Can you believe this? He'd probably end up back at the store but, finally, he cleared the woods onto a backyard much farther to the right of the clamshell than he wanted. At least he could scope it out from here…

…Yep, lots of people running around now. And a very familiar van backed against the playground. Merlin's here.

"About time," Butch groused and skirted the backyard until he reached the road and, cautiously, looked around. He saw clumps of people coming down the road towards the clamshell, moving from one streetlight island to another, appear, disappear, appear, by their stance and motion all Pineys of various tribes and clans. Lots of other Pineys roiled about the clamshell floor, boys and girls mixing it up, pushing and slapping at each other and the music hadn't even started yet.

Man, this is going to be fun. Or dangerous.

What's the diff?

He scrutinized each car within sight but did not recognize any of them. Didn't matter; the El Camino could be on the other side of the lot. Or up on a side street. He focused on the van and saw Opie leaning in the back fooling around with something. No Don, at least, not yet.

One last reconnaissance to assure himself and he scooted out of the woods in front of a group of approaching and boisterous Pineys, surprising them into silence. Butch waved cheerily and then ran across and up to Opie.

"Need some help?"

Opie almost broke his head on the top of the van, which was hilarious, turned and stared at Butch, confused for a moment.

"Oh! Hey, man!" he said and gave him a bear hug. "You scared me there for a moment. Thought you were a cop."

Butch grunted in pain at the sudden assault and then pulled at his blouse as Opie stepped back.

"Does look like that, doesn't it?"

"Sure does. You could make good bank taking dope off

people tonight."

Butch considered. Might be a righteous hustle but, no, had enough trouble already.

"Is Don here?"

"Haven't seen him."

Opie gave Butch an intense up-and-down, shook his head, then put disapproving hands on hips.

"Dooby said you'd gone and done it."

A pause.

"You poor bastard."

And then, "What the hell man, did you fall down a flight of stairs or something?"

"Or something."

"Damn. Do you need to go to a hospital?"

"Probably."

Opie's brows skewed and then he shrugged.

"Let me know."

He went back in the van and shifted stuff around and tugged on something.

"Grab that, would ya?"

Butch helped Opie pull out some cymbals.

"Heard you acquired a new drum set by giving a free concert."

"Yeah!" Opie laughed. "This is it. Help me bring it to the stage."

Butch grabbed a couple of stands and more cymbals and some wires and hauled them over, staying right behind Opie, who hoisted a snare drum. Gave Butch cover from the growing crowd. They cleared the lip of the cement pad laughingly called a dance floor and up the stairs to the raised platform. Dave and Wendell were already up there fooling with guitars and amps. Dooby stood on the floor in front of the stage.

"So, you made it!" he said and burst into that insane Dooby laugh.

"I did. Is Don here?"

"Not yet."

"Look at you!" Dave said, slapping him several times on the name tag, almost driving him off the stage.

"Yeah!" Wendell snatched the cap off Butch's head. "See you made Eagle Scout."

"Hardy har-har," Butch said and snatched it back.

Thing was not going to survive the night, that's for sure.

A sudden searing beam of white-hot light, so powerful it actually knocked him back, blinded him. Dooby, braced against the stage, aimed a spotlight at Butch with one hand while flipping a microphone in the other. "Ladies and gentlemaan," he announced over a PA system filled with feedback, "the newest member of our armed forces."

And there Butch was, all lit up like Berlin during a bombing raid.

A chorus of boos and curses rose from the floor and the mass surged his way before Dooby put the light out, the unexpected shock of darkness stopping the mass cold.

"Why don't you draw a fucking target on my back?" Butch snarled at Dooby, that is, when the spots cleared from his vision enough to locate the jerk.

"Pish." Dooby dismissed. "Like no one knew you were coming. Looked like an elephant floundering out there in the trees. You'll be all right. You're with the band. Speaking of which, help us get this stuff plugged in." And threw cords at him.

Butch unwound them and plugged things into things, not really sure what things exactly plugged into what but familiar enough with the process to avoid a fire. Butch figured he'd make a fairly decent roadie when Merlin hit the big time. And they would. The band was that good.

Dooby and he struggled a giant spool of heavy-duty wire out to the telephone pole where several switch boxes hung. By now, Butch was nothing but a constant ache and this part of the setup was a bit beyond him, so he watched Dooby thread plugs and chords into various slots and then lean back, satisfied.

"Think we're set."

"Good," Butch said, casting a look back at the pad, "because the natives are getting restless."

Judging by the shadows-within-shadows boiling over the pad and into the parking lot, it was quite the crowd now, with clumps of Pineys and hardguys and babes and chicks flowing back and forth, colliding, mixing and still throwing uncoordinated punches at each other, then different combinations of the same beer- and dope-fueled people reformed and repeated the whole cycle, staggering and swaying. A sober Piney was bad enough; spurred by legal and illegal substances, a Piney riot was just one wrong word or stumble away.

"Yeah!" Dooby said, grinning and watching the same show, "This is gonna be fun." A blink. "Or dangerous. But, what's the diff?"

Butch gaped.

"What?"

Dooby chuckled and headed to the stage.

Butch stuck close to him, weaving through the small tornadoes angling his way, attracted to the uniform like lightning to a metal roof. Fingers plucked at it. "Fucking dick!" "Fascist!" "Baby killer!" interspersed with "Cool!" "General Patton!" "Kill a commie for mommy!" assailed him from all sides and Butch wasn't sure if this was a hostile crowd or not. Not a good idea to stand here and clarify so he stayed on Dooby, telegraphing the immunity that a band member earned at one of these things.

Dooby hopped on stage and Butch continued around it until he was behind the speakers, putting lots of hardware between him and the crowd. Like a tide hitting a breakwater, the crowd broke at the stage and washed back into the pad where it met another onrushing tide of Pineys and drunks and drunk Pineys demanding the music start. Now.

Butch scrutinized the tides but didn't spot Don. He frowned. The guy should be here, right here, in the back near the van with Butch. Made no sense that he wasn't. Don wouldn't miss this, just wouldn't, a strong indicator that the note was true.

"I got a bad feeling about this," he whispered in his best Bogart.

"Hello!" Dooby's voice suddenly exploded across the pad, followed by a wave of squealing feedback so loud that at least three people grabbed their heads and screamed in pain. Eardrums must have shattered. Dooby did something at a glowing box covered with dials sitting beside him and the feedback dropped.

"Sorry 'bout that," Dooby chuckled. "Let's try something else."

His voice swelled as he picked up his guitar and settled it across his stomach.

"Hi, everyone! We're Merlin, out of Trenton!"

The crowd roared because they were popular down here, popular everywhere in between, for that matter, and Dooby hit the opening chords of 'Smoke on the Water.'

Pandemonium.

The guitar screamed across the pad, a banshee soundwave blasting the Pineys and the hardguys and babes right out of their shoes, Opie's cymbal roll and Wendell's bass and Mike's Hammond B rolling up behind like sonic tsunamis scouring all before them. The crowd was suddenly blood red and cobalt blue and supernova white as the spotlights blasted them from the front of the stage, somehow pulsing in the same rhythm as the chords, stage magic courtesy of one of those red blinking boxes at Dooby's side. Thrown back on their heels, the crowd's mouths dropped open, all hands clapped to sides of heads, their collective scream of joy drowned because the instruments took over the entire sound spectrum.

At the break between the first and second set of chords the crowd rocked forward, the sonic dam having dissipated, and they ran towards the band, the screams scaled in pitch from the high soprano of the girls to the basso roars of the boys and the tide smashed against the stage, the hardguys hammering the floor with their fists and the girls grabbing at Dooby's feet. He kicked them off and drove everyone back with more chords.

Butch raised his arms above his head and bellowed and jumped and swayed all by himself against the van, the bruises forgotten, demon possessed, the anarchy of youth, this teenage wasteland on an August night with the stars wheeling in their forever tracks and demanding the ancient sacrifice of song and blood. The chords blasted and the faithful swung and danced with the rage of it, the power, the demands of life and parents and cops and school kicked in the balls.

At least for the next couple of hours.

'Water' segued effortlessly into 'Highway Star' and this was a Deep Purple crowd and it almost fell over en masse in ecstasy because nobody will take my car, absolutely nobody, and somehow the amp volume increased into pure guitar assault, Mike screaming the lyrics in a semblance of singing. He was the only band member who could do a semblance, so he got the duties. Dooby was the greatest guitar player in America, but he couldn't carry a tune in a baggie. Odd, that, him being a son of a Del Viking and all, but talent usually skipped a generation.

Sins didn't.

Somehow Butch ended up in front of the stage as Mike rolled the bridge with those wondrous, descending notes, Dooby following, and hands slapped him on the back and Butch turned and there were seven or eight PL girls pulling at him, eyes wild and off-world and taken by the dance frenzy. Butch was never going to win a dance contest but he could hold a rhythm and girls just wanted to dance, they just did, so he jumped right in. Hardguys stared at him because they didn't dance, they stood in groups and yelled incomprehensible challenges and punched each other in the mouth and threw beer cans but they never, ever, danced; Butch used that to his advantage, ending up in daughters' bedrooms at midnight with one and sometimes two PL girls grateful for a dancing boy.

The girls love a man in uniform, too, and were all over him screaming and grabbing as their boyfriends punched each other in the mouth and threw beer cans and yelled quite clearly, "I ain't gonna join no Army and march and take no orders!" But the girls wanted a sure man with a guaranteed job and paycheck and a chance to get out of New Jersey who also danced and he was popular right now. For how long, he had no idea.

Apparently, not very.

One of the girls, a stringy-haired blonde with the strangely big nose that seemed a characteristic of PL females, stopped her booty shake and stared hard at him.

"Hey, don't I know you?"

"Maybe." Butch kept up the controlled flail that uninitiates might consider dancing.

She went still, a non-action immediately out of place on the dance floor, cocked her head and narrowed albino eyes at him.

"Yeah," she said, shaking a finger. "You're Don's friend."

Butch stopped dancing, the two of them now an island of stillness, out of place, attracting hardguy attention. "Do you know where he is?"

"Yeah."

At that moment, Merlin flowed into 'Bang a Gong,' a rather incongruous shift in style and tone that puzzled the hell out of the hardguys but Butch understood because it was a dance beat and Dooby could read a crowd and knew what this one wanted.

Dooby never made the set ahead of time; he kept the interwoven song lists in his head until he'd figured out what the crowd wanted and then signaled the others when to shift and what to shift to because he was the greatest guitar player in America and could manage a band so, fine, let's go with it.

Butch crowed his joy, couldn't help it because this girl had a hubcap diamond star halo and he was descending knee-level on a twist and smiling at her, c'mon, dance, girl, just dance.

"So where is he?" he asked as he reached his lowest limit.

She did not answer, stepped back in the crowd and was gone, replaced by more stringy-haired big-nosed PL girls who were dirty and sweet clad in black don't look back but Butch did look back, shields up, phasers on stun. He scanned the knots of hardguys and Pineys ringing the dancers, all of them hitting each other and crushing beer cans against each other's foreheads and looking at Dooby with blank expressions of "What's this shit?" when he spotted the girl talking to a separate group of hardguys, their murderous expressions following right down her index finger pointed directly at his face. All of them wearing biker jackets. Breed biker jackets.

Uh oh.

Butch slid backwards, hoping to put some stringy-haired big-nosed girls in the line of sight between him and the Breed but that was useless because he was taller than all of them and was a skinhead in a sea of both girl-and-boy-stringy hair and, to top it all, was wearing a uniform. As inconspicuous as a lighthouse on a pitch-black coast.

Feeling his way through the stringy hairs, he almost reached the stage and the quasi-protection of Dooby's big red guitar, a weapon the guy was willing to swing at anyone who came after Butch (as previous incidents attested), when two powerful hands seized his shoulders from behind, literally lifted him off the ground and turned him.

Eddie.

Not a Breed, but the closest a person could get without actually being one. Eddie was a Piney lumberjack, infamous for his Herculean strength – hence the ability to lift Butch off his feet – and a Hulk temper worse than Butch's, two qualities that led to his frequent hiring by various groups to conduct activities involving mayhem and bone breakage. He knew Butch by sight, which enhanced his value to recently interested parties, so Butch was not surprised by this but was surprised by Eddie's sudden appearance.

Shoulda spotted him a lot earlier.

After all, Eddie was hardly inconspicuous: well over six feet tall and six feet wide with bright blond hair and bloodshot eyes that made him look like a cheesy Dracula.

"Hi, Butchie boy," Eddie said and grinned, revealing the three or four teeth left in his head. Result of previous contracts.

"Hi, Eddie," Butch said and kicked him as hard as he could in the crotch.

Desperate times spur desperate acts, and crotch-kicking the Hulk was about as desperate as they come, but Butch, fortunately, got the reaction he needed: Eddie's eyes bulged out of his head, he gasped an impressively deep and long "*Oof!*" and dropped Butch to the floor as he collapsed.

Unfortunately, he collapsed right on top of Butch. Now it was Butch's turn to go "*Oof,*" all the air driven out of his body. At least he was still in control of his limbs, unlike Eddie, who suffered the crotch-kick equivalent of an epileptic fit, spraying and bleating and jerking his arms like a marionette.

Should take advantage.

Struggling for breath against the anvil laid across his chest, Butch wedged his elbows under Eddie's stomach and shoved. That gave Butch breathing room and he grabbed a lungful of air and rolled to his right. He immediately smacked into several pairs of scrambling legs, most of them belonging to stringy-haired big-nosed and now hysterical girls trying to get out of the way while yelling for their boyfriends or cousins or someone to help them. Butch got to his knees and pushed off, fending slaps on the way up and then spun around to take in the situation.

Merlin had come to a full stop mid-note, Dooby staring at him in complete shock, as was the rest of the band except for Opie, who had a big grin on his face and had risen to his feet behind the drum stand. Girls scattered from Butch like raindrops off a spun rope, careening to every corner. Hardguys took their places, their expressions ranging from open-mouthed amazement to jaw-clamped rage. That was bad enough. But the wall of Breed tidal-waving in his direction from the back of the floor was worse.

And then it got worse.

A vise gripped his ankle, almost snapping it in half. Looking down, Butch saw the red-eyed Eddie Hulk attached to him, the other arm swinging over to grab his remaining ankle.

"I am going to kill you," Eddie said, quite clearly and calmly, and Butch knew the man spoke with conviction.

Butch did two things. He raised his entrapped ankle and brought it down as hard as he could on Eddie's little finger, then turned to Dooby and said, quite clearly and calmly, "Help."

Dooby whipped the Gibson off his shoulder but, instead of braining Eddie with it, carefully placed it in the stand…

Hmm. Must be new.

…then leaped off the stage, head first, into an onrushing pile of hardguys who had no idea what was going on but knew a fight when they saw it and decided Butch was the epicenter of this mess, so let's get him. Wendell and Mike were still too astonished to move, but Opie swan-dived right after Dooby, more as wingman than anything.

That took care of an immediate threat. Now to finish off another. Butch looked down at the howling Eddie, who had grabbed the stomped hand, checking his finger for compound fractures. Butch drew back a leg as far as he could and drove it into the point of Eddie's chin. Low quarters were good for something. Eddie's head snapped back hard into the concrete floor and his red eyes rolled to white and he went limp. Butch wasn't sure if he was knocked out or just stunned but he didn't plan to stay around and find out. He jumped over Eddie and landed next to Dooby struggling with some hardguy trying to tear Dooby's hair out. Butch round-kicked the hardguy right in his exposed ribs and the guy yelled and dropped like a PL girl's panties on a Saturday night.

"Thanks!" Dooby said and laughed at something going on behind Butch. Butch looked. Opie was punching the crap out of some huge hardguy while other hardguys stood transfixed by a guy this little wielding so much power.

Hardguys, meet Opie, one of the best street fighters in New Jersey.

By this time, everyone in the five concentric rings was in full combat, hardguys against hardguys, stringy girls against stringy girls, stringys versus hards. It was impossible to resolve the fighting into its individual components, reminding Butch of a Bugs Bunny cartoon where everyone clawed at each other in a tornado of fists and feet. One advantage: the wall of Breed had been stopped cold on the perimeter. But, there was also a downside: Dooby and Opie and Butch were trapped.

"To the van!" Butch yelled and dove over the stage lip, grabbing Dooby's Gibson on the way.

Dooby was hot on him, a Marshall head and amp somehow stacked in his arms while Wendell and Mike carried equal amounts of amp and whatnot. Opie was still on the floor enjoying himself too much.

"C'mon, man!" Butch yelled as Dooby and the others stacked equipment in a rather orderly fashion in the back, Amazing how expensive stuff will generate instinctive dexterity in the midst of crisis.

Opie turned, a big smile on his face, to see what they were doing and got a fist into the side of his head.

"Oh, hell," Butch muttered and cleared to the front of the stage as Dooby and the others grabbed more equipment and hauled it into the van.

Looks like we'll be all packed up and ready to go in the next few seconds, just need Opie.

Butch slammed both hands down like hammers onto whatever heads and shoulders were bent over the place he'd last seen Opie drop; those heads smacked into each other and bounced away. Opie was flat on his back, arms crossed over his face to protect himself.

Butch grabbed the front of his shirt.

"Move!" he yelled and hauled him up, aided by a very motivated Opie.

"Thanks, man!" he said and slapped Butch on the back as he sped by, leaping for the van.

Butch gathered his knees to follow when he was ripped off the stage and thrown back on the floor.

By Eddie.

"You sonofabitch," Eddie said, in the same quiet and calm manner he'd previously used to promise Butch's death, and then punched Butch right in the head. Butch's vision shook like a paint mixer and stars flew by as he collapsed to the pad but he saw Eddie winding up for the next punch. A few more like that first one and Butch's skull would moosh like a melon. He whipped up both arms to try to block the coming blows, but Eddie would blast right through them. He braced, wincing in expectation of a broken nose. He'd never broken his nose, even after hundreds of karate fights. This was going to hurt.

And then Eddie was gone.

Blinking through his crossed fingertips, Butch was momentarily confused because Eddie was actually still there but now a foot or so taller, if that were possible, and struggling against a set of huge arms. Familiar giant bicep arms.

Boulder.

Boulder had Eddie in a bear hug, hoisted in the air, testament to Butch's earlier evaluation of how strong the guy was. Even more testament, he tossed Eddie aside like a sack of garbage, taking out a whole row of hardguys as he did so. He then reached down, the silver teeth grinning at Butch, and pulled him straight to his feet.

"I thought I had till Friday!" Butch pleaded his case, figuring Boulder's next action would be to remove one or both of Butch's arms. All Boulder did was look at him blankly, shrug, then turn around and backhand another hardguy throwing punches at him.

What the hell?

Either Boulder was making sure Butch lived until Friday so he could kill him himself, or he was a Merlin fan and here for the music. Whatever, Butch was glad the guy showed up. At least, for the moment. Perhaps now would be the appropriate time to make himself scarce before Boulder decided Friday was too long to wait. He turned.

Right into Professor.

"Hello," Professor said.

"Uh…"

Professor grabbed Butch's stunned hand and shook it. "Sorry about the earlier misunderstanding. Things are good now."

"You talked to my sister?"

"Among others."

"So… you know her well enough that things are now cool, but you threatened her."

Professor raised eyebrows.

"Earlier. When we had our discussion."

Professor shrugged. "That's life in a bike gang. One moment, you're threatening to kill your friends. The next, you're killing another gang." And he thumbed over his shoulder.

Butch looked. Fishkill and Home Run, now joined by Boulder

and about seven or eight Pagans, stood in the middle of the pad as the tidal wave of Breed slammed into them. It was like watching the ocean rage against a sea wall and the two groups beat the holy hell out of each other. Knives and bats and chains and fists flew, as did sprays and ribbons of blood and teeth.

Pagans and Warlocks fighting side by side against Breed… guess that's life in a bike gang.

Butch watched, gobsmacked. Professor grinned, waggled his eyebrows and turned for the scrum.

"What does it mean?" Butch asked.

Professor turned a blank look on him. "Oh," he said, after a moment, "that. 'Let them hate as long as they fear.' It was Caligula's foreign policy." And he smiled and pulled out a switchblade and launched into the fray.

Butch wheeled because he didn't want to see someone's ears fly through the air. Bright red lights half-blinded him and he blinked hard and cleared his vision in enough time to see the van speeding off, slinging dirt and gravel at the hardguys clawing at the back door. That was pretty funny and Butch laughed as the hardguys fell off, getting rock tattoos all over their faces in the process, but then realized the van had sped off. Leaving him here. Alone.

Thanks, guys.

And then Dooby came sailing over the stage knocking hardguys out of his way, laughing insanely, Opie right beside him laughing insanely, and they cleared a path up to him. "Best concert ever!" Opie crowed.

"Thought you guys left me."

"And miss all this?" Dooby said, "We just moved the stuff out of harm's way. Mike and Wendell will be here in a minute. At least, Mike will." Dooby cackled and punched a Piney in the throat.

Oh man, this is great, this is just too great and these guys are my brothers forever and ever.

The sun sprang to full brightness in Butch's heart and it was time to put all that Oak training to good use. He slapped a big Piney across the face and then drove a fist deep into his stomach, screaming a 'Kia!' at the same time and doubling the Piney in half. He then round-kicked another Piney right in the neck and the guy went straight down on top of the Piney he'd just doubled and

Butch rose in the air and executed a perfect flying spinning-heel kick, catching someone, who knows who, right in the face, and landed with perfect balance back in position, probably the only time in history such a technique was ever successful in an actual fight, kung fu movies notwithstanding. He spun in the opposite direction and dropped his hands on the pad, and broomed someone down with a leg sweep; the guy cracked his head on the concrete, immediate knockout.

"Go, man, go!" Dooby yelled and it was on. Butch punched and kicked and screamed like Bruce Lee gone crazy, the surge of power and war blasting through his veins and limbs, turning them into iron. He was a steel whip, slashing and cutting and trapping the enemy, the hardguys and the Pineys and the burnouts and the greasers who saw the uniform and thought it an easy kill, until they had the misfortune of getting into range. His TI would be proud of him, taking out whole rows of hippie assholes disrespecting the uniform…

But that wasn't the reason for it, Sergeant Butler, oh no.

…It was the pure joy of combat.

Butch foot-swept someone's ankle while striking the chest and the guy went flying. Someone grabbed his shoulder and Butch hooked an elbow around the available wrist and twisted the fingers and threw the guy over his hip, the guy yelling the whole time. The bruises and scrapes from Professor and Boulder disappeared as adrenalin rendered him invulnerable. Someone else grabbed the back of his neck and Butch reached back and grasped the arms with both hands and spun and twisted the Piney's elbow right over his head and kicked the legs out and the guy went down, landing on his elbow to a crack of bone and the guy screamed and someone drove a fist right into Butch's sternum and he lost all his air.

All of it.

He collapsed, gasping, wheezing, his breath so short he couldn't get anything into his lungs and his throat closed and someone whapped him across the forehead and Butch fell back, landing hard on his tailbone. A couple of fists from different people hit him across the shoulders. If he was counting accurately, this was the third beating he would endure today, that is, if he gave April credit for the slapfest in the Pontiac. So far, he'd held up fairly well, although the Professor's beat down had been somewhat restrained. Not so the one he was now facing, as the Pineys and hardguys and dopers and losers all realized the Bruce Lee Army Air Force guy was down and this was the opportunity to do him in. Butch felt the blows and kicks increasing, like a tropical storm making landfall, and was sure the surviving Breed would converge on him and finish the job.

"Get off him, motherfuckers!" roared over his head and Viking was there, throwing Pineys off Butch left and right. HP jumped in next to his brother, pummeling some hardguy across the stomach with machine-gun fists. Joan Baez grasped some stringy-haired girl by the stringy hair, waltzing her around the floor. Even the Enduro twins were in the middle of it, kicking and scratching back to back. Butch blinked in amazement.

HP grinned at him from above. "Good party!" he yelled and slammed a Piney across the mouth. Butch laughed and laughed and gathered his feet, ready to vault upwards for round two.

Sirens.

There was a stunned and immediate cessation of all activities, as if a switch were thrown and time frozen; even the fists careening across Butch's back stopped in mid-strike.

"Cops!" someone screamed.

"Scatter!" someone else screamed and time reversed.

Fists retracted and persons spun away and, like a stink bomb thrown in the middle of a prom, there was a giant rush of people in all directions, all falling over themselves and over each other in the scramble to clear out. Never had so many moved so fast on all fours and twos to get off the pad and off the beach and out of the country. Knees and legs drove into Butch from all directions but it was inadvertent, a victim of the stampede. Still hurt, though.

HP and Joan Baez exchanged looks.

"Gotta go!" he said as he shook Butch's hand, "Thanks for the invite!" and the Moon Crater gang vanished.

"Let's go!" Dooby, at his ear, pulled on Butch's shoulder.

Butch still didn't have his breath and he waved Dooby in closer.

"Can't. Breathe," he wheezed. "You. Go."

"Man, I ain't leaving you here!"

Butch gulped air.

"Gotta get… Mom's car." He waved in the general direction of the beach. "You guys go. Now."

The sirens were increments closer, indicating the cops had made the entrance to PL on two wheels and racing for the beach. Dooby hesitated.

"You sure?"

Butch waved him on.

"Take Deep Hollow."

"Right!" Dooby stood and headed to where the van had suddenly appeared next to the dance floor.

"Hey!" Butch called.

Dooby stopped in mid-stride.

"Where's Don?"

Dooby threw out 'who knows?' hands and Butch watched as he leaped in the back of the already running van, Opie and Mike urging him on and the back wheels smoked and the van canted on its right side and almost flipped over burning rubber for the Deep Hollow bridge, the back door flapping from the G forces and Dooby and Opie grabbed at it and the van was gone, the lights out, silhouetted against the pines and heading towards the bridge.

Red flashing lights blazed through the backyards and trees lining the main road, which meant the cops were just seconds away. Best not be here when they arrived. He looked around for his cunt cap but it was nowhere to be seen.

Great.

He'd have to wear his wheel hat when he arrived for school, which meant he'd look like a complete dork, er, more of a dork than usual.

Let's not worry about that right now, shall we?

Taking as much of a breath as his aching lungs would allow, Butch propped on his hands and pushed and somehow was on his feet, swaying, red spots before his eyes… no, that was the first set of cop cars making the turn. Lurching across the pad, Butch accelerated to full speed in nanoseconds, urgency overcoming his breathlessness, and hit the road just as the first cop car, one from Perkins Township, screamed into the parking lot where the van had been. Two staties screeched behind it.

Butch marveled.

Man, this was serious enough to get troopers involved?

The cops burst out of their cars, not even bothering to close the doors as they unslung billy clubs and rushed the clamshell.

Not everyone had unassed the pad: The Breed. The Pagans.

The Warlocks. Moments before, bent on killing each other, now they stood shoulder to shoulder, Boulder and Professor anchoring the ends of the biker line, a phalanx waiting for the rushing wave of uniforms. Butch stopped on the edge of the woods and watched, fascinated.

Cavalry charge.

The first wave of cops struck the wall of bikers like King Richard's heavy horse on Saladin's line, smashing and swinging and breaking through, but not scattering the tribes. The biker line reformed and launched a charge of its own, medieval combat, chains and metal against club and fist, a shrieking roil of savages and knights and more cop cars piled up and more uniforms rushed and battle cries and just plain cries escalated and he really, really needed to get the hell out of there.

Reluctantly, Butch backed into the woods, watching the battle that ebbed and surged with one side then the other gaining advantage but more cops were showing up every second and, despite the valiant effort of the valiant biker few, this would be a cop victory, as always, and a couple of staties turned and looked in his direction so, go. Go.

Butch raised a hand in benediction to Professor and melted into the dark.

Still dazzled by the flashing lights and the pageant, Butch stumbled over roots and limbs and through the godawful underbrush, heading for the darkest part of the trees because Dooby said how easily he'd been seen approaching, so imagine now. Once he was sure he was invisible, he'd figure out where the store was. Should be simple enough; orientate to the sounds of battle and move ninety degrees to the right of it. At some point, he'd reach the parking lot. Or the sand. Whatever. So he pushed on.

He was in the center of the darkness when he heard a puzzling sound. Water. Flowing hard and fast. Sounded like it was raining and Butch put a hand out but no raindrops and he was confused. There's no creek out here... wait, that's not a creek. That's someone pissing against a tree, long and hard and Niagara Falls-like. And it went on and on and there was only one person with the legendary ability to urinate with such power and duration...

Pee Sea.

"Hi, Butch," Pee said, a trick of the flashing cop cars and

streetlights converging at that moment to show him standing with his back to Butch as he shook the last remaining drops against the tree he'd been using. He zipped up and turned and faced him.

"Your car's over there." He chin-pointed off to the right. "Let's go for a ride."

Butch slowly backed up. "I don't think—"

Pee pulled back his lumberjack shirt and Butch saw the pearl handle of the .45 tucked there.

"Wasn't asking," he said.

Butch nodded and headed towards the store. Pee Sea fell in behind.

Chapter 20

Butch stumbled out of the underbrush to the left of the Pontiac. Now how that happened he had no idea; must have made a big circle through the woods. Measure of his disorientation, or Pee Sea's uncanny sense of direction. Probably both.

"Keys," Pee said and Butch wordlessly handed them over.

"Get in," and Butch headed towards the driver's side.

"No," and Butch right-faced and left-faced as smartly as parade and dropped in the passenger's seat.

Should really start locking the doors. Could have avoided April's slapfest. Could now (a) run away or (b) wrestle the gun away as Pee Sea unlocked the door for him and (c) get shot. Forget it. He wanted to escape, not commit suicide.

As if reading his mind, Pee's hand drifted about the pistol as he settled behind the wheel. Butch remained docile, that whole 'better part of valor' thing. Pee fumbled with the keys, stuck them in and turned. The engine caught. Billy, don't be a hero, some singer pleaded on behalf of some girl.

"What the hell is this shit?" Pee Sea, incredulous, stared at the radio.

Butch turned out palms. "What can I say? It's my mom's car."

"Doesn't she have FM?"

"No."

"You're shitting me." Pee Sea shook his head in wonder. "New car. You'd expect better."

"Ridge wouldn't spring for it."

Pee Sea chuckled. "That Ridge is one cheap bastard."

Butch was somewhat surprised.

"You guessing, or you actually know?"

Pee Sea turned fully on him, his face eerie green and cancerous in the dashboard lights. "I know a lot of things, motherfucker." He glared.

Butch began to sweat.

"Look, Pee, it wasn't me."

"What wasn't you?"

"Who screwed you over. That was Jape and Truck."

"And yet," Pee Sea said, "you're the one who showed up."

"I didn't know what they'd done."

"You not only showed up," Pee Sea continued as if Butch had said nothing, "you handled everything. In fact." Pee Sea cocked his head, a look of satisfaction on his face. "You arranged it. You came to me with the deal." He leaned back against the window, a move that cleared the distance between his hand and the pistol handle, which shone eerie green and cancerous in the lights.

"I'm not the one who packed the bag."

"But you were the last one with it."

"Jape packed it," Butch insisted.

"Funny," Pee Sea said, feigning indifference, "Jape said *you* did. Said the whole idea was yours."

A cold wind blew up Butch's spine.

"You talked to him?"

Pee's eyes turned cold and murderous and brooked no further questions. More moments went by and Butch squirmed, desperation pooling in his stomach.

"You know you can't believe anything he says." Butch paused. "Said."

"Yeah, I know." Pee Sea drummed on the steering wheel. "People will say anything, just to get out of anything."

And he bored into Butch.

"But I'm telling the truth!" Desperation locked him into a full nelson. "You know it!"

"Do I?" Pee Sea regarded him mildly. "Ain't been much truth out of you lately. Just ask that girl of yours, April."

Butch sighed with exasperation.

"She's not my girl anymore. Hasn't been since April, and I'm not trying to be funny. She's mad at me, and you know how that goes."

Pee shrugged.

"Yeah, I do. Women backstab you faster than anyone. But you straight-up lied to her. Said you were gonna marry her, and then you blew town. And her pregnant and everything."

Pee Sea shook a finger at him.

"*Tsk.*"

Butch was flabbergasted.

"How do you know about that?"

"Tolja, I know everything."

Butch sat back heavily.

"What the fuck?" More to himself than Pee.

Pee Sea shook his head in mock horror, continuing this line of torture.

"Just up and left. Didn't tell her anything. Or her dad and your mom and Cindy and everyone! Run off to the Air Force, of all places."

He finger-slapped Butch's sleeve.

"Oh, by the way."

Pee Sea fished into his pants pocket.

"I think this is yours."

He pitched Butch's cunt cap into his lap.

Butch frowned at it. It was muddy and wrecked and obviously unwearable.

"Thanks," he muttered.

"Don't mention it. So, look at this from my perspective, man. You ran away. After you and your pals screwed me, you took off. You didn't try to make it right. You didn't come to me and explain, say, 'Hey, Pee, Jape and Truck did this, not me, I want to fix it.' No. You ran. So what am I to think?"

Butch said nothing, simply stared out of the windshield. Pee Sea was wrong, but then again he wasn't, and it was frustrating and unfair because Butch was going to die for something he did not do, or, at least, did not intend.

Did not foresee.

Okay, let's settle for that. Two other idiots caused all this and, in Butch's hasty scramble to distance himself from their idiocy, he did things now construed as proof of guilt. The way things look trump the way things are. David Jansen fled the train looking for the one-armed man, a necessary action on his part but one that underscored everyone's mistaken belief in his guilt. Fortunately, it all worked out for him but Butch didn't think he would get the same resolution. Even if Pee Sea believed him innocent of the double-cross, there was the principle of the thing: a man in his position simply could not be seen as weak.

Or forgiving.

Damn, damn, damn. Unfair, unfair, unfair.

But what did he expect? Life so far was nothing but damnation and unfairness. He was the long-term victim of forces he could not control, of the evil intents of others, a reed in the whirlwind. Off in the distance, he heard Dad's laughter.

Pee Sea sat patiently, giving Butch enough time to come up with a reasonable explanation and when he didn't, said, "Uh huh," and put the car in reverse. Slowly he pulled out of the spot, a man in no hurry, and coasted to the lot entrance. Butch calculated his chances and concluded those were, surprisingly, better than fifty-fifty. He was still in combat mode, having been fairly successful during the clamshell riot, and he was more than a match physically for Pee Sea, although the guy was strong and a very experienced street fighter. Yes, there was the gun, but all Butch needed was some speed and a little bit of luck. There it is. The situation. So?

So.

Butch did nothing because it was his fault. All his fault. He should never have come up with this hare-brained idea in the first place. This all happened because he wasn't man enough to face his responsibilities and marry April and submit to plans made for him and yeah, yeah, master of your fate and no one tells you what to do so what gives them the right to take your life completely over but, hey, don't give me that crap you did fuck her, didnja? You convinced her to move in and play house because you wanted nooky and the pretense of adulthood without the actual work. Look at me, I'm living with some chick and we're partying and I got my own place and I was cool in San Francisco and I'm cool again, I'm cool.

What did you think was going to happen?

And, yeah, yeah, April turned out more black widow-ish than he'd realized, but that's his fault, too. Instead of rushing into mutual living arrangements, maybe kept separate and merely dated? For a few months, say? Then you might have seen what a control freak she was, how much of a Daddy's Girl she was, how wrong she was for you; or, at least, had the opportunity to discover those things before becoming so entwined. But, no, gotta be cool, man.

And then, to top it off... a drug deal? Seriously?

You miserable bastard.

Butch hung his head, which would probably end up on a pike somewhere in Lebanon State Park in the next ten minutes or so. Exactly as deserved, because you're such a loser. Such an idiot. Such a miserable bastard, you miserable bastard. And that's because you're dead weight. You're not even supposed to be here, are you? You weren't supposed to be born. And God is about to correct that error, in a manner and method commensurate with your sordid, sad mistake of a life.

The cops had overrun the clamshell and placed a couple of patrol cars front-to-front on the beach road, blocking the way back into the Lakes. Pee Sea couldn't go there without getting caught, but he turned and headed towards the barrier anyway. Puzzling. And reckless. All Butch needed to do was make some kind of commotion and the cops would end this kidnapping attempt *tout de suite*. Not even Pee Sea was crazy enough to shoot him in front of cops...

Right?

...So what's this? Did Pee Sea think he was that much of a pussy he'd stay quiet?

Well, I am, but desperate times spur desperate measures, dude. Just ask Eddie.

He took in a big breath and braced. Get ready.

Handcuffed Pineys draped cop car hoods, about to join several other Pineys already stuffed in the back of cop cars, including, speak of the devil, Eddie, who stared at Butch through the windshield of one of the barrier cars with murderous intent. Butch almost busted out laughing.

Well, that's one less craphead to deal with, so let's get rid of another one.

And he stoked a big "Help me!" breath in preparation when both barrier cars suddenly parted, giving the Pontiac room to pass between them.

"Hey, Pee!" one of the staties yelled from the driver's side.

"Hey, Jonesy!" Pee Sea yelled back.

"You comin' to the barbecue?"

"Wouldn't miss it," and Pee Sea drove slowly past as Trooper Jonesy stared hard at Butch with murderous intent.

Butch's "Help me!" died in his throat.

Trooper Jonesy would help Butch, all right, slapping him into the backseat with Eddie, and leave them both there for about five minutes of quiet conversation.

No thanks.

Pee Sea continued, leisurely waving and calling out to various other boro and state cops who were happy to see him as they happily clubbed the Pineys and the hardguys who'd been too stupid to run when the sirens first sounded. Pee leisurely acquired the road and headed for the Deep Hollow bridge.

"Jesus," Butch said.

"Business," Pee Sea replied.

They bumped over the bridge as Eric Clapton came on the radio bragging about shooting sheriffs, Pee Sea singing right along.

"Did you?" Butch asked.

"Hmm?"

"That deputy shot in Tabernacle, was that you?"

Pee Sea chuckled. "Think the song says I didn't shoot the deputy."

"So… you didn't?"

"Nobody got shot. Somebody with a badge got shot *at*, but there's a big difference."

"So, back to the original question, was that you?"

Pee Sea shrugged. "Some people refuse to cooperate."

Waddyaknow, there's still a few honest cops h'yeah'bouts. Too bad none of them were h'yeah'bouts.

Butch blew a raspberry, resigned to his fate. Pee said nothing, merely smiled.

They cleared the bridge onto Deep Hollow and, despite the situation, Butch stirred. Back on his Street of Joy. But it was about to turn into his Street of Death. Maybe not. Maybe Dooby and the boys had stopped up the road somewhere, like they used to do after a Merlin concert, waiting for him and Don and whoever decided to tag along to catch up. Party with the elves and wood sprites until dawn or a ranger chased them out.

That increased his odds of survival… or increased the number of his friends who will end up with heads on pikes in some forest clearing. Better if Dooby and the boys were halfway to Trenton by now, completely unaware of Butch's impending demise. It meant fewer casualties.

Speaking of which. "Where's Don?"

Pee Sea, slowing down for the road's quick transition from asphalt to dirt, shrugged his shoulders. "Dunno."

"What'd you do with him?"

"I didn't do anything with him."

Butch snorted.

"Like you didn't do anything with Jape."

"I didn't say I did anything with Jape," Pee Sea responded coolly.

"Right," Butch continued the snort, "just that you," air quotes, "talked to him."

"I did talk to him."

"And?"

"And what?"

Butch blew out a breath.

"What did you do to Don?" he repeated.

"I didn't do anything to Don."

The conversation had become circular as the Pontiac adjusted to the soft road, canting a bit here and there but taking it well.

"Then why'd you leave the note?"

Pee Sea looked over, one eyebrow cocked.

"What note?"

"This one!" Butch snarled and whipped it out of his pocket and practically shoved it in Pee Sea's face.

Pee stood on the brakes, which the Pontiac didn't appreciate and the back end came around, blocking the entire road, as Pee Sea grabbed Butch's wrist with one hand while shoving the pistol against his head.

"Are you fuckin' crazy, man?" he roared.

Butch gritted his teeth, sure his brain was seconds away from decorating the windows, but kept the note pressed in front of Pee Sea's eyes. Both of them held position for a bit and then Pee Sea took the picture while keeping the pistol's barrel in place, fumbled around until he found the interior light, turned it on and examined the note.

"That's ominous," he concluded.

"So you killed Don, the same way you killed Jape, the same

way you're going to kill me," Butch summarized, his voice more mournful than he liked.

Pee Sea flipped the note back at him.

"I didn't kill Don. I didn't kill Jape… as far as you and the cops know, anyway. And I'm not going to kill you."

The pistol remained against his head, belying the last statement, and there was the note and Jape's headless body and a shot sheriff, or deputy, whatever, and Butch beheld the last moments of his life.

Let's go down swinging.

"Bullshit!" he said and braced for the bullet.

Which did not come.

Pee Sea laughed and tucked the pistol back in his belt and goosed the Pontiac and expertly straightened it out and headed deeper into the magic forest and Butch was confused and cautiously optimistic because nothing was going the way he feared it would. Yet.

What the fuck is happening?

"Where'd you get that, anyway?" Pee gestured at the note now on Butch's lap.

"You know damn well where."

"And yet I asked the question." Pee Sea *tsk*ed. "You know you're supposed to be this really smart guy but I'm thinking you're dumber than a rock."

"So you didn't leave this in my locker?"

"Your locker?"

"At Perkins."

Pee Sea re-raised his eyebrow.

"We've been out of high school awhile, ain't we? So, you don't really have a locker anymore, right?"

"My old locker. During senior year."

"I have no fucking idea what you're talking about. And I don't have a problem with Don."

"You don't?"

"No."

"But—" and Butch realized it was somewhat foolish to point out that Don accompanied him on the ill-fated drug run and that Pee Sea's principles meant Don's headless body was mouldering somewhere in the woods to Butch's right, or should be, but maybe it wasn't a good idea to plant ideas not in evidence, so he stopped talking.

"He was being a pal," Pee said, indicating he had, indeed, considered the idea, "I admire that."

He stopped the car in the middle of the turn towards Magnolia.

"And I'm a reasonable guy."

That was hardly a word Butch would have used to describe Pee Sea, but he kept that to himself because there was no need to exacerbate matters. Pee was looking towards Magnolia, away from Butch, and this would be as good a time as any to smash him upside the head and make his escape into the magic forest but something stayed his hand. Maybe it was how relaxed Pee was. Maybe he was always relaxed before beheading someone, but that seemed incongruous, so Butch waited to see what would happen next.

"So here it is." Pee turned back to him. "I know you didn't have anything to do with Jape's dumbass decision. I made that up. You passed. Good job."

He patted Butch on the shoulder.

"Still leaves me with a problem because there's a lot of other dumbasses out there who need lessons. And I'm still out the money. So, what to do?"

He eyed Butch, cold and murderous, then said, "Get out."

Butch blinked.

"What?"

"Get. Out."

And the pistol was pointed at his stomach.

So, here, by the side of the road where other midnight travelers of the magic forest would find him, shot and bleeding and gasping his last breath, comforted by the knowledge that he was not dying for a mistaken belief but to serve as a caution. Finally, his life meant something.

Really don't want that as my legacy. One last desperate effort...

"I thought you said you weren't going to kill me."

"I'm not, but I will shoot your fucking dick off."

Which amounted to the same thing but Pee Sea might make a distinction so Butch hastily slapped the door open and scooted out and stood there, inadvertently making the shooting of his dick much easier and he involuntarily tightened his hips, waiting for it.

"You wanna close the door?"

Pee Sea waved the pistol irritably.

Butch did. "What are you doing?"

"I'm taking the car."

"But—"

"This pays your portion. Not all of it 'cause this is a cheap shit car but I'll get a couple thou for it. Jape and Truck already paid theirs. And where you're light."

He let that sit there.

"Report it stolen in a couple of days. Your idiot stepfather can file the insurance."

"But—"

Pee Sea turned the wheels towards Magnolia.

"You know why you ain't dead?" he suddenly asked through the window.

Butch shook his head.

"'Cause you joined the Air Force. Don't need trouble with the Feds, I don't."

He tapped the side of his head.

"Smart."

He leaned over and fished around on the floor and pitched the cunt cap out of the window at Butch's feet, the note floating out seconds later, and slowly drove away. Butch watched the brake lights flash and then the car turned left, back to the Barrens.

Butch stood quietly for a moment, then stooped down and picked up the note and put it in his pocket and then the cunt cap and put it on his head even though it was a complete mess and would get him court-martialed should some Air Force officer happen by. Which, given how this day had gone, was more likely than normal circumstances would dictate. Butch took a surrendering look down the road expecting to see a staff car's headlights bearing down on him, but nothing.

First time anyone said he was smart to join the Air Force but, given the situation, Butch didn't consider it a compliment. It was a good example of unintended consequences. Which were the guiding physics of his life.

Let's review.

Due to the odd events of the past two months, he was now at the intersection of Deep Hollow and Magnolia on an August night in a trashed uniform, having gained a reprieve on his life at the expense of his freedom, all of his friends dead or missing, no money and no car, the mystical woods he loved regarding him with amusement.

If he had actively planned this, it would never have happened. Too many disparate items, people, and events would have to be manipulated and coordinated with split-second timing to even get halfway here. He blinked at the alley of stars visible above the road. "I'm God's hackey sack," he said to the heavens.

One day, he should write a novel.

But for now, he should get out of here, before some local drug dealer with a beef changed his recently changed mind and came back. Miles from nowhere he was, and hummed a few bars of the Cat Stevens' song. If he wanted to get home before dawn, he should start walking.

Where exactly was home, again?

Butch sighed and flipped a mental coin and decided it was the apartment, primarily because the last place he wanted to be at sunrise was standing in Ridge's empty driveway explaining why the car was missing. He wasn't so sure he could explain. He checked his pockets and, fortunately, he still had the door keys.

Let's get going.

He took one step and a tidal wave of weariness and pain, both physical and psychic, overwhelmed him and he dropped to his knees.

Oh, man. I'm not going to make it. I shouldn't make it. I've fucked up too many things. For years. Pee Sea did me no favor.

He looked up at the moonlit trees, which swayed in sympathy. They knew him, but things pass and his day passed and the woods had seen many days and many people pass and it was his time to go and let others take his place. So he could limp along and arrive at the apartment as the sun rose or maybe earlier if he could hitch a ride with someone crazy enough to stop at midnight and pick up a disheveled airman stumbling along the side of the road, or he could forget all that and remain kneeling and wait for the current generation of crazy kids to come barreling along Deep Hollow, stoned and laughing with all the world right here and right now, and run him over.

A car turned into Magnolia.

At first, Butch thought it was Pee Sea, who had, indeed, changed his mind and now regarded Butch as an enemy and coming back to machete his head and leave it on a pike but the car turned from the Perkins direction and unless Pee Sea made a complete loop around the area in less than a minute, no. Maybe it was a ranger intent on running off the teenagers necking in their cars in the parking lot next to Magnolia but it was coming straight on, so no, it was someone heading back to the Lakes or into the woods for something or other and they would accelerate and plow him over before they spotted him and that was good.

The car slowed as it approached. Moonlight exposed it. The Batmobile.

It paused, canted around, and pulled up next to him. The driver's window was down.

"Get in," Don said.

Chapter 21

"Where the hell you been, man?"

"Here and there. You gettin' in, or what?"

Butch let out a long breath and shook his head and stood up and came around the car and reached for the handle and Don bumped it forward, almost throwing Butch off balance.

"Very funny," Butch said and moved towards the handle again and, bump forward.

"Hardy har har," and another reach and another bump and Butch said, "Dude."

"All right, all right," Don sniggered and Butch half expected him to bump just one more time for yuk's sake, but he didn't and Butch hastily slid in before the comedic opportunity became too rich to ignore. Don hit the pedal and the front of the Batmobile rose and they careened left and were hurtling into the magic forest.

"Remember this?" Don said and turned the headlights off.

Magic.

The moon silvered the road and the trees and fairy dust glowed and sparkled as they zipped along, pucks and elves scrambling out of the way shrieking with laughter. Butch saw unicorn herds galloping through the brush and ogres and trolls raise dull heads to watch the car pass by and the firebirds and pixies swarmed the hood and he could not help it, he laughed. Seeing all this and he wasn't even high…

"You been smoking?" Butch asked suspiciously.

"Maybe. Why?"

"I'm getting contact."

"Excellent!"

Don laughed and held up a partially smoked joint.

"Light it up and go full-bore."

"I can't, man." Butch warded him. "They'll catch me."

"Who?"

"The Air Force. They pee test."

"Bummer," Don said and expertly flipped the joint into his mouth while striking a match one-handed.

Butch blew it out.

"Hey!" Don yelled.

"You can't, either. The test is good enough to catch someone smoking next to me."

"Double bummer," Don observed and kept the joint in his mouth as the moon took point, leading them on. The unicorns disappeared, thank God, and Butch settled into the seat. "You know, I've been looking for you all day."

"I know."

Butch raised 'what-the-eff?' hands. "You know? So where the hell—"

Don whipped the wheel hard to the left and the Batmobile bounced once on a particularly rough part of the road, the back end changing places with the front; Don stomped on it and the car flew, recovering already passed ground, the road silver and magic and clear all the way back to the bridge.

"Woo Hoo!" Don yahooed as Butch uncrammed himself from the little space between the door and the seat.

"Warn a guy, will ya?"

"Shut up, wuss."

And he sped up, if that were possible.

Butch laughed, despite his impending death because what better way and what better place and he leaned forward, anticipating. A little drift to either side and *bam*! Teenage legends, just like Cornell and pals. Stoned kids driving through here over the next ten generations, slowing down and pointing, "Here, man! It happened right here!" Exchange of wide-eyed looks. "And they're still haunting the woods, man."

Like they'd always been.

"Before you kill us," Butch said, "I want to apologize."

"For what?" Don's lips were so tense and concentrated the

joint was sticking almost straight up.

"Getting you involved."

Don shrugged. "I'd have done the same."

"Well, yeah, but… I didn't mean for things to get so out of hand."

"No one does. But things just do."

"Yeah, okay, they do… frankly, I thought you were dead."

Don laughed.

"Well, here I am, so obviously not."

"Not so sure about that anymore," Butch said wryly and glanced into the back seat. No Frank. Thank God.

"Hold on," Don said as they crested the rise, the bridge before them. Cut the wheel to the right, this time, and a little slower so it was a gradual, almost regal fishtail around the pivot and they were pointed back at the moon and the woods and off again, fast but not as fast as the first run. Butch swore he saw an orc scramble away.

"Jesus," he breathed, "what's in that dope?"

"Dust," Don said and settled on the moon.

Butch frowned.

Can you contact-high dust?

"Anyway, I also wanted to tell you, you were right."

Don was nonchalant. "I'm always right. But about what, specifically?"

"About running away. Turns out, there was no need." He paused. "It's like, everything settled on its own. That it's all okay. April's found the man she really wanted. Cindy's finding the men she really wanted. Pee Sea isn't mad at me. Or at you. I overreacted."

"How?"

"Joining the Air Force."

Without a word, Don cut hard and they bounced once again and the tail came around again and they were facing back towards the bridge and Butch was prying himself out of the door jamb while muttering imprecations when Don stopped. Dead. Right in the middle of the road, the silver way before them.

"You didn't react enough," he toned.

"Huh?"

"Because, I am dead." And he stared at Butch.

Butch blinked.

"Are you messing with me?"

Don turned back to the road, facing the distant bridge with an unreadable expression. "No, I'm not. I've been dead since we graduated. So's Dooby. So's all this." He waved a hand at the magic woods. "Dead. Buried. Rotted away."

"Is this a metaphor? Because, dude, you're freaking me out."

"Good!" Don turned on him, wild-eyed. "Good, motherfucker! Freak out! And get the fuck out!"

"Like, right here?" Butch fumbled, confused, at the door handle.

"No, idiot!" Don head-slapped him. A pretty good one, making Butch's ears ring. "Get out of *here*. The Lakes. New Jersey. This life. Get the fuck out and don't ever come back."

Butch gaped at him, rubbing his head. "What the hell?"

"This." Don passed an encompassing hand across the windshield. "Is nothing. All of this is nothing. It's small. It's petty. It's soul-sucking. You're all dried out, man, just from a few years' exposure. You have to understand. It's all nothing. It's all dead." He shook his head. "Like I am. You stay here, and you're next."

You're next?

Butch whipped the note out of his pocket. "You did this."

Don said nothing.

"You put this in the locker. Why?"

Don looked sad. "'Cause I knew you'd go back there. You always do."

"What?" Butch was incredulous. "No I don't! First time I ever went back to my locker since we graduated!"

"But you always go back to the school. In your mind, in your attitude, it's where you want to be. Knew you'd find a way into the locker. Knew it."

Butch stared at the note.

"But, dude, this is pretty harsh."

"What other way to wake you up, man?"

Butch didn't know whether to be mad or amused. "I thought Pee Sea had done you like Jape."

"What makes you think he didn't?"

The air grew cold, unnatural, and Butch felt an undertone to it like a distant tolling bell, a rift in the silent night. The interior of the car dimmed to pitch, the only light coming from the silver-coated road , a road leading away, far away, to a land Butch did not recognize. Other things stirred in the woods, fell things, and they were hungry. A terror gripped him, reflexively making him grip the seat. This was borderlands, the far country, the home of dark and shadow,

"You're trying to resurrect the dead, man."

Don's voice from a blackness that enshrouded the driver's seat.

"You can't. And if you ever come back here, ever, after you're done with the Air Force, after you're done with whatever, then all this—" a dark hand silhouetted by the silver woods. "—all this… magic… disappears."

"What are you talking about?" The terror became panic. "You're not making any sense!"

Ghost hands seized his lapels.

"You *know* what I'm talking about!" Don shouted. "It's all gone. Already! All of it! It's! All! Gone!" Don slamming him against the seat with each word. "You can't bring it back. You can't."

"Dude!" Butch struggled against Don's iron grip, unable to break it, no matter what techniques he tried.

"You come back, you'll just be another south Jersey loser," Don's voice, mournful. "Headless body out in the woods somewhere. Forgotten. And no one else will remember us."

"You have to remember us," Frank said.

"Gah!"

Butch almost leaped through the roof. Both Don and Frank, both slightly lighter silhouettes against the pitch-black interior, faced him, one from the back seat, one next to him. It was obvious, though, from the tilt of their shadow heads that they were tickled about scaring him half to death.

"No one else will," Don said.

"No one else cares," Frank added.

"And that's not fair." Don.

"And you know what that's like," Frank admonished, rocking a silhouette baby in his arms.

And the car was gone. Just gone.

Butch sat in the middle of the sand road, the moon witch-silver and ancient and binding the spirits of pain and loneliness with grief spells and he leaned forward and tears fell.

"Come back," he whispered to the woods. "Don't leave me. I

don't have anyone else."

The trees cried, too. But no one came.

After a couple of years, he stood up slowly and carefully brushed himself off and raised a sympathetic hand to the trees and found his cunt cap attached to his belt and put it on. He checked his pocket but the note was gone.

Of course. It's on the floor of the Batmobile.

The trees stopped crying and the real night returned and Butch wondered how much of whatever substance did this to him was still in his system and wondered how in the hell it had been introduced and by whom. For the life of him, he couldn't remember eating or drinking anything that could cause this, just the beers with HP.

Was that it?

When the Air Force busted him over the pee test, he could tell them he'd been slipped a mickey, or whatever its modern equivalent.

Like they'd believe me.

He turned about thoughtfully, taking in the woods and the road. He was halfway between the two entrances. One brought him closer to Perkins and the end of all things, the other closer to the Lakes and the bridge and all the magic. But the magic was gone.

Just like that… well, no. Don was right, again. It's been gone since graduation.

All day he'd tried to resurrect the dead. And he might have succeeded, for a moment. For only a moment. His heart ached.

Time to go.

He turned towards the Perkins side and trudged through the sand, the moon now benevolent and sympathetic and showing the way out. Not the way home. Home was gone; at least, all the places he'd been told were home. They're haunted, now. If he went to any of them, he'd be a haint himself, a ghost on the edge, some far figure barely glimpsed out of the corners of eyes, flitting about the dusty corners trying to raise the other dead, immediately dismissed, immediately forgotten. He couldn't do that to himself. He wouldn't do that to those guys. To Don and Dooby. To Frank.

No one else carried the memories and the boys would all drown, dissipate, get lost in the big whirling mess of space and time that was the universe and no one would ever know them.

And it would be his fault.

Jeez.

He stopped and looked at the woods. "I am really tired of being blamed for everything."

No response.

"Really tired," he said again and resumed the trudge.

A voice floated out to him, "Then stop doing stupid things."

Could have been Don or Frank. Could have been God.

"I get blamed for things I didn't do."

"Then do the things you should."

Butch mused.

That made sense. Simple. Elegant.

And impossible.

Because he had no clue what those things were.

It took about twenty more minutes to reach the road and the night had deepened in that time. The dark was darker and the moon brighter…

Commit to memory, commit, because

…Remembrance is bigger, tinged with magic. Butch heard a troll snicker and caught a pixie flit out of the corner of his eye and stepped onto the shoulder and faced Perkins then slowly 360-d, photographing everything, memorizing every leaf and branch and pebble and the death light and time, time.

"Remember," someone pleaded.

I'll try.

He started walking.

About ten minutes or ten hours later, Butch heard the rush and tire whine of a car coming from the direction of 70 and he moved off the shoulder onto the berm and stuck his thumb out but kept walking. This late at night, there was a better than even chance the car would clip him rather than see him or would stop and ten or twelve Breed would jump out and beat his ass. So he kept one foot pointed towards the woods should he need to run.

The shoulder glowed in the headlights as the car slowed, the surprise of the driver evident by the quick deceleration. Butch didn't look over but felt the front of the car keep pace with him. He heard a window roll down and braced for a bullet or a curse.

"Hey, man, what are you doing out here?"

HP.

Butch stopped and turned.

"Lost my car."

HP's smiling face framed the passenger window. Joan Baez was driving, looking over HP's shoulder.

"Lost?"

"Long story."

They laughed.

"I'll bet. Get in."

"Not until you tell me what did you do to me."

HP nodded, a knowing smile on his face.

"We helped. Like we're doing now." And he pointed at the back door.

Butch hesitated then reached for the door. The twins and the Viking all pushed and wrestled to make room and Butch squeezed in.

And was gone.

ACKNOWLEDGMENTS…

…are for non-fiction books, histories, encyclopedias, cookbooks, etc., not fiction. Lots of researchers and librarians and editors and SMEs get involved with a non-fiction book and deserve the author's recognition and thanks. A novel springs fully armoured from the author's forehead so who is he acknowledging? Himself? What hubris. A last (or in some recent cases, first) page gushing thanks to wives and lovers and dogs and members of the writing group is a poor attempt to sound humble. They're like Academy Awards speeches, the self-absorbed writer acting like his novel was a group effort. No, it wasn't. It was a self-regarding exercise, an arrogant use of time better spent with the wives and lovers and dogs so cavalierly dismissed during the novel's writing and then belatedly mentioned in some throwaway appendix. Spare us.

Yet, I've added one because some things need 'splainin'. I guess this is more accurately a Notes section, a Clarification, what have you. It may drift into some acknowledgments but as part of the clarity.

This is the last of the Frank Vaughn books, which may sound like it was a trilogy but it wasn't. I even call it a trilogy but that's not accurate. A trilogy is a continuing story that needs three novels to tell it properly, like *Lord of the Rings* and Alastair Reynold's *Revelation Space*… which yeah, I know, has a fourth novel to it but you can safely ignore that one and yeah, I know, *Lord of the Rings* was originally one novel and was cut up by the publisher. Which means it still fits my definition. Trilogies have an object – like a house – or a destination, like Mars. Or a mission, like destroying the evil ring or finding an absent God (WARNING! Shameless promotion ahead!), as in my *Ship to Look for God* trilogy. *Partholon*, by the way, is not a trilogy… well, the first three books are but it's actually a series with three, possibly four, more novels to go and I swear I will get to them one day. The

Frank Vaughn novels are too slapdash for a quest or goal. The only thing they share are the same members of a family, and a ghost. Maybe a ghost. Not sure.

The *Frank Vaughn* books are fiction. They are not a memoir. They *are* based on true events: on the last day of school, 1965, in Lawton, Oklahoma, a mother beat her son to death with a baseball bat. Whether that was prompted by the boy forgetting to bring his report card home or not is unknown, but every local kid believed that was the reason and so it became part of the lore. No more than a week after, my family blew apart and I found myself riding across the South in a white Rambler station wagon at the mercy of my rather violent and unpredictable dad. That's pretty much the plot of *Frank Vaughn Killed by his Mom,* so why isn't it a memoir? Because the events in the book either (a) did not happen in the sequence presented (b) did not include the people depicted or (c) did not happen at all. No one would believe the true story, so I wrote it as fiction, which is more believable.

Southern Gothic is completely fiction, with a caveat. It depicts rather accurately how everyone turned out, without any accuracy of how they got there. None of the events in *Southern Gothic* happened… well, at least, none of the main events. There are no bodies, at least, ones that I had anything to do with, so don't go looking. You might stir up things better left alone.

Looking for Don is a paean to a place and time now lost in the mists of history, but one that anybody who was a teenager anywhere south of Trenton from 1970-1975 remembers with great fondness and astonishment. It was absolutely the best place and time to be a teenager in America. If you don't believe me, just crank up Bruce Springsteen's first three albums, all done when he was still one of us, before he went all Hollywood. I, also, got stuck in the swamps of Jersey and had at least one 10th Avenue freeze out. All of us did.

Many, many of the events in *Don* are true. Names have been changed to protect the innocent. And the guilty. If you were there, you'll recognize some things and may think you recognize some people, but, you don't: these characters ain't real. They're like the pixies and the unicorn herds in Lebanon State Forest, the ones that used to cross Deep Hollow at midnight when the moon was full. We all saw them. But they don't exist.

I suppose.

Many, many of the places described in *Don* do exist. The Train Wreck, the Moon Crater, the Carranza Memorial are still in the Barrens. Somewhere. Please stay away from the blue holes unless you know what you're doing. People disappear in them. Please stay out of the Barrens altogether unless you know what you're doing. I am halfway convinced that the Barrens constitute a portal to other dimensions. I saw way too many weird things out there, including something the size and shape of Bigfoot that stalked our campfire one night at the Crater. Could have been a Piney, but even the shyest couldn't resist the Rolling Rock we offered. Could have been substance abuse, but I don't think so.

A word on terms: hardguys are those steroid abusers who draped themselves wide-legged and red-eyed over the hallway lockers yelling "Waddaulookinat?" at everybody trying to either get to class or into the locker over which said hardguys were currently draped. You know the type. Basically harmless, unless provoked. And everything provoked them, like you trying to get into your locker. "Greasers" is not a racial epithet: all kinds of racial and ethnic groups were greasers. They were the car nuts, self-taught mechanics who could take the wreck of a 1964 Impala and, within a week, have a chrome fuel-injected muscle car stepping out over the line. Other regions call them gearheads, but 'greasers' was our term. You know, from the grease?

Pineys…

…are unique. I don't know of an equivalent subspecies in America. No, they're not hillbillies, although they can cook up some mighty fine 'shine. They're not Okies or swampers or any other degenerate inbred group you'd care to mention. They're not inbred, for one thing. Well, most of them aren't, although just about every Piney is a cousin of some kind or another. They're highly educated. Lots of Piney doctors out there. And they are absolutely dangerous, probably one of the most clannish self-supporting self-protecting criminal enterprises in America, so organized and effective that the Mafia could take lessons. They *want* you to believe they are back-swamp hayseeds. That is a mistake you will make only once. If you survive. I'm not kidding when I say stay out of the Barrens unless you know what you're doing. Or unless you pick up a Piney in Tabernacle to ride along with you.

I got to south Jersey in 1970, and, over the next five years had the best of times, worst of times, yadda yadda, and I still recall it all with great fondness, great trepidation, and am slightly stunned that I lived through it. I have been around the world at least three times since, been in very dangerous and very cool situations, met some of the best people on earth, got myself into lots of trouble, got out of a lot of trouble, was present for some very earth-shaking historical events, stood alone against the hordes and shoulder to shoulder with brother Vikings, and still have never loved any of it as much as I did the universes of south Jersey. Nothing else ever compared. Whenever asked where I'm from, I name it.

And I will never, ever live there again.

I left in 1975. By that time, the spirit was gone. Drugs killed it, as it killed a lot of things and lots of people. We all thought we could handle it, and we couldn't. No one can. I have been back several times since, of course, but that was prompted by familial obligations, not desire. See, it's all gone. Don, the real Don, died a few years ago and everyone else who was part of that wonderful crazy gang o'mine has, too, or simply disappeared. Deep Hollow is a shadow of its former self, tamed by suburbia, and there is so much encroachment on the Barrens that the Pineys have to go deeper and darker. Stay out of there.

But, when the moon is right and the salt air is blowing and somehow you find yourself in a 1960s vintage automobile, take a ride off Deep Hollow, past the Magnolia cutoff, and look. You'll see unicorns.

…Okay, yeah, some shout-outs. Shout out. Just one: to Jayne Southern, my editor, Genghis Jayne, is of passive voice the slayer, was the one standing firm and willing to embrace the slings and arrows of outraged author proclaiming the past progressive is still a viable format. And it is, dammit.

You made it better.

OTHER BOOKS BY D. KRAUSS

The Frank Vaughn Trilogy
Frank Vaughn, Killed by His Mom
Southern Gothic
Looking for Don

The Partholon Trilogy
Partholon
Tu'An
Col'm

The Ship Trilogy
The Ship to Look for God
The Ship Looking for God
The Ship Finding God

Story Collections
The Moonlight in Genevieve's Eyes
and other Strange Stories
The Last Man in the World Explains All
and other strange tales

ABOUT THE AUTHOR

D. Krauss currently resides in the Shenandoah Valley. He's been a cottonpicker, a sod buster, a surgical orderly, the guy who paints the little white line down the middle of the road, a weatherman, a gun-totin' door-kickin' lawman, a layabout, and a bus driver, in that order.

Website:
http://www.dustyskull.com

Goodreads:
https://bit.ly/3bkPDCm

YouTube: Old Guy Reviews Books
https://bit.ly/3y3KHLY

MeWe: dkrauss

www.ingramcontent.com/pod-product-compliance
Lightning Source LLC
Chambersburg PA
CBHW070637100726
47907CB00007B/2022